Haunted by You

Praise for *Haunted by You*

"*Haunted by You* is a compelling and compulsive read with heart and an enigmatic love story that will keep you reading until the very last page."
—**Ashley Mansour**, International Bestselling Author

"Young Adult romantic suspense and thriller fans, get ready to add Louise Davis's debut, *Haunted by You*, to your TBR pile. Set in Moncks Corner, South Carolina, Davis expertly weaves the story of two teens, Genevieve and Steve, as they learn to navigate young love and loss amidst family secrets. Part romance, part mystery and suspense, with a few real ghost stories for good measure, *Haunted by You* is one hundred percent an enjoyable read and I look forward to more books from Louise Davis."
—**Jessica Reino**, Author, Author Coach and Senior Literary Agent

"In a haunting portrayal of what it means to love in the midst of uncertainty, Davis was able to take the realities of doomed hope and create a masterpiece where the characters must learn to trust each other and pick up the pieces together. *Haunted by You* will grab your attention from the first page and will stay with you long after the last word."
—**Erin Huntley**, Author, Freelance Editor

"Louise takes a real location with interesting facts and history and successfully weaves it into the plot of her story. *Haunted by You* is a strong, tragic tale that will leave you looking over your shoulder. Not all ghosts come from the dead …"
—**Susan Shepard**, Author of *The Gardiens Series*

"*Haunted by You* is full of mystery and suspense, the storyline kept me on the edge of my seat the entire time! I felt connected with the characters immediately and couldn't wait to see how their stories played out. *Haunted by You* is for anyone who wants an easy, thrilling read!"
—**Morgan Martin**, Author of *Healing Empty Hands*

"Louise Davis spins a web of intrigue mixed with young love in a town known for spooky jails and dungeons of folklore, but the ghosts her well-constructed characters face are more harrowing than any tour guide can convey. Louise's expert writing haunts you, forbidding you to put down the book until you've read every last word."

—**Jennifer Keith**, Author of *Fixing the Funny Bone:*
The G.R.I.T. Method to Heal with Humor

"Louse Davis expertly intertwines spine-chilling ghost stories from Charleston's history and the suspense of frightening threats in this intriguing, yet fun thriller. *Haunted by You* plunges readers into the lives of characters you will quickly fall in love with as they navigate the pressures of teenage life while also dealing with real life and death situations. If you're looking for a creepy and anxiety-filled ride, *Haunted by You* delivers just that!"

—**JoAnna McSpadden**, Author of the upcoming series
The Lumos Gems Chronicles

A NOVEL

HAUNTED BY YOU

LOUISE DAVIS

NEW YORK

LONDON • NASHVILLE • MELBOURNE • VANCOUVER

HAUNTED BY YOU

Published in New York, New York, by Morgan James Publishing. Morgan James is a trademark of Morgan James, LLC. www.MorganJamesPublishing.com

Publisher's Note: This novel is a work of fiction. Names, characters, places, and incidents are either products of the author's imagination or used fictitiously. All characters are fictional, and any similarity to people living or dead is purely coincidental.

Proudly distributed by Publishers Group West®

A **FREE** ebook edition is available for you
or a friend with the purchase of this print book.

CLEARLY SIGN YOUR NAME ABOVE

Instructions to claim your free ebook edition:
1. Visit MorganJamesBOGO.com
2. Sign your name CLEARLY in the space above
3. Complete the form and submit a photo
   of this entire page
4. You or your friend can download the ebook
   to your preferred device

ISBN 9781636981727 paperback
ISBN 9781636981734 ebook
Library of Congress Control Number:
2023934513

Cover Design by:
Rylan Bird
www.voodooartsstudio.com

Interior Design by:
Chris Treccani
www.3dogcreative.net

Morgan James is a proud partner of Habitat for Humanity Peninsula
and Greater Williamsburg. Partners in building since 2006.

Get involved today! Visit: www.morgan-james-publishing.com/giving-back

For my own Steve,
who encourages me to chase my dreams and sees me for me,
flaws and all. I love you.

And to my mom,
this book quite literally would not be here without you.

Prologue

The rain is cold and bites at my warm cheeks. The mist rising from the ground is so thick it looks almost unnatural and reminds me of the funerals. The mist, the rain, the hole in my chest, all of it is like reliving the day we put them in the ground. There are some mornings that as I wake, I am sure it was all a horrible nightmare, then reality crashes into me.

My life has been forever changed.

I am empty and full of pain at the same time. How is that even possible? Everything reminds me of them.

Standing on the empty street, rain distorts my vision of what was once my home. It looks exactly the same: still painted eggshell white with the big, happy, yellow shutters that Mom insisted the house needed. The lawn is still mowed and the beautiful flowers still bloom along the front of the house. More flowers line the stone walkway that winds its way from the front door to the driveway.

The gigantic willow tree in one corner of the front lawn brings painful memories: days spent climbing the tree, and the slumber parties with my friends and sisters in the tree house Dad built for us.

The tree house is still there, firmly attached like it has always been. Dad spent months making blueprints to build the perfect tree house for his daughters. Mom was so excited to paint it and hang curtains, but was so upset when none of us girls wanted to paint it bubblegum pink. After a heated debate, we all finally agreed on a lighter maroon. It was enough to satisfy Mom.

Memories continue to flood my mind, like the one hot day my younger sister came up with the idea to make our own swimming pool. I wasn't sure we were going to survive when Dad got home from work and saw the muddy hole we had dug right in the middle of the front lawn.

I watch for any sign of life in the house now, even though I know there won't be any. There are no lights, no happy sounds of a family eating dinner together, no music coming from the garage where my older sister had once tried to start a band.

The rain is coming down hard now. My sweatshirt hood isn't doing much to keep me dry and the cold, wet fabric clings to my skin. I try to swipe the wet strands of my long hair behind my ears, but they fall back across my eyes almost instantly.

The rain pelts my face like slivers of ice, which makes the hot tears sting my cheeks.

Wishing I could go inside and get a warm, comforting hug from Mom, or listen to one of Dad's horrible jokes, I turn my back on the only place I have ever felt safe and start toward the unknown.

End of August

Seven months earlier

Chapter 1

Genevieve

Looks are everything on the first day of school; first impressions can make or break you. Thankfully, my hair falls in just the right place and my first-day-of-school look is coming together nicely. I check my river-washed jeans and fitted burgundy T-shirt one more time in the full-length mirror hanging on the back of my bedroom door.

My mom's high-pitched order rises from downstairs. "Genevieve, you better come eat or you're going to be late!"

Charlotte, my mom, looks like an older version of me. We share the same auburn hair, dark green eyes, and are both covered in freckles. Mom is gorgeous, freckles and all, but my freckles make me look younger than my seventeen, almost eighteen, years.

She spent most of her adult years staying at home with my two sisters and me. When Violet, my older sister, started college this year, Mom decided to go back to work. She is a real estate agent, so she can schedule around things if she feels like one of us needs her to be somewhere.

A horn blast from the driveway sounds the arrival of Livi, my best friend. With one last look at my long, vibrant, auburn hair, I grab my backpack and run down the stairs and out the door, yelling, "Bye, Mom!" over my shoulder. Mom rolls her eyes and cleans up the uneaten breakfast. I hop into the front seat of the car and throw my backpack into the back, almost hitting my little sister, Konnie, who is already in the backseat. Livi backs out of the driveway and speeds toward Berkeley High School where Livi and I are seniors, and Konnie is a sophomore. It's weird starting the school year without Violet.

"What in the world are you wearing, Livi?" I say, taking in Livi's outfit. "There's no way your mom let you walk out of the house looking like that." Her skirt is so short, I'm not sure it can classify as one, and her top looks more like a sports bra than a shirt. "You do remember our school has a dress code, right?"

Livi grins. "Mom had to work a double shift at the hospital so she didn't see me this morning. Being the only child of a single mom has its perks sometimes." She throws a glance toward Konnie in the back seat. "Most of the time," she adds.

Konnie glares at Livi. "I don't know why you're looking at me. You know I don't go and tattle everything I hear. You'd always be in trouble if I did."

"Anyway," Livi interrupts, "as for the dress code, that's what the jacket in the back seat is for."

I raise my eyebrows. "I still think they might notice you're missing pants, even if you're wearing a jacket, Liv."

Livi glares at me as she pulls into the school parking lot and parks. "Get out of my car, you party pooper."

"What would you do without me, you heathen?" I laugh.

"Well, I'd have a lot more fun, for starters," Livi grumbles. "You're like having my mom tag along with us all the time." Konnie and I burst out laughing.

"At least you don't have to live with her," Konnie pipes up, earning a glare from me as we climb out of Livi's brand new, red, Mustang convertible.

Livi's dad had it delivered for her birthday this summer. He isn't super wealthy, but he seems to be trying to buy himself back into her good graces after missing over a decade of her life. She still refuses to talk to him, but regardless of what she says I know she loves the car, even if she did grumble about it when it showed up.

I follow behind Konnie on the sidewalk. Her dark brown, shoulder length hair is braided tightly into two French braids. I may be a carbon copy of Mom, but Konnie and Violet are female versions of Dad; olive-toned skin, brown eyes, and dark brown hair. Konnie even inherited Dad's poor eyesight, they both wear glasses, which makes them look even more similar. In true Konnie fashion, she doesn't look nervous at all as she waves a goodbye and heads into the school.

Livi bumps my shoulder with hers. "Are you up for some fun?"

"What kind of fun?" I ask warily, as we enter the red-brick, two-story building.

My friendship with Livi baffles me. We are best friends, yet we are polar opposites. Maybe it is because we balance each other out, keeping each other in check. I try hard to stay out of trouble and do what my parents and teachers expect of me, and Livi likes to push buttons and get a reaction out of people. She does what she wants, when she wants to, no matter the consequences.

Livi rolls her eyes and lets out an exasperated sigh. "The fun kind of fun, Genevieve. What other kind is there?"

"You know exactly the kind of fun I'm talking about. If your fun is going to some lame guy's apartment to do who knows what, I'd rather stay home, thanks."

"Ugh! You're so boring sometimes. But as a matter of fact, Miss Goody-Two-Shoes, no, that is not the kind of fun I was talking about. I want to go on a ghost tour in Charleston. I'll even pay, just this once, if you'll come with me."

Great. Apparently, the sudden interest in ghost hunting T.V. shows these last few weeks isn't going to pass as quickly as I had hoped. Livi always looks for something new and exciting, sometimes obsessing over her latest interest until she's exhausted her focus. Most of her passions fizzle out pretty quickly; I hope this supernatural one doesn't stick around for long. I hate getting scared.

I give Livi a skeptical look. "What is with your new obsession with the supernatural? And didn't we already go on a tour this summer?"

"The tour this summer was a walking historical tour, it wasn't a ghost tour. How do you not remember this? It was, like, two months ago."

Despite Livi jumping from one passion to the next, history has always been a constant interest. Not the type of history you learn in school; she loves the hidden stories of the forgotten people who came before us.

"And you say I am the nerd," I laugh. "Has anyone told you that you have quite the addiction to history? The supernatural I get. That is right up your alley, but the history just doesn't go with your whole 'screw the world' motif."

Navigating through groups of students catching up after summer break in the senior hall, everyone looks so grown up. I have known most of these kids since kindergarten. They still clump together in the same groups: the jocks, the overachievers, the kids who don't follow the rules. It is weird to think that if we hadn't become best friends when we were three, Livi and I would be in different groups at school.

We pass our teacher, Mrs. Gnighting, wearing a below-the-knee pencil skirt and professional looking blouse. I have always thought she looks more like a lawyer than a high school teacher. Mrs. Gnighting raises her eyebrows at Livi and tells her that her skirt is too short. We continue down the hall with Livi acting like she didn't hear a thing, weaving through students on their way to class in the packed hallway. How she gets away with her defiant attitude is beyond me. We stop at our freshly painted lockers and grab what we need for first period.

Livi flaunts down the hallway, a group of football players parting as she walks through the middle of their group toward her first class. "Oh, and Genevieve, just so you know, a lot of history and the supernatural go hand in hand, so you and your opinions can go stuff it."

"See you at lunch!" I call after Livi, trying to hide my smirk.

— • —

Finding Livi at lunch is never a difficult task. Today is no exception. After a brutal first day in AP English, I walk into the lunchroom and see Livi sitting on top of one of the tables picking through her tray of food. The bright pink streak through her ebony hair catches attention. The color changes at least once a month.

"Where's your food?" she asks, oblivious to all the sidelong glances that almost every male in the vicinity is throwing her way.

"English ran late, I'll wait for the line to die down a bit," I sigh as I sit down next to her. "Remind me why I decided to take so many hard classes this year?"

"Because you're brilliant and are going to be halfway done with college by the time you graduate." She slides her tray over to me. "Here, eat mine. The protein bar in my backpack sounds better than whatever that is."

I laugh and look down trying to figure out what is on the tray. It might be an enchilada, maybe? At least that's what I hope it is taking my first bite. Despite its unappealing look, the food tastes pretty decent, still not sure what it is though.

"Look at this picture that Chad posted." Livi leans over and shows me her phone screen. "I look hideous."

I roll my eyes. Livi couldn't look hideous if she tried. She has perfect skin; I don't think I have ever seen her get a zit. Her makeup is always exquisite and she pulls off her drastic A-line hairstyle flawlessly.

"You look great, Liv," I say in between bites.

"I still don't get why your parents won't let you guys have any sort of social media. It's stupid."

"I don't really think I'm missing out on much."

Livi takes a bite out of her protein bar. "I still think it's ridiculous. Everyone has social media."

"My parents don't have social media, either," I point out.

Livi gives me an irritated look. "Okay, everyone in the world besides the Clark family has social media. You guys are just weirdos."

The bell rings. Laughing, I gulp down my food and finish eating. Livi slides off the table and heads to class with a backward glance and a wave. Gathering my stuff, I drop my tray off and wonder if my teachers are trying to set a record for how much homework can be assigned on the first day of school.

— • —

After school, Konnie and I find Livi lying on the hood of her Mustang, sunbathing in the South Carolina sun.

"How long have you been working on that tan, Livi?" I ask.

Livi's skin is pale and never tans during the summer, no matter how hard she tries, but she also never burns or gets a million freckles like I do if I am in the sun too long. She almost looks like a porcelain doll.

"I haven't been out here that long. Mrs. Gnighting told Mr. Hollman about my skirt and he said I needed to change my clothes." Livi rolls her eyes. "I went home to change and never went back to class."

I am pretty sure Mr. Hollman, our principal, has Livi's mom, Darla, on speed dial. I feel bad for Darla, who's always getting calls about Livi and her behavior. I'm sure she will be getting a call today if she hasn't already.

I look at Livi and raise my eyebrows. "Skipping class on the first day. That must be a new record for you."

Livi slides off the hood and climbs into the driver's seat. Taking a peek at her makeup in the mirror, she tucks her ebony hair behind her ear.

"Have to make sure I soak up these last days of summer. Did you decide about the ghost tour?"

"A ghost tour sounds fun. Can I come with?" asks Konnie.

"Sorry Konn, ghost tours are for big girls. We'll take you next time we go out for ice cream," Livi says with a snide smile.

Konnie looks irate. It drives me crazy that Livi treats her like she's a baby. It's irritating she always wants to tag along, but I don't want to hurt her feelings. Before Livi can say anything else, I jump in with, "Sorry Konnie. Liv is paying, and with all the new additions to her wardrobe I'm pretty sure her allowance is dwindling." Turning to Livi, I say, "She isn't two anymore, so stop being a brat. As a matter of fact, why don't you take Konnie on the tour with you? She actually wants to go."

Livi just laughs. "Do you guys want a ride home or not?" Konnie looks at me with a hurt expression, but we throw our backpacks into the back seat and pile into the car.

"Have you made a decision about the ghost tour?" Livi asks again.

I shrug my shoulders. "Sure, as long as my mom says I can go, and you promise you aren't going to try to sneak into any college parties."

I think back to the first week of summer break. Livi and I decided to kick our summer off right with a day at the beach, which ended up with Livi trying to get into a party. A big crowd of college kids were having a huge summer kickoff event at one of the beach houses. We didn't even make it through the door. Livi in her skimpy scarlet bikini probably would have been able to sweet talk her way in if she didn't have me tagging along in my black polka dot one piece and a huge sun hat with terror etched onto my face.

The sunhat has been a cause of contention between us for years. Livi hates it, but I would rather avoid adding more freckles on my already freckled face. Not to mention that I burn anytime I am out in the sun if I don't slather on an extreme amount of sunscreen. Livi regularly teases me that I could get sunburned if someone leaves a lamp on too long.

Livi's voice brings me back to the present. "Oh my gosh, I did that one time, and we didn't even get into the party. I promise we'll drive straight to the ghost tour and then home afterward." She pulls up to my house. "Now, get your butts out of my car."

Konnie and I have just enough time to get out of the car and shut the door before Livi speeds away. Konnie gives me a skeptical look. "I doubt Livi is going straight to the tour and back."

I sigh. "I know, but at least if I'm with her she won't get into as much trouble."

"Who are you kidding? Nobody can get into trouble if you're there," Konnie giggles.

I give Konnie a shove toward the house. "Whose side are you on, anyway?"

"Neither. You're both crazy," Konnie jokes, as she dodges another shove, and runs inside the house.

Chapter 2

Steve

If you would have asked me last year where I would be my senior year of high school, I wouldn't have been able to imagine the reality I am living in.

Drying my hair after a quick shower I sigh, remembering that wearing a uniform is required here. I never would have thought that I would be starting my senior year of high school at a boarding school, but here I am. Don't get me wrong, the Charleston Academy campus is awesome, it has really cool, old brick buildings nestled near the ocean. The glistening water can be seen over the tops of the buildings when I look out my Boone Hall Dormitory room window. Boone Hall is an old building that has been completely updated. Everything is pristine and new, but it is so far away from home.

Away from Gran.

Groaning, I look around my musty dorm room and the stacks of boxes piled everywhere. I really should finish unpacking. Probably should have spent more time unpacking during the weekend instead of going to all the welcome parties. Good thing I don't have a roommate to worry about; I can leave my unpacked boxes on the empty side of the room for the whole school year. That way, when I convince Gran to let me come home, I don't have to pack anything back up.

Guilt hits me again as I walk to my first class at Charleston Academy. It's my own fault that I'm so far away. If I hadn't gotten expelled from Brookhaven High, I wouldn't be here. Gran made it really clear that this is my last chance.

I better make it work.

Last year I was able to stay home and do school online. I thought it was fun; I got to wake up when I wanted to, do my school whenever, and still hang out with my friends when I wanted. It was fun, until I realized that it's easy to miss things with online school if you don't read every word the teacher posts. I thought I was doing okay until I flunked out of the first online school. Gran thought it wasn't the right fit for me, so we tried another online school. I flunked out of that one too. That is when Gran had the idea to get a hold of an old friend, Mr. Langston, who taught at a boarding school in Charleston, South Carolina.

At first I thought she was joking, trying to make me take school more seriously. I didn't think she would actually send me away. Next thing I knew, Gran was packing up her things along with mine and getting her house ready to rent out to tourists. I fought her like crazy; I still don't understand why she moved into an assisted living facility. I know she was struggling with a lot of her regular daily activities, but I was there and I was helping her with anything she needed help with. She told me I should be out living my life while I am young, not taking care of an old lady.

I would rather take care of an old lady than be 737 miles away from her. She is all I have left.

A fancy foreign sports car speeds past me and parks next to my old, beat-up, green Jeep, pulling me out of my self-torture. I watch Troy, a new classmate I met at one of the parties over the weekend, climb out and look at my Jeep with a disgusted look on his face.

"Hey, Troy, nice car."

His face changes as soon as he sees me. "Is that your Jeep?" he asks pointing over his shoulder toward my car as he walks toward me.

"Yep. Paid for it myself." I was so excited when I saved up enough money to get my own car. It may be old, but I love it.

"Cool. Vintage."

I laugh. "That's one way to look at it I guess."

"I don't know why I even bother bringing my car to school. It's almost impossible to get a pass to drive off campus."

My already foul mood plummets even further. "Really? I was hoping to be able to explore the area a little bit."

"Yeah, it's really hard to get a pass. They usually only approve passes if a parent requests it, and if you get caught leaving without a pass it's not good.

A senior last year got expelled for driving to the beach at Isle of Palms without permission."

"Well, that sucks."

"At least we're allowed to walk off campus without a pass, as long as we're back before curfew."

Charleston Academy is only a short walk from the historic downtown Charleston. At least I will be able to do a little bit of exploring. I watch as Troy pulls out the newest iPhone to check the time; another reminder I don't fit in here. All the students here have the newest, fanciest versions of everything. Phones, clothes, cars—you name it, and they have the model that comes out next year. There is no way Gran would be able to afford tuition here. The only reason I got into Charleston Academy is because Mr. Langston pulled some strings to get me in and helped me apply for some scholarships. How he even found scholarships to apply for with my grades baffles me.

All of that doesn't matter, though. The truth is I should be home helping Gran. She shouldn't be living in an assisted living facility.

Right after the accident that killed my parents, my paternal grandparents, and my little brother, Jeremy, Gran came to the hospital. She held my hand and told me not to worry; she was there and everything would be okay. I didn't know then that my entire world had changed.

"Where are you from again?" Troy's questions snaps me back to the present. He slides his new shiny phone back in his pocket and gives me his full attention.

"Brookhaven, Mississippi." Moving after the accident, from the bustling city of Atlanta to a quiet little town in Mississippi, was a big change. Gran usually came to visit us; I barely remembered her house when it suddenly became my home. Gran made that little house feel like the best place on Earth.

"I have no idea where that is." Troy chuckles. "Sounds cool though. What made you transfer schools for your senior year?"

"I was an idiot and punched my principal in the face. In my defense, he deserved it."

Troy's eyebrows shoot up. "Really?"

I nod. "Don't worry, I'm not planning on making a habit out of punching authority figures."

Laughing, Troy slaps me on the back. "Not going to lie, there are some faculty members here that I would love to see you punch in the face, but try and stick around a while. I like you."

I follow Troy into my first class of the day and wonder why I always seem to find trouble. I swear I try to avoid it, but trouble likes to find me. Poor Gran. I love her with everything that I am, but I have definitely been a problem child. I don't try to get into these crazy situations, they just happen. Like when Gran took me to the beach when I was eleven.

I don't even remember what beach we went to, but one morning Gran woke me up bright and early and told me to get into the car. We drove for what seemed like forever and then there it was right in front of us. I had never seen the ocean before and seeing the endless water, feeling the salty mist on my face, was the best thing I could remember ever experiencing. We unloaded the car and walked down by the water where Gran spread out our towels and stuck a big umbrella in the sand for shade. We spent the day playing in the water and building big elaborate sand castles.

When your grandma is an artist, only a masterpiece is acceptable.

Gran read a book, while I dug a trench where the waves washed up onto the beach. Sand coated me from head to toe, knowing the waves could rinse it off I decided to wade out into the ocean. Soon the water was so deep my toes couldn't touch the ground, instead of going back to shallow water I continued to swim around for a bit. There was quite the current sweeping down the shoreline so when I came back to shore to dig in the sand some more, Gran wasn't there. Nothing looked the same. Panicked I searched all the faces on the beach for Gran, unfortunately walking in the wrong direction. Long story short, it was already dark when another family helped me find a lifeguard, who was able to help locate my frantic grandma. I thought she was going to break at least one of my bones in her vice-grip hug when she saw me.

Now I don't have to take a long drive to see the ocean, I just have to look out my window. The bell rings and I follow the rest of the students out of the classroom and pull out my schedule. My next class is History of Charleston with Gran's friend, Mr. Langston, as my teacher. I find his classroom and pick a desk in the back row next to Troy. I'm not sure how I ended up with a history class as an elective; a downfall of having Mr. Langston help me with my schedule, I guess.

Mr. Langston appears at the front of the room. I didn't even see him walk in. He smiles at the whole class and finds me at the back with his eyes before continuing. "Welcome to your History of Charleston course. Most of you have been at Charleston Academy for several years now. Can any of you tell me some of the main historical facts about Charleston?"

A girl at the front raises her hand. "Charleston is the oldest city in South Carolina."

"That is correct. It was founded in 1670; it was named Charles Town and actually located where Charles Towne Landing is now. It didn't move to its current location until 1680."

Troy raises his hand next to me. "Wasn't it, like, one of the biggest cities or something?"

"Yes. It was the fourth largest colonial city and the wealthiest. Anyone else?"

"I think a war started in Charleston," another student says.

"A war did start in Charleston. On April 12, 1861 the Civil War officially started at Fort Sumter in the Charleston Harbor."

Mr. Langston pauses and looks around the room for a minute before continuing. "Charleston had the privilege of having the first playhouse, the first museum, the first golf club and the first public college in the United States. It's also known as being one of the most haunted cities in America. How many of you went on one of the ghost tours in town this weekend?"

I raise my hand with several other students. I have never really cared for history class in school before. Spouting off facts and reading textbooks never appealed to me, but I was surprised with how much I liked the tour I went on over the weekend. Turns out that listening to true stories—especially *creepy* true stories—while walking around the actual places the stories took place is really interesting.

When I got to campus on Friday, Mr. Langston helped me get settled in my dorm and gave me a tour of campus, then helped me find all the welcome-to-campus activities that were going on. He told me about the ghost tour multiple times, so I figured I should check it out.

"If any of you liked the ghost tour, I help out a local tour company that does ghost tours around the historic part of Charleston. Every semester a few kids from my classes have the opportunity to work for the tour company. You get paid and you get extra credit in my class if you sign up."

That sounds interesting. It would be a good way to get off campus, get myself some spending money, and help with my grades. Well, my grade in history class, at least.

The rest of the class goes by quickly. Mr. Langston has a way of making history super interesting and I am surprised to realize I am enjoying my time in class. I am actually a little disappointed when it ends.

On my way out, I stop at Mr. Langston's desk. "I want to sign up for helping with the tours, if I can."

"I was hoping you would sign up. How is your first day going?"

"Okay. Just trying to find my way to all my classes without being late."

Mr. Langston chuckles. "Yeah, Charleston Academy is a bit more spread out than most high school campuses. We'll be meeting for training for the ghost tours this afternoon. I'll email you all the information."

"Thanks. I'm looking forward to it." I hurry out of the classroom and toward where I think my next class is.

— • —

After my last class I have a little break between school and when I am supposed to meet for the tour training. I call Gran while I walk to the tour office. She answers on the first ring, as usual.

"How was your first day of school, Hun?"

The sound of her kind voice makes me miss her even more. "It was good. This campus is crazy though. Some of the classes are so spread out I have to run from one to the other or I'll be late."

"Tell me all about the campus! Can you hear the ocean everywhere you go?"

After answering her first question she bombards me with more questions about my classes, campus, and the students.

"Are there any girls that have caught your eye?" she asks.

"Gran, I've been here for three and a half days, and most of that has been going on walking tours with Mr. Langston, or welcome parties. When would I have had time to pay attention to the girls around here?"

She laughs. "I know you; you don't have to pay attention to them, they find you all on their own. How is Xavier?"

"Mr. Langston is good, Gran. How do you know him again?"

"That's old news, Stevie Boy, but I have to run. They're going to start Bingo without me if I don't get over there soon. Love you!"

She hangs up before I can respond. She keeps bringing up all the activities she is doing to make me feel better about her moving into the facility. I hope she is truly loving it and not just putting on a show for me.

After the tour training ends I am excited for my job to start, even if the thought of giving my own tour still makes me a little nervous. Not only are the stories interesting, but it is fun to see the reactions from the people in the tour groups as the stories are being told. Other than my worries about Gran, I think I may like this new city.

Chapter 3

Genevieve

I get my love of architecture from my dad, Tony. He says that even when he was a kid he was always doodling design ideas on everything. Growing up in the system, my dad didn't have anywhere to go when he turned eighteen, so he joined the Navy. Foster care was rough on him. He had a bad attitude about life and joining the Navy helped him get back on track. He has loved his career in the Navy and he does get to design things as a propulsion systems technical advisor, but I think that sometimes he wonders what life would have been like if he had pursued his architectural dreams.

I was little when Dad drew up the blueprints for the tree house, but I remember being enthralled watching it come together on paper, and I was even more excited when what Dad drew on the paper was actually there in the big willow tree in our front yard. After that, Dad and I have shared a mutual love of architecture, and I have known from the day I got to sit in that tree house that I wanted to be an architect. Dad and I started designing my dream house last year, and every spare minute we have is spent on the plans to add more. My favorite room so far is the gorgeous library; if there is anything that can compete with my love of architecture it is my love of reading.

I doodle a mini version of the library on the side of my homework before I realize what I'm doing, and try to get my focus back on the task at hand. Learning history from textbooks and memorizing dates really doesn't hold my attention. I hear the front door open and close while I try to memorize information about the invention of the steam engine and other important facts about the industrial revolution for my quiz tomorrow.

Dad walks in and kisses the top of my head. "Hey, Genna Bear. Want to work on those blueprints for a while?"

"Sure, Dad. That sounds great; I'm pretty much done with these chapter notes anyway."

Closing the book, I load everything that was on the table into my backpack before I follow Dad into his office where he is opening his safe and pulling out the blueprints we have been drafting. They aren't worth any money but Dad has always said if something happened to the house, he would want them protected. Soon we are both sucked into the designs and all the ideas we want to add.

"Wouldn't it be awesome if we actually got to build this house one day?" I ask.

Dad's brown eyes light up and a smile spreads across his face. "I have no doubt that one day you will build this dream house of yours, Genevieve."

Smiling, I think about how fun it was to watch the tree house move from paper to the front yard and I can't even imagine what it will be like to have this amazing house we are designing become a reality. Our concentration is interrupted by the doorbell and the sounds of Livi arriving. Mom has told Livi that she is welcome anytime, no need to knock, but she still rings the doorbell on her way into the house.

Livi walks in through the office door with a scowl on her face, fifteen minutes late, dressed much more conservatively than she was earlier in the day. "Are you ready to go?" she grumbles.

She is in a mood. Apparently, something has happened between school and now. I will have to get the full story on our drive to Charleston.

"Neither of you are going anywhere until you eat something," Mom says, pointing toward the table where Konnie is already sitting.

"Let's pick this back up tomorrow, Genna Bear," Dad says as he rolls up the blueprints and puts them away.

I follow Livi into the dining room, where she sits down and starts grabbing food. With a mouth full of biscuit she says, "M'kay, but we have to hurry, Mrs. C., or we'll be late for our tour."

I sit down and fill my plate.

"Where are you girls off to tonight?" Dad asks in between bites.

"Charleston, for a ghost tour," Livi says, with excitement in her voice. "It's going to be epic!"

Dad looks at me with raised eyebrows. He knows how much I hate getting scared. I couldn't even finish watching Jumanji with him. "Livi has a new love for anything haunted, and she said she was paying, so I figured I might as well tag along," I say.

"No need for that; I can give you girls some money for the tour. That sounds like fun."

Livi gulps her food down. "Thanks, Mr. T.! You're the best."

Dad has been in the Navy my entire life—I think it's been something, like, thirty-one years. He is a Chief Warrant Officer and works at the Naval Weapons Station, Joint Base Charleston. I have no idea what he actually does; he doesn't really talk about it. I think a lot of what he works on he isn't allowed to talk about. Even though Dad likes to keep his home and work life separate, we do get together for BBQ's and such with his fellow officers regularly. We have known his commanding officer, Admiral Smith, for as long as I can remember.

My dad is an expert in what he does, and he is gone a lot, but still active in parenting us. He makes it a point to be home for family dinner whenever possible. Apparently, whatever he does has made it so that he doesn't get transferred much anymore. Most of the moving around was done before my parents decided to start a family. They had kids later in life; Dad had just turned thirty-two the week before my older sister Violet was born. He was deployed on a ship so much when we were little that Mom decided to stay in Moncks Corner by her parents for support. Until we started school we would be with Dad anytime he was on land, but when he was on the ship we were at Grandma and Grandpa's house.

We would travel to see Dad when possible but home was always Moncks Corner. When the house next to my grandparents went up for sale my parents decided to buy it. We lived next to Grandma and Grandpa until they passed away; Grandpa five years ago and Grandma just last year. It has been hard on Mom, losing her parents and then watching her childhood house next door sell and new people move in. The new neighbors seem nice enough, but it is weird not being able to walk into Grandma's house to say 'hi' and grab a cookie whenever I want.

Mom was super close with Grandma. They did everything together and after Grandpa died, Grandma spent most of her time at our house. I honestly don't know why she didn't just move in with us. I guess she wanted her own space, but enjoyed our company. I have so many memories of all of us girls going to get pedicures together. Grandma always had perfect nails. She went to get them done once a week and sometimes Mom would tag along and bring us with her. Mom was Grandma and Grandpa's only child, so poor Grandpa was outnumbered by the ladies of the family.

Grandma is actually why Livi and I met. She was always doing things to help others out and helping the ladies at church with anything they needed. She really was an amazing role model.

Livi and her mom, Darla, moved to Moncks Corner after a nasty divorce. Darla didn't have much. She had just graduated nursing school and got a job at our small hospital. She had never been to Moncks Corner before and didn't know anyone. Grandma took her under her wing and watched Livi for Darla while she worked. Mom and Darla became fast friends and I had an instant best friend. Livi was three, I had just turned four, and we have been inseparable ever since. Livi and I were always attached at the hip and Violet was always with us when she wasn't dancing.

"Genevieve, did you call your sister?" Mom asks, startling me out of my thoughts.

I shake my head. It has been a busy few days and I completely forgot to call Violet. We usually sit and give each other a play-by-play of the first day of school after we get home. Hers is mostly about boys and what happened with the other students during the day, mine is usually about my classes. This year is different though. I am still home and she is at Julliard in New York City.

Violet and I are Irish twins. She was born in December and I surprised everyone by coming a month earlier than I was supposed to the next year in October, making us only ten months apart. Where I seem to have gotten all the book smarts, Violet has all of the talent. She is the best dancer I have ever seen. I know I am biased, but she is amazing. I wasn't surprised at all when she got her acceptance into Julliard. I think my parents were hoping for a school that was a little more affordable, but when your daughter makes it into Julliard, you figure it out.

"I think she's feeling weird," Mom says. "She's out of her element being without you and starting college all at the same time."

"It's Violet, Mom, she'll be totally fine. When has she ever needed anyone to help her out?"

"She's still human Genevieve, and I know she's missing everyone as much as we're missing her."

"I'll call her tomorrow," I say. Mom gives me a look that only a mother can give. "I promise."

Everyone is quiet for a minute while we inhale Mom's delicious fried chicken. She can pretty much cook anything she sets her mind to, and it is always sooooooo good. Not only is her food delicious, but it is beautiful too. Her talent for making things beautiful doesn't stop at food; she also has an amazing eye for decorating.

Our house is always decorated perfectly, like, magazine worthy decor. I never realized it until I started going to friends' houses and they actually looked lived in. Certain rooms in our house do look lived in, just not any of the front rooms that company can see.

Mom loves to entertain. Our birthday parties growing up were epic. I think Mom finds us boring now that we are teenagers and just want our friends and pizza on our birthdays. Where Mom is a social butterfly, Dad is a little bit awkward.

He is the best Dad and always up for whatever any of us girls want to do, almost like he is one of the kids. So many times he has gotten in trouble right along with us, for joining in some of our shenanigans. One time, Violet and I got into a food fight in the kitchen when we were supposed to put the dinner leftovers in the fridge. When he walked in and caught us, we were terrified, then shocked when he picked up a spoonful of mashed potatoes and joined right in. Mom was NOT happy when she found us. Dad was on the floor with us, scrubbing until the kitchen was back to its usual shiny perfection. He is also the type of person who isn't a fan of silence and always needs to fill a lull in the conversation. Today is no exception.

"I've got a new one for you girls," he says.

Konnie, Livi, and I all groan. Dad loves corny dad jokes. Like really, really loves them. I have no idea where he comes up with them. I half wonder if he sits and searches the internet for them instead of working.

"After an unsuccessful harvest, why did the farmer decide to try a career in music?" he asks.

We all just stare at him while we continue to chew our food.

"Oh, come on guys!" he says.

"I don't know, why?" Konnie finally responds.

Dad's face lights up. "Because he had a ton of sick beets."

I can't help it. I chuckle a little bit. "That was pretty bad, Dad."

He laughs and takes another bite of chicken.

Livi looks at her cell phone and jumps up. "If we don't leave right now, we won't make it on time."

I take a few more bites, grab my hoodie, follow Livi out the door, and climb into her car. Dad runs out of the house to catch up to us and hands Livi a fifty-dollar bill through the window.

"You girls have fun tonight. Make sure you both stay together and keep track of each other."

"Don't worry about us getting into any trouble. You've met your daughter, right?"

Dad laughs. "You have a point there, Livi."

"You know, Dad, most parents would be grateful they have a daughter that likes to follow all the rules. Not give them grief about it," I sigh.

"Oh, I am grateful, Genna Bear, but I have to be able to tease you about something, don't I?" Dad rumples my hair and plants a kiss on my head before Livi starts to back out of the driveway.

Chapter 4

Steve

The fog is so thick it looks like we're driving through white cotton candy. Jeremy thinks if we stick our hands out the window, we could grab some and eat it. I've never seen anything like it, almost like we're driving through the clouds up in the sky. I always wondered if you could sit on a cloud like they do in the cartoons.

Mom seems really nervous; she tells Dad to slow down and pull over until the fog lifts. Dad tells her we just need to get through it; we're following Grandpa and Grandma and there is no cell service to tell them if we were to stop. It's so crazy; I know Grandma and Grandpa are in the car just in front of us but I can't see them at all.

I think the fog is neat, but Mom is really scared now and I am starting to wonder if I should be scared too. Mom doesn't normally get so upset with Dad.

All of a sudden, I can see Grandma and Grandpa's car. It's too late for Dad to stop and I can hear the screeching tires and crunching metal as we plow into the back of their car.

Mom is screaming, asking if we're okay and trying to wake Dad up.

Dad lays on the steering wheel, like he's asleep, except he's bleeding. The blood runs down his head, over his cheek, and starts to drip onto the floor.

More tires screeching, metal screaming, our car is shoved even farther into Grandma and Grandpa's car. Mom isn't screaming anymore. I can't hear anything but a loud ringing coming from inside my own head. Somehow, over the ringing, I can still hear the drip, drip, drip of Dad's blood. Or maybe it's my own blood now.

Then everything goes black.

I startle awake and try to calm myself down. I must have fallen asleep while doing my homework. My heart is beating so hard I can feel my pulse in my fingers and toes. Definitely need a shower; sweat is dripping off of my body. It has been such a long time since the last nightmare of the accident. I still wonder why I survived. Why did I have to stay behind and live my life without them, and why were the best people I knew taken away from me?

My training for the tours is finished and tonight is my first solo tour. I won't even have another tour guide with me if I forget part of a story. My stomach is in knots, and I can't figure out why. Sure, it will be my first time doing a tour by myself, but I am used to being in front of a crowd.

Playing in front of crowds with my band was an almost-every-weekend occurrence, and freshman year at Brookhaven High the student body elected me as class president. Heck, half the time I didn't even know what was going to come out of my mouth. Standing up in front of the whole school during assemblies and just winging it was never hard and I never really worried about looking dumb in front of everyone.

I guess it is easy not to be embarrassed when you know that everyone likes you. It also helps that I've known all my Brookhaven classmates since I moved to Gran's when I was ten. I am sure I am not everyone's cup of tea (for instance, my old principal at Brookhaven High), but so far I haven't really had to work that hard to make someone smile.

I guess I should probably put some of this nervous energy to work and finish unpacking my dorm room. I want to make this feel like my space, but at the same time there is a part of me that hopes Gran will call and say that she hates her new living situation and she wants me to come home immediately. It's not going to happen. I already tried convincing her to just let me get my GED. She would have none of that.

"Stevie Boy, you need to have a senior year—experience dances, football games, and graduation. Don't just sit around with a decrepit old lady, wasting your life away."

I laugh thinking of Gran and her spunk. How anyone could think she was decrepit is beyond me. That lady has more fire and spunk in her than anyone I know. I don't understand why she feels like I would be wasting any time spent with her. I think the main reason she doesn't want me to see her this frail is her own pride.

I open a box and right on top are the photos I brought from home. Gran bought me frames for all the pictures that I wanted to take. I pull them out one at a time: Gran and I at the Fourth of July celebration last year; Jake, my old band mate, and I playing on stage, him on guitar and me on the drums; the last family photo that I took with my parents and little brother.

I close the box. Maybe I should try to do my homework again instead. I pull my math book out of my backpack and start working on today's work.

The alarm on my phone snaps me back to reality. Time to walk to work; the anxiety of my first solo tour comes back in full force. I pull on my shoes and make my way to the tour office. It is only about a five-minute walk and I get there quickly. While waiting to find out what tour groups I will have today I look through the tourist brochures in the office. I am definitely going to have to check out the Magnolia Plantation; it looks super cool. Cypress Gardens is in a place called Moncks Corner; I might have to check that out, too. It says it is a black water swamp. Sounds interesting and weird at the same time, I'm not too sure about black water.

Mr. Langston walks up. "You're giving two Charleston Haunts tours today. The first one starts in twenty minutes."

I let out my breath; I didn't even know I was holding it. "Well, I guess I'm glad I only have two tours on my first solo day."

Mr. Langston squeezes my shoulder. "You'll do great."

I walk to the meeting spot for the tour and gather the small group. It consists of two couples and a family of four. I stand in front of the group and introduce myself. "Hi everyone! My name is Steve, and I'll be your guide tonight. Are you guys ready for a terrifying time?"

After a chorus of yeses, we walk down the street toward White Point Gardens. I tell some interesting and some spooky facts about different places as we walk by. When we get to White Point Gardens, we walk into the shady park. The reprieve from the sweltering South Carolina sun is a relief, but doesn't do much to alleviate the relentless heat and humidity.

The park is beautiful and the walkways are lined with old oak trees covered with Spanish moss. There is something about the long lines of tress with moss hanging from them that makes you feel like you are in a different world. It is eerie and magical.

We walk past numerous monuments until we reach the northeast corner of the park. There is no one in this part of the park; I don't think I have ever seen anyone over here on all the tours I have gone on. It just feels wrong over here.

We gather around a weathered monument. "This monument is dedicated to Stede Bonnett, a pirate nicknamed the Gentleman Pirate. He was a wealthy man and a landowner. According to rumors his marriage was not the healthiest and drove him over the edge, turning his high society life into a life of crime."

I let the group inspect the monument for a few minutes before continuing the story. "He was a terror all along the East Coast plundering ships until his capture in 1718. After his capture he and his entire crew were sentenced to be hanged. All thirty pirates were hung in this area of the park and their bodies were buried right next to the park in the marsh, just past the low water mark."

"The pirates weren't the only unfortunate souls to be hanged in this beautiful space. Between 1718 and 1849 there were almost two hundred documented hangings and at least two people listed as being gibbeted. Gibbeting is when they would hang a dying or dead criminal in a cage-like contraption, leaving them on display as they decayed to deter others from turning to crime."

We walk back toward the tour office. "It's hard to imagine this beautiful park being anything but serene, but it's far from peaceful as the restless ghosts of the past haunt these grounds. There have been reports of orbs, cold spots, and apparitions. But the most seen and heard ghosts are those of the Gentleman Pirate and his crew, wandering the park, waiting for their ship to return."

As the group disperses several of the members tell me that they really enjoyed the tour. Smiling, I thank them. I'm not sure what I was so worried about, once the tour started it was easy, and even fun. Hopefully, those poor little kids don't have nightmares.

My body relaxes and I go sit in the tour office to cool down before my next tour. It's another Charleston Haunts tour. I feel calm; this next tour will be easy.

Chapter 5

Genevieve

I love the playful banter between Livi and I, but I also love that we can talk about anything. We know everything about each other but, if we need to, we can sit in comfortable silence without feeling awkward.

"You didn't look very happy when you picked me up tonight. Wanna talk about it?" I ask.

Livi runs her fingers through her hair. "Not really. Mr. Hollman called my mom. It didn't go over so well. She threw the skirt I wore on the first day of school in the trash. It cost me over forty dollars!"

"How on earth could something with that little fabric cost forty dollars? And why on earth would you spend that much money on it?"

I squeal, while trying to dodge whatever Livi can get her hands on to throw at me. It worked though. Soon, we're both laughing.

"It was cute, that's why. Plus, I'm going to get the hottest boyfriend possible for senior year."

"Liv, I have a feeling that you aren't going to attract the kind of attention you want if you're waltzing around in practically your underwear everywhere you go."

Livi lets out a long breath. "Ugh. If I tell you that I think you might be right, will it go straight to your head?"

"Probably," I laugh. "Unless I die of shock first."

"Well, I'm not planning on dressing like you anytime soon, but I did get whistled at by a guy who was missing most of his teeth while I was filling up my car with gas. So, you might be right." Livi giggles and I can't help but join in.

Livi cranks up the music and we spend the rest of the drive singing at the top of our lungs with the convertible top down.

It takes almost an hour to drive the roughly thirty-five miles from my house to the historic part of downtown Charleston. Driving down Hwy 52 is mostly dense trees on both sides of the highway. The trees are so thick it almost feels like you are driving through a tunnel.

The warm, humid air whips my hair around my face as we drive. I love the feel of the wind on my face. It makes me feel free. It isn't until our speed increases as we get onto the interstate that I wish the convertible's top was up.

The trees give way to buildings as we get closer to the ocean. Charleston's historic downtown really is beautiful, nestled right up against the water. Rainbow Row is one of my favorite places to look at. Beautiful historic mansions, painted all sorts of different bright colors, line the coast. Livi doesn't drive down to Rainbow Row this time though. We drive past Charleston Academy and start looking for a parking space near the Charleston Historic City Market.

We find a place to park (which, is almost impossible.) Livi squeezes into a spot, I'm not even sure it's a real parking space, and starts touching up her makeup in the mirror. I roll my eyes. Livi adores her makeup. She has a perfect complexion, colorful eyes, and bronzed cheeks. I wear mascara and the occasional eyeliner. It drives Livi crazy that I could care less about makeup. She is always trying to convince me to let her do my makeup anytime we go anywhere. We climb out of the car and walk toward the tour office.

"What tour are we going on?" I ask.

"The Charleston Haunts tour. Doesn't it sound awesome?" She turns to me and grabs my arm. "I hope I get super spooked. Wouldn't it be the best night ever if we see a ghost?"

Livi regularly doesn't wait for anyone to answer before she asks her next question when she gets excited. Sometimes it is hard to get a word in at all.

"Not gonna lie, Livi, I'm totally okay with not seeing a ghost or getting spooked. I still don't know how I let you talk me into this."

Livi glares at me. "Oh, lighten up, would you? It'll be fun! And it's supposed to be scary; if it isn't spooky then we wasted our money."

"You wasted my dad's money, you mean."

Livi stalks ahead and gets in line at the ticket office. After we buy our tickets, we have a few minutes before the tour starts and we sit down to wait.

26

"Don't be mad Livi; you know I don't like being scared. This should just prove I care about your interests and want you to have fun." I look at Livi. "Truce?"

"Truce, but I'm not going to refrain from laughing if you scream like a little girl on the tour. Especially if we see a ghost!" Livi giggles.

People start to gather at the meeting spot, so we join them. Livi is bouncing with excitement. I try not to roll my eyes at her.

The tour guide comes out of the office and walks up to our group. "Hi everyone! My name is Steve and I'll be your guide tonight. Are you guys ready for a terrifying time?"

My jaw drops. Steve is the most gorgeous guy I have ever seen. He has light brown hair cut short, a goatee, and the most piercing blue eyes. I missed most of what he said because I was so distracted by those eyes.

They have to be contacts right? Nobody's eyes could actually be that bright blue, I think to myself.

Livi looks over at me and smirks. "Has someone caught Genevieve's attention? He's definitely hot, but not my type. Not enough tattoos," Livi laughs. "You might want to close your mouth, though, and stop staring; you look like a creeper."

I snap my mouth shut and feel a ferocious blush appear on my cheeks. "Shut up, Livi. He may be hot, but he's obviously too old for us."

"Too old for you maybe. I need to find out if he has some cute friends," Livi says, and gives me a look that means she is up to something. "Come on, let's go introduce ourselves!"

Livi grabs my arm and pulls me along with her to meet him. My stomach drops. It is the closest thing to pure terror I have ever felt.

What in the world is going on? I talk to boys at school every day. I have adequate skills to communicate with the opposite sex in my daily life, so why do I feel like Livi is marching me to my execution?

"Please no, Livi! Please stop. Let's just stay at the back of the group," I plead. "It will be scarier if we are in the back with no one behind us. Probably more likely to see a ghost!"

Livi bursts out laughing while continuing to drag me toward the front of the group. "You've got it bad, girl. I don't want to miss anything, so we need to be up front and center where all the action is."

In seconds, we are at the front of the group and Livi is introducing herself. My brain shuts off when he looks directly at me.

They have to be contacts. Or he isn't human. One or the other, I think.

I have no idea what Livi is rambling on about. It's like I am underwater and no sound can reach me except the deafening noise of my heart pounding.

I can see his mouth moving, but the thumping in my ears makes it difficult to interpret what he is saying. I should say something.

Why are his eyes so stinking blue? I ask myself.

What did he say?

OH MY GOSH. I think I might die of embarrassment. Can you die from embarrassment?

Livi elbows me. "Dude, he asked you where you're from and if you've ever been on a ghost walk before."

My poor brain is still having trouble translating words into something that I can understand. Why can I understand what Livi is saying, but not Steve?

"What?" I mumble.

Livi rolls her eyes. "We live in Moncks Corner and this is our first ghost tour. We're super excited!"

Steve looks at me, a question in his eyes, and smiles. It happens again, complete brain shut down. He turns away from us and leads the tour group down the street. I don't move.

"What in the heck is wrong with you?" Livi growls, while pulling on my arm to get me walking. "We lost our spot at the front of the group! Would you move your feet please?"

We follow Steve down the sidewalk. He is telling the group about famous ghosts that have been spotted in the different areas that we pass. I am trying hard to pay attention, but I just can't focus. School today must have worn me out a lot more than I thought it did.

Steve is still talking about ghosts and ushers us into White Point Gardens. He stops the group around an old monument and starts talking again. Normally, I would be scared listening to ghost stories. I'm not. Steve has a nice sounding deep voice, it is soothing. I don't think anything could be scary while he is talking. Maybe if I actually understood the words he was saying it would be a lot scarier, but my brain is still having trouble interpreting the English language. At least I am still walking. Right? My brain is still functioning a little bit at least.

Too soon, the tour is over and we are back at the corner that we started on. I look at my phone and see that the tour lasted about an hour and a half. What?! I can hardly remember a single thing that was said, or anything that I looked at, if I'm being honest. It's like I'm missing a chunk of time in my memory. I can, however, remember exactly what our tour guide's eyes look like and the soothing sound of his deep voice as he told us about all of the stuff I didn't pay any attention to on the tour.

Next thing I know, we are back at the office and the group is dispersing. Steve walks up to us with that gorgeous smile and says, "It was nice to meet you two. I've never made it up to Cypress Gardens. That's in Moncks Corner, right? I want to check it out sometime."

I mumble something incoherent.

"Well, here you go, ladies." He hands us each a coupon. "Come back for another tour. I work every Tuesday, Thursday, and Friday evenings. Oh, and every other Saturday."

I just stare at him. Maybe I'm having a mental breakdown. My mom is always telling me that I take too many hard classes at one time. You would think it would take more than a few days of my senior year before losing my mind, but I cannot put anything together to form a coherent thought. He turns and walks toward the office.

"Well, apparently he's into weirdos." Livi looks at me like I am an alien. "Because you're being such a weirdo tonight."

"What do you mean?"

"Genevieve, were you not paying attention at all? He was talking to you multiple times during the tour. Not that you ever responded to him, you were walking around like a zombie."

"He did?" Oh man! I must have looked like such an idiot. Did he really ask me questions and I didn't respond? I guess it isn't that far-fetched since he just asked me questions and I couldn't remember how to talk. How embarrassing.

"Ummmm yeah, and then he gave us coupons to come back."

"He probably gave everyone coupons."

"Definitely didn't. Not to mention, he told you what days he works." Livi smacks my shoulder. "Ugh, Genevieve, what is your deal?"

I look at Livi and try hard to focus. "I don't know, Liv. I don't even remember a single word that was said on the tour. Was it scary? Did you see his eyes?"

Livi bursts out laughing. "No, it wasn't freaking scary because I was more worried about you going brain dead the whole time. 'His eyes!' Holy cow, girl, when you crush, you crush *hard*. I thought we might go our entire high school career without you wanting to date at all."

I sigh. "I don't have a crush on him; I was just a little distracted. Plus, he's too old for me to date anyway."

Livi looks at me like I have two heads. "He told the group that he's a senior at Charleston Academy. In case you forgot, we're seniors too."

I don't say anything and Livi continues her rant. "Even if he was out of high school, you turn eighteen in October. Jealous about that, by the way. Why does my birthday have to be in July?" Livi lets out an exaggerated sigh.

"I'll admit he's good looking, but that's about it. I wasn't really paying attention because I didn't want to get scared. We were on a tour that was supposed to scare us, you know."

Livi eyes me skeptically as she unlocks the car. "Uh-huh. Sure. Whatever you say, weirdo."

Once again I can feel the blush creeping up my cheeks. Without making a sound, I get into the car and buckle up.

Chapter 6

Steve

A cool breeze off the ocean is a welcome relief from the muggy heat. There is something about the sound of the waves that calms me. The salt in the air sticking to your skin, the steady rhythm of the waves, and the vastness of the water, there really is no comparable feeling to standing near the ocean. I really enjoy spending so much time in the historic downtown part of the city and the fact that I can see the water for most of my day makes it even better.

My first day of solo tours went well, kinda. I remembered all the stories and the groups seemed like they were enjoying the tours, but my last tour tonight was interesting. I have always been pretty confident when talking to girls and, not to toot my own horn or anything, I've never had issues with girls being interested in me and have never been turned down when asking someone on a date. Maybe it gave me a big head. At some point I was going to run into someone who didn't want anything to do with me. I just wasn't expecting it to be the most beautiful girl I have ever seen. When the two girls walked up to the tour group tonight I had to catch my breath.

Her friend introduced her as Genevieve. She wasn't wearing very much makeup and almost looked a little bit nerdy with her Bermuda shorts and T-shirt with a hoodie tied around her waist. But her long auburn hair and deep green eyes were intoxicating. When she threw her head back and laughed at something her friend, Livi, said I was hooked.

Except, I tried to talk to her the entire tour and she didn't even respond most of the time. Livi was quite the chatter box. I was a little bit hesitant to ask them to come back, but I couldn't let them leave without trying to catch her attention. I gave them coupons for another tour and told them my work schedule. She didn't even smile. Livi grabbed them and thanked me and pulled Genevieve down the street.

It is starting to get dark and the lights from the city are shimmering on the water. I didn't expect Genevieve to stick with me like this. She didn't even talk to me and I can't get her off my mind. Maybe it's because she is the first girl who wouldn't give me the time of day.

Why in the heck did I not ask for a number? I am sure Livi would have given me hers, but I didn't and I have no way of getting a hold of them, I don't even know their last names. And I am not holding my breath that they will be back.

I start walking back to campus but before I make it to my dorm building, I run into some of my new classmates. I can't remember their names. Names always stress me out. It takes forever for me to remember someone's name; I usually have to put a reminder of how I know them in my phone until I have been around them for a long time.

But Genevieve's name is already permanently engraved into my mind. I remember Livi's name too, not normal for me.

"Hey! You're Steve, right?" a petite blonde asks.

"Yeah, sorry, remind me of your name?"

"Kinsley, and this is Ava," she says, pointing to the girl next to her.

"That's right! Sorry, I'm trying to remember a lot of new names."

She smiles. "I'll let it slide this time. We're headed to a party at Magnolia Hall. Want to join?"

For a school that makes you get a pass to drive anywhere, they sure do allow a lot of parties. I should probably go back to my dorm and do more homework, or finish unpacking, but a party definitely sounds like more fun.

I follow them to Magnolia Hall's common area. There are a lot of students crammed into the space and the music is loud. Loud enough to make me forget about the girl who wouldn't give me the time of day and my worries about Gran.

I see Troy, he ended up being in most of my classes, but I haven't really talked to him much since that first day walking to class. He seems like a fun person. Troy is throwing darts at a dart board hung on the common room wall. I stand next to him and watch him throw.

"Not bad," I say.

He looks at me and smirks. "You think you can do better?"

"Well, it's worth giving it a try," I say. "Want to play 41?"

"Sure. Loser has to do a dare of the winner's choosing."

"Deal."

A crowd starts to form around us. 41 is a pretty simple game, you start with a score of forty-one and you have to get to zero. You can't go into the negatives and your last dart has to be a double. I win in three throws with a single nine and a double sixteen.

Thankfully Troy is a good sport. "All right, what's my dare?"

"Have you heard of the gallon challenge?"

Troy shakes his head.

"You have to chug a gallon of milk and try not to throw up."

"Sounds easy enough," Troy says, as Ava hands him a gallon of milk she pulled from one of the dorm refrigerators.

I am impressed when he almost gets the whole gallon down before throwing it back up. This starts a whole bunch of guys challenging me to games of 41.

I decide to take a break and go sit on one of the couches. It is too soft and almost swallows me when I sit on it. A group of girls makes their way over to introduce themselves. The ringleader is Kinsley and I am starting to realize she might be at the top of the social ladder here.

"So, Steve, do you have a girlfriend back home?" Kinsley asks.

"Not at the moment."

The whole group giggles and Genevieve pops back into my head. Dang it! I literally have a whole group of girls giving me attention and my brain decides to think about the one girl who ignored me. There has got to be something wrong with me.

Kinsley smiles. "Any girls back home that are missing you? Are you a heartbreaker?"

"Maybe a few. I usually had a girlfriend, but they never lasted very long."

"Well, maybe you were just dating the wrong girls." Kinsley winks.

"Yeah, probably." I try to give her a genuine smile.

I probably sound like a huge jerk. I have fun going on dates and hanging out with girls, but I have never had a relationship that I really wanted to continue after a couple of months. There just always seems to be something missing, and there was always someone new ready to take their place when I was ready to move on. I didn't try to sabotage the relationships, and I genuinely feel bad when I have to break up with someone, but I just can't seem to form a lasting connection to anyone.

Like Evie, my last girlfriend in Brookhaven. She was gorgeous and flirty and fun, but every time I tried to talk about anything other than gossip from school her eyes would glaze over. It got old after a while and I was glad for a reason to break up when I left for Charleston.

I have a feeling that Kinsley is a lot like Evie, but with more money. I'm not even sure why I am already getting so much attention here. Probably mostly because I am the new kid, or maybe it is the fact that I already grow an impressive amount of facial hair. That is nothing new; I had to start shaving in eighth grade. I think it helps, mostly because it makes me look older than a senior in high school.

It sounds super weird, but I wish I could find someone like Gran. She is a spitfire and always up for an adventure. She doesn't take crap from anyone, but she can have great conversations, deep conversations. She makes whoever she is talking to feel like they are the most important person in the world and she has always been my biggest fan in anything I do.

Even when I decided I wanted to play the drums in a garage band she came to every one of our gigs. When I joined a band called "The Barf Bags" I probably should have realized that we weren't ever going to be that great. We thought the name was funny at the time. But Gran was always there cheering us on. Girls from school would flock to the stage, but I don't think any of them really liked the music; they just wanted to be with guys in a band. The fact that our biggest fan—who am I kidding, our only real fan—was a seventy-four-year-old woman, probably should have given us a clue that we weren't going to make it big. It was fun while it lasted, but I won't be bringing up the topic of "The Barf Bags" at Charleston Academy. I guess it wouldn't hurt to say I played the drums in a band and hope nobody asks any questions.

Sitting on the couch surrounded by a group of girls, I realize that a lot of people back in Brookhaven and here at Charleston Academy know who I am. I am the fun guy, the guy who can always make everyone laugh, but it is just now dawning on me that I don't actually have any close friends.

I have only been in Charleston for a week, so it would be weird for me to have a close friend here already, but even in Brookhaven I don't have any close friends. I have a lot of people that I call friends, and my closest friend is my band mate Jake. We hung out almost every day in Brookhaven and we still text each other stupid memes almost daily, but I have never really talked to Jake about anything below the surface.

Now that I am thinking about it, the only person that I truly confide in about my actual thoughts and how I feel, is Gran. I am surrounded by a sea of people and I have never felt so alone.

I stand up. "Sorry ladies, I need to get back to my dorm to finish unpacking."

Kinsley looks irritated. Against a chorus of protests I leave the party and walk to my dorm.

The sound of the cicadas outside is loud enough tonight that I can't hear the sound of the ocean. I walk into my empty dorm room and shut the door behind me. My eyes wander over the room, full of boxes that I have yet to unpack. It reminds me of my life, never standing still long enough to get attached to anything. Deep down I think I feel like anything that I love will be taken away from me. The one family member I have left is hundreds of miles away and I have never missed anyone as much as I miss Gran and her feisty attitude in this moment.

September

Chapter 7

Genevieve

With my eyes still closed I groan and grope around on my nightstand to silence the obnoxious ringing of my phone. It takes a minute for me to realize that it's Violet, my older sister, calling.

"Why are you calling me so early, Vi?" I yawn into the phone. "Is everything okay?"

"Are you sick or something? You're usually up and ready for school by now."

"My dual credit classes are intense and I've been up late studying every night." I decide to leave out that studying had been more difficult than normal. My brain has waited for the most inconvenient time of my high school years to start daydreaming. Every time I see any shade of blue, I'm reminded of the tour guide's eyes. *What is wrong with me?*

"Well, don't burn yourself out, Sis. I thought you would call me after your first day, but didn't school start, like, two weeks ago?"

Oh crap! Has it really been two weeks already? I promised Mom I would call Violet the day after the ghost tour and totally spaced it. In my defense, it has been two weeks of the hardest classes I have ever taken. What happened to teachers starting off slow? Really bad timing for me not to be focused.

"I was planning on it Vi, sorry, I am struggling with my classes. I might need to get a tutor or something."

There is a long pause on the other end of the phone.

"Okay, spill. What is going on? You *are* the tutor. You have been helping me with my homework since you were in kindergarten. Which doesn't make me feel super smart, by the way. I'm the older sister. I should be helping you with your homework."

I groan. "I don't even know what's going on. So, I don't know what to tell you."

"Did something happen? Do I need to come home and kick someone's butt?" She continues, "What did Livi do? It must be Livi, right? Did she drug you?"

"Whoa, calm down, Vi," I laugh. "No, Livi didn't drug me. I'm fine. I've just been a little distracted. It's making it hard to focus."

Violet grunts. "Well, what did Livi do that has you so distracted?"

"Livi didn't do anything. Why do you always assume everything is Livi's fault?"

"Because I'm not there and the only time you get into any trouble is when you're trying to keep me or Livi out of trouble." She sighs. "It's kinda weird that you haven't called to check up on me, make sure I'm going to class and stuff all by myself."

"Well, are you going to class?"

"Most of the time."

"If I have to babysit you from five states away to make sure you're going to your college classes, I don't have a whole lot of confidence in you graduating. Do you want me to call you every morning and make sure you go to work after you graduate, too?" I snap.

"Ouch. That hurts. Of course, I'm going to class, I was kidding." She sounds hurt and I feel bad for snapping at her. "And no, I can wake myself up in the mornings now and after I graduate, thank you very much."

I sigh. "I didn't mean to snap at you, Vi."

"I was just calling to check in; we haven't gone this long without talking. Ever. But I don't know what you've done with my sister, so when she shows back up, can you have her give me a call? That would be great." Violet hangs up on me.

I groan. I need to get things together. This is supposed to be the best year of high school, right? So far, I am falling behind in my classes, I haven't seen Livi much and I just pissed off my sister, who has always been there for me. Instead, I am daydreaming about a guy I have only seen once.

Livi and Violet have had boyfriends come and go, but I have always been more worried about getting good grades and extracurricular activities that will look good on my college applications. I have never had, nor been interested in having, a boyfriend.

And there I go again. Thinking about maybe having a boyfriend, when I don't even know if he noticed me. I know nothing about this guy. Definitely out of character for 'follow the rules Genevieve,' I should probably avoid any more tours in the future. Maybe see if there are any cute guys in our high school. Are there? I have never really noticed before.

Guess that is what happens when you spend most your time doing extra credit work. Now that I think about it, some of my lab partners might have been a little bit cute, a bit nerdy, but cute. After seeing Steve, they seem like little kids though, which is weird. Steve looks older than us, but Livi said he is a senior at Charleston Academy. It's probably the goatee. Maybe he is a super senior, doing senior year twice?

I'm jarred out of my thoughts by my cell phone ringing again. Thinking it's probably Violet calling back to yell at me some more, I am surprised to see that it is Livi calling. If Violet was surprised that I was still sleeping, I am equally surprised that Livi is awake.

"Hey, what's up, Liv? Why are you up already?"

"My mom has decided that we're going walking together early every morning. I think she's lost it." I can practically hear Livi rolling her eyes over the phone. "You want to go on another ghost tour on Saturday? Maybe 'Blue Eyes' will be there."

"Ugh. Stop. I think I'll pass," I groan.

"Oh, come on. It'll be fun. Maybe you can speak this time."

"Shut up, Livi. I told you last time I wasn't paying attention because I didn't want to get scared and I still don't want to get scared, so … pass."

Livi sighs. "Please, Genevieve. My mom won't let me go to Charleston if you don't go and I really want to go on another tour. This one is called the Haunted Jail Tour and it sounds awesome! I can even call and ask if 'Blue Eyes' is working and see if we can get on his tour."

"No!" I snap. "And you really have to stop calling him that. I have seen the guy once and I didn't even talk to him."

"Trust me, I know," Livi says, unable to control her laughter. "You were hilarious. He asked you direct questions and you just stared off into space. Can you try to be more normal this time so that I can enjoy the tour?"

I don't respond. I want to see if I can catch a glimpse of Steve again, and at the same time I really don't want to.

"We can go out to eat somewhere after. I'll even let you pick where we go."

And now Livi has resorted to bribery. I think about it for a minute. Well, so much for avoiding going on another tour, thinking about seeing Steve again is almost scarier than thinking about getting scared on the tour. On the other hand, he only works every other Saturday, so we have a fifty-fifty chance of him not being there.

"Okay, fine. But you have to promise not to try and scare me. Can we try to go on one of the tours that start before it's dark?"

"Deal. You're the best friend ever!"

I hang up and put my cell back on the nightstand, then plop my face back into my pillow. "Livi, you have no idea how much you owe me," I mumble to myself. I pick my phone back up and send a text to Violet.

> Vi. I am sorry! Please don't be mad.

I don't even have to wait for a response.

> I'm not mad, Sis. Just wish you would let me know what's going on. I can tell something is bothering you. I'm here. Plus, I may need you to make sure I go to class.

> LOL. You love dancing. I doubt you need to be told to go to class. I'll call soon. I promise.

I get up and try to tame my bed head into a ponytail, get dressed, and head downstairs to find something to eat before Livi picks us up for school.

Soft voices float up the stairs from the hallway.

"I got a weird text this morning. I think someone might be trying to black-mail me," Dad whispers.

"What in the world would someone be able to blackmail you with?" Mom whispers back.

"I can't talk about it. I don't even know if it is legit or some sort of a sick prank Charlotte."

Did Dad just say someone is trying to blackmail him? I walk down the stairs as quietly as I can and slip into the kitchen without being noticed. I was, apparently, not as quiet as I thought I was, Mom and Dad have both stopped talking.

Digging through the cereal in the pantry, I find a box of Cinnamon Toast Crunch, pull it out and fill a bowl.

"I thought I heard someone in the kitchen. Good morning, Sleepy Head," Mom teases. "I figured it was you since Konnie already ate."

I'm surprised that Mom is acting so happy; maybe I misheard her conversation with Dad. "Good morning, Mom. Do we have any plans this weekend? Livi wants to go on another ghost tour on Saturday and wants me to go with her."

"That should be fine, Sweetie. Just let me know the details before you go." She smiles but has a worried look on her face.

"Is everything okay, Mom?" I ask.

She looks startled that I asked. "Everything is fine. Your dad seems to be working more than normal and seems stressed, but that isn't anything out of the ordinary with his job at times." She turns to look at me. "I have noticed that you seem to be a little more uptight than usual, is everything okay with you?"

"I'm good. I just think I overdid it a little bit on the dual credit classes. They are tough this trimester."

"Well, let me know if I need to go into the school with you to adjust your schedule. I do want you to have some fun your senior year. Don't overwhelm yourself."

I smile. "Thanks, Mom. I think I'll be fine; I just need to get into a better routine." *And get my brain functioning again*, I think to myself.

I have a feeling maybe I shouldn't go with Livi to Charleston this weekend. I should stay home and spend some time with Mom and Dad instead. They both seem so stressed, and I swear I heard Dad say someone is trying to blackmail him, but I am distracted as I hear Livi pull into the driveway and honk the horn. Ignoring my thoughts, I grab my bag and walk out the door with Konnie.

Chapter 8

Steve

The loud banging on my door pulls me out of my dream. Now that I am awake, I can hear my muffled alarm going off. I must have snoozed it and put it under my pillow without even waking all the way up. I crawl out of bed and answer the door to an irritated looking dorm parent.

"You missed first period and you're late for your next class, Steve."

"Yeah, sorry, I slept through my alarm."

With a look that only a disappointed adult can give he turns around and starts walking down the hall. "You better hurry."

That is an understatement. I would have needed to hurry if I woke up two hours ago. Now I am screwed. What happens when you skip a class and you are super late for your next one at a strict boarding school? I guess I am about to find out. I didn't get my homework done last night and I am not doing great in my classes. Like Gran said, this is my last chance. I really need to get more serious about getting good grades. Well, at least passing grades. Let's not get too crazy.

To make matters even worse I had been dreaming about Genevieve before I woke up. Why? Why in the heck am I dreaming about the girl who completely ignored me? Irritated, I start shoving my books into my backpack and throw on my uniform.

I am so tired; I really shouldn't have gone to that party last night. I left the party early, but I couldn't concentrate on my homework and when I finally decided to try to go to sleep I couldn't. I ended up scrolling through my social media accounts until who knows what time. I tried looking Genevieve up, but couldn't find her anywhere. I did find Livi though, I thought about sending her a friend request, but decided against it. I am pretty sure that would be creepy, they didn't even tell me their last names and we hardly even spoke. Although, judging by the amount of friends Livi has on there, I am assuming she wouldn't think twice about adding another one.

I sprint to class and try to sneak in the back. No such luck. At least Mr. Langston is my teacher for second period.

"Nice of you to join us," he says with a smirk.

"Sorry, Mr. Langston," I mumble before sliding into my desk.

He goes back to the white board and starts talking about our big history project that we will be working on all semester. And it hits me. I forgot to even start on my outline for the project. The outline that is due today. I groan and put my head on the desk. Why am I incapable of keeping track of my schoolwork?

"Everything okay back there, Mr. Adler?"

I snap my head back up. "Yep, totally good."

I hear snickers around the classroom. Mr. Langston turns back to the board. What a crappy start to the day.

Every other class isn't much better. I need a break. Maybe I can use my history project as an excuse to get a pass and go explore some other areas of Charleston. Maybe drive up toward Moncks Corner a little bit. *Nope, don't even go there.* I need to do homework. I will probably be doing homework until early in the morning just to catch up.

After the last bell, Troy catches up to me as I make my way back to my dorm. "Where were you this morning?"

"I slept through my alarm. Do you know what happens if you miss a class?"

"I'm sure you will be getting a call from the Dean of Students. I think since you were asleep and not just skipping class, they might just let you off with a warning. I'm not sure though."

I groan. "Great. I hope they don't call Gran. I can't get into trouble here."

"Speaking of which, you have got to tell me the whole punching your principal in the face story. Did you just wake up one day thinking it might be a good day to commit battery?"

I laugh. "No definitely not planned. I don't even remember what started the whole thing. I did something and he started ranting about how horrible of a job my grandma had done raising me. The rude comments about me I could take, but when he started saying horrible things about Gran, I didn't even think before I punched him."

"Did you get arrested?"

"No, thanks to Gran. She talked to Mr. Lincoln and he didn't press charges. I know I shouldn't have punched him, but it felt good at the time. Until I got expelled."

It hurts to think about missing my junior and senior year at Brookhaven High. All my classmates that I grew up with are moving on without me. It feels worse than I thought it would.

Troy and I part ways when we get to Boone Hall. He waves as I disappear into the building and walk into my room, plopping down into my desk. Might as well start with my outline for Mr. Langston. The problem is, I still don't even know what I want to do my history project on. I wonder if he would let me do my whole project on one of the ghost stories? At least that would be interesting. My cell phone ringing breaks my concentration. It's Gran, she starts talking as soon as I answer.

"Skipping class already?"

So much for Gran not getting a call. "I swear I didn't mean to Gran, I slept through my alarm."

"Sounds like you need to spend more time sleeping and less time socializing."

"I actually came home before curfew last night, I just couldn't sleep."

"Are you doing okay? You really need to focus on your schoolwork, Stevie Boy."

"I know Gran, I promise I'm trying."

"Okay, if I get another call about you missing class we are going to have some words. Don't make me come to Charleston to make sure you're going to class."

I laugh thinking about my feisty Grandma walking me to class. I miss her so much it really doesn't seem like a punishment. "You promise?"

"Oh stop. You know you wouldn't want me interfering with all your fun."

"I think you'd like Charleston Academy. There would be a lot here in Charleston for you to paint."

"Describe what you can see right now for me."

I chuckle. "Well, Gran, it's not too exciting. I see a desk, books, and way too much homework that I have to get done."

"Well, that was anticlimactic. Guess what I can see right now?"

"Should I be afraid to ask?"

"Probably," she replies mischievously.

"Maybe I don't want to know then."

Gran breaks into hearty laughter. "You can always put a smile on my face, but honestly you probably don't want me to describe what I'm seeing. I'm on an outing to the hot pools with a group from the facility. The hot pools feel nice, but I don't think anyone wants to see the amount of saggy skin that is floating around in here."

I almost spit the water out that I just took a drink of. "Yeah, I am okay. Thanks though."

She sounds in good spirits, but she sounds off a little bit too. I miss home so much right now, I would even go soak in the hot pools with a group of people that could all be my grandparents if I could see Gran right now.

"You feeling okay, Gran? You sound tired or something."

"I'm fine, Stevie Boy, don't worry about me. Just concentrate on school; I can't wait to come see you graduate. You're going to graduate, right?"

I sigh. "Don't you think it's a little bit early for me to be flunking out already?"

"Maybe, but with your ambition of seeing how many schools you can attend in two years, I wouldn't put it past you."

"Ha ha, so funny. I've gotten a little bit behind, but I'm working hard to catch up."

"I love you more than anything in this world, but I also know you better than anyone else. You need to make sure that you put your schooling as your number one priority and fun with friends second."

I groan. "I know, Gran."

"Hang in there, Stevie Boy; you are going to do great things in this world."

She disconnects the call. Gran is funny about saying goodbye. She always hangs up before anyone can say goodbye, she says she only likes hellos.

I am able to get quite a bit of my homework done, so when some friends stop by to see if I want to go to a movie with them, I decide to go. I did do a lot of homework and I work all day tomorrow—it is crazy how many tours they try to fit in on Saturdays—so I think I deserve at least a little fun.

Chapter 9

Genevieve

The drive to Charleston goes by way too quickly. I still can't decide whether or not I am hoping Steve is working today. On one hand, I feel like I should keep my distance and focus on school, but on the other hand, I definitely wouldn't mind seeing him again. Maybe I will get lucky and catch a glimpse of him, but he won't be our tour guide. I don't really know how I can recover from the embarrassment of the last tour. Better to just avoid seeing him again all together.

"You have been awfully quiet on our drive," Livi pointed out as we walk toward the tour office. "Anything you want to talk about? Or anyone?"

"Nope, I'm good; just have a lot on my mind."

"Are you hoping we get 'Blue Eyes' as a tour guide?"

"Liv, I told you not to call him that, and I honestly don't know if I want to see him again." I sigh, "I really need to focus on school right now. He has already caused enough problems for me."

"I knew it! You like him way more than you are letting on. You should totally get his number. You need to have some fun senior year."

Ugh! Why does everyone keep telling me that? I have fun; I just get all of my schoolwork done first.

"I plan on having fun this year, but I don't need any distractions. If I'm going to get a good scholarship, I need good grades."

Livi grins. "I have complete faith in you, Gen. Is it even possible for you to get bad grades? Come on, live a little!"

"He may not even be working today, and even if he is, what are the odds that he is the guide for the tour you want to go on?"

Livi looks at me with a mischievous grin. "Well come on, let's go find out."

The office is in sight and my heart pounds, a nervous wave of energy flooding my stomach with every beat it makes against my ribs. I feel like maybe I should take a run around the block. I don't even like to run. I scan the area. No Steve so far. Maybe I can actually pay attention to the tour this time. *Please give us a woman this time, or at least an overweight, balding middle-aged man,* I silently plead.

We get up to the front of the ticket line and Livi asks for two tickets for the next Haunted Jail Tour.

The lady at the counter looks at her computer. "The next available Haunted Jail Tour isn't until three o'clock, is that okay?" Livi looks at me and I nod. "Please meet your guide in front of the Old City Jail fifteen minutes before your tour's start time." The lady says as she hands Livi the tickets.

Livi thanks her and we walk back out into the hot muggy air and decide to find something within walking distance to eat, no need to have to try and find parking again. We decide to grab some food from one of the vendors in the market. After walking through the market for a few minutes, we decide on a vendor and I order some fried catfish with a side of hushpuppies. We find a place to sit in the shade.

"Does it say who our tour guide is on the ticket?" I ask as I pop another hush puppy into my mouth.

Livi pulls out the tickets and inspects them. "Not that I can see." She hands them to me.

I read every word on the tickets, even the fine print. Nowhere does it say anything about the name of the tour guide. Even though I am not sure I want to see Steve again, the suspense is doing a number on me. I am not a big fan of surprises, I would much rather know what is happening in advance. My family and Livi like to tease me about my planning tendencies. I am the type of person who has all my Christmas presents bought before the season even starts.

But when you're best friends with a girl like Livi, surprises are inevitable. You would think I would be more used to them by now.

We finish eating our food and wander around for a while before it is time for us to head toward the Old City Jail. With every step closer my stomach does more summersaults. *Why did I eat so many hush puppies?* I ask myself, contemplating on whether or not I am actually going to be sick.

Livi notices and raises her eyebrows. "You don't look so good. You okay?" she asks as we walk up to the building.

There is already a group forming, but I don't see anyone wearing the tour company's shirt, apparently our tour guide hasn't arrived yet. We sit down on a small decorative wall to wait and I pull out my phone to keep my mind occupied. As I am looking at some fun pictures Violet text me today, while exploring New York, I hear Livi giggle next to me.

"Don't forget to talk this time," she teases.

I look up just in time to see Steve sauntering toward the group. *You have got to be kidding me!*

"Seriously!" I groan. "There are tours every half hour on Saturdays. I thought for sure there was no way he would be our guide again."

"Well, today is your lucky day."

"Or my unlucky day," I mumble. "Please don't embarrass me."

Livi looks at me. The mischievous gleam in her eyes sets my heart on a race that I have no control over.

"Livi please!" I beg as she stands up and waves.

"Hey Steve. Remember us?" Livi asks.

Steve turns to look at us and to my amazement his face lights up with a huge grin. "Of course. Livi and Genevieve, right?"

"That's us." Livi smiles.

She turns to look at me.

"Hey," I manage to squeak out.

Livi just rolls her eyes and turns her attention back to Steve.

"Have you ladies ever been on the Haunted Jail Tour before?" he asks me. The full attention of those brilliant blue eyes is almost too much to handle. *Don't be a weirdo. Don't be a weirdo. Don't be a weirdo.* I chant to myself and hope that it somehow can kick start my brain into some form of its usual function.

Livi is watching me, no doubt wondering if she is going to have to jump in and tell him I am a mute. But I recover and smile. Hoping it is a normal smile and I don't look like I am about to end up in the paper. "Nope, we have never been on this tour. The last tour you took us on was our first ghost tour. Livi's obsession with the supernatural is her latest passion."

He looks surprised that I spoke. I can only imagine what I looked like during the last tour. "Livi's latest passion? What about you? Not into the ghost tours?"

"I would rather not be scared out of my wits. I still don't know how Livi has talked me into going on two tours."

"A blue-eyed tour guide might have something to do with it." Livi tries to look innocent while I shoot daggers at her with my eyes. I can feel the heat creeping into my cheeks and hope that my blush isn't too dramatic. To my surprise, when I look at Steve he also has a hint of pink on his perfectly tan cheeks.

"I doubt that." He laughs.

Livi smiles. "Don't you have a tour to start or something?"

"Right," Steve says and then turns toward the rest of the group. "Hi everyone! My name is Steve, and I'll be your guide tonight. Are you guys ready for a terrifying time?"

A chorus of excited yeses comes from the group. I groan. How in the world do I get myself into these situations? Thankfully, my brain doesn't shut completely off this time. The tour is actually pretty interesting, even if it is creepy. I notice that every time we stop in a different room and Steve starts to tell another story, he always finds me and makes eye contact. *Don't get too excited,* I tell myself. *He is probably making eye contact with everyone in the group. That literally is his job.* But I can't help notice that it seems like he is talking directly to Livi and I most of the time.

Steve ushers the group into a jail cell and I swear the temperature in this room is several degrees colder than the room we just left. "We are currently in the cell of the late Lavinia Fisher," he says in a serious voice. "She is famous for being the first female serial killer in the United States of America and is our most seen ghost on the tour." I swallow hard. I think I liked the tour that I didn't pay any attention to better.

Steve continues his creepy story. "She and her husband John Fisher owned a hotel six miles outside of Charleston called the Six Mile Wayfarer House. Guests would stay at the inn and Lavinia and John would kill them, steal all their valuables, and dispose of the bodies. They were first suspected when several guests went missing after their stay, but because John and Lavinia were so well liked in the community, the suspicions were ignored."

I look at Livi and whisper, "Why did I let you talk me into this?"

51

"Because you are the best friend ever! I hope we see her ghost," Livi whispers back with excitement lacing her voice.

I sure hope not, I think as panic starts to well up inside of me. I am pretty sure I have made a horrible mistake letting Livi talk me into this. Not only am I going to make a fool of myself if I get scared out of my mind, but I will be making a fool of myself in front of—let's face it—the most attractive guy I have ever seen. I swallow hard and try to get a grip on my panic. I try to only partially listen to Steve as he finishes the story, but I can't help but take it all in.

"In February of 1819, Lavinia and John made a fatal mistake by letting one guest get away and they now had an eyewitness. They were arrested and brought to the Old City Jail where they were held until their trial where they pleaded not guilty."

How can any human being be so evil? I think to myself.

Steve continues. "However, they were found guilty and sentenced to be hanged on February 18, 1820. Lavinia wore her wedding gown to the execution and her last words before they were both hung were, 'If you have a message you want to send to hell, give it to me—I'll carry it.'"

As Steve finishes probably the most disturbing story I have ever heard, Livi grabs my arm and startles me. I let out a scream that could wake the dead and Livi bursts out laughing. Once again, I feel the uncontrollable heat rising to my cheeks as I look toward Steve, who has a huge smile on his smug face.

"I am never going on one of these tours with you again," I threaten Livi.

"I doubt that," Livi says before bursting into another fit of giggles. "I don't think I have ever heard you scream like that before. Best day ever!"

I shove Livi in front of me. There is no way she is going to walk behind me for the rest of the tour. As we continue through the jail, which is now my least favorite place on the planet, paranoia starts to take over.

The hair on the back of my neck stands up, it feels like we are being watched. Hearing distinct footsteps behind us, I reach for Livi's hand and grab it harder than I mean to.

"Do you hear footsteps?" I whisper.

"There is a whole tour group of people walking, Genevieve. Yeah, I hear footsteps."

All those little hairs on the back of my neck start to tingle. "No, do you hear footsteps behind us?"

Livi stops to listen for a minute. While she is listening, the group gets farther ahead of us than I am comfortable with. My gaze is torn between watching Livi, listening for footsteps behind us, and watching the group get farther and farther away from us. I hear more footsteps behind us and when I look at Livi and see her eyes go wide, I know she can hear them too.

"Oh my gosh!" Livi squeals. "We're totally going to see a ghost!"

I whimper. There is no other way to explain the sound my body involuntarily makes. I think I might be starting to hyperventilate.

"Livi, I really don't want to see a ghost. Can we please catch up to the group?"

"Just a couple more seconds. I want to see what is making those footsteps."

"It's Lavinia Fisher! Didn't he say she's the most seen ghost? And we just left her cell. There is NO WAY I am staying here waiting for her to show up. Are you crazy?"

Livi peers into the dimly lit hall outside of the cell we just came from. I can't decide whether I should look behind us to see what is coming, or turn around and drag Livi as fast as I can back to the group before we are murdered by a ghost. *Can you be murdered by a ghost?* The logical part of my brain wonders.

Both of us are so focused on looking toward Lavinia's cell that neither of us hears Steve as he walks up behind us.

"What are we looking at?" his deep voice asks.

My heart stops.

Livi lets out a scream that puts my earlier scream to shame and Steve bursts out laughing.

"Well, my job here is done." He chuckles.

I am not sure if my heart is beating so fast because I am terrified or because of the close proximity to Steve, but either way, I am ready to get out of this creepy building.

"How close is the exit?" I ask. "I need to get out of here now!"

Livi has recovered and is laughing with Steve until she sees my face, which I am pretty sure has absolutely no color left in it at all. Her eyes fill with worry as she takes it in.

"Are you okay?" she asks me. Then turns to Steve and asks, "How much more of the tour do we have left?"

"It's over. The rest of the group has already gone their separate ways. I came back to find you two when I realized you were missing from the group."

"You ready to go, Genevieve?" Livi asks.

I nod and we start walking toward the exit. After we walk out the doors and the hot humid air hits my face, I start to feel better. I didn't realize how cold I was. We wait for Steve to lock the door and the three of us start walking back toward the tour office.

"Do you ladies want to come back for another tour next week?" Steve asks us.

Livi looks over at me. "Maybe we should do your least scary ghost tour next."

"Maybe we shouldn't do any ghost tours," I mumble.

Steve and Livi both burst out laughing and I glare at both of them.

Livi hooks her arm through mine. "Oh come on, Genevieve. You had to have had a little bit of fun." I give her a skeptical look.

Steve walks up on my other side. "Just stick by me and I'll make sure you don't get too scared."

And that does it. Despite my better judgment, we make plans to go on the Dock Street Theatre Tour with Steve as our guide on Thursday.

"See you Thursday," Steve says as he heads to his next tour.

I am in so much trouble, I think to myself as I mentally try to calculate just how many hours I will have to wait until Thursday.

Chapter 10

Steve

Focusing on my homework is near impossible this afternoon. Knowing Genevieve and Livi are coming on my tour this afternoon has me feeling antsy, which annoys me. At least I *think* they are coming on the tour this afternoon. We made the plans, but I never asked for either of their numbers. I hope they are coming; it's all I have been able to think about since Saturday.

Giving up on trying to study, I decide to walk to work early. My plan is to go walk along the shoreline for a little bit and then check in at work, but I am on autopilot and end up walking to work to check in first. Instead of walking down to the water, I just go sit at the starting point of the tour. I am forty-five minutes early, not sure what I am going to do until the tour starts.

Hearing the scuffle of shoes, I turn to look down the street and can't believe what I am seeing. Genevieve and Livi are walking toward me!

"You're early," I say. *Way to go, Captain Obvious.*

Genevieve smiles. "So are you."

"We decided to drive here straight from school," Livi says.

I just stare at them. I NEVER have trouble coming up with something to say, but there is a first time for everything and today is apparently that day for me. The already warm day starts to feel sweltering. *What am I doing?* I should at least look away if I am not going to say something. *Right?* I just can't stop looking. Genevieve looks gorgeous, and different from anyone I would usually find attractive. She once again is wearing Bermuda shorts and a T-shirt with a sweatshirt tied around her waist. Her auburn hair is pulled into a tight ponytail. How can she look so average and so extraordinary at the same time? And why does she always have a sweatshirt with her, it is almost eighty degrees outside.

"Awkward," whispers Livi.

I can feel the heat creeping into my cheeks. Genevieve looks mortified and she is giving Livi a look that I am assuming means *shut your mouth.*

"What in the heck are you doing with your face?" Livi asks Genevieve.

"Trying to get you to shut up," Genevieve grumbles.

"Why would you want me to shut up? I'm the only one talking," Livi points out.

Well, can't really argue with that point.

Livi looks at both of us like we have lost our minds and asks, "Soooooooo, ummm Steve, which tour is the scariest?"

Finally, something I can focus on. "Probably the Haunted Jail Tour in my opinion, but each tour is different and depending on how each tour goes, some are a lot spookier than others."

"Have you actually seen a real ghost?" Genevieve asks.

"I haven't actually seen a ghost, but there have definitely been some unexplainable things happen at the tour sites that give me the creeps."

"Sweet! I want to see a ghost," Livi says, at the same time Genevieve says, "I am totally okay if nothing creepy happens while I am on a tour."

I laugh. "How are you two best friends?"

Genevieve and Livi look at each other, shrug their shoulders and laugh. There is another awkward silence before Genevieve asks, "So how do you like going to a boarding school?"

"Charleston Academy is really nice and all, but I would rather be home. I do like the school and most of my teachers, so I can't really complain."

"Are you planning on going to college after you graduate?" Genevieve asks.

"I don't know, maybe? Yes? I mean that is kinda what my grandma always told me I would be doing after high school, but I don't really know what I want to be when I 'grow up.'"

I put air quotes around the 'grow up' part. I wonder if I will ever actually grow up. I mean, I know I will physically, but will I ever be able to focus on what I need to, or will I always be distracted by something that looks more fun than what I am doing?

"Gen has her whole life planned out. Get into an awesome school and become a super-star architect. She is crazy smart," Livi says.

Raising my eyebrows, I turn my attention to Genevieve and she blushes.

"I don't have my whole life planned out," she says, glaring at Livi.

Livi giggles. "Only most of it."

Genevieve rolls her eyes and changes the subject. "How did you start doing ghost tours?"

"My history teacher helps out with the tours and gives his students the option of helping out too. Getting paid for doing extra credit seemed like a no brainer. Not to mention that I really like giving the tours."

"Do you really need extra money? I mean you go to Charleston Academy," Livi points out.

Man, this girl really doesn't have a filter. "Let's just say I'm not like most of the other students at Charleston Academy."

While we have been talking, other people who signed up for the tour have been trickling in. A decent-sized group is now waiting; I look at my phone and see that I am a couple of minutes past when I should have started the tour. Oops. I give the girls a smile before I jump up and get the group's attention.

"Hi everyone! My name is Steve, and I'll be your guide tonight. Are you guys ready for a terrifying time?"

Leading the group down the street toward the Dock Street Theatre, I can't help but keep glancing at Genevieve and Livi who are walking at the back of the tour. We stop in front of the historical theater. The front of the theater boasts six intricately carved pillars that hold up a balcony with a green railing and pillars that have a busy intertwining design. I let the group take a look before I start talking. Genevieve looks enthralled by the designs.

"The Dock Street Theatre was the first theater built in America. Its grand opening was in 1736. Just four years later the Dock Street Theatre, along with most of Charleston's other historical buildings were destroyed in the Great Fire of 1740. In 1809, Mr. and Mrs. Alexander Calder built a hotel where the Dock Street Theatre used to reside. They named it Planter's Hotel after a family who came to stay during horse racing season each year."

I look around to make sure I still have everyone's attention before continuing. "The hotel needed a great deal of repairs after the Civil War, and to top it off, the earthquake in 1886 caused even more damage. The building was abandoned and it wasn't until almost fifty years later that it became a project to create jobs during the Great Depression. The hotel was the base for the new theater that they once again named the Dock Street Theatre after the historic theater that burnt to the ground in 1740."

I lead the group into the theater. The inside is majestic with large wooden pillars and dark green curtains covering not only the stage, but each theater box on the second level. Genevieve's eyes light up as she takes it all in.

"The Dock Street Theatre has been called Charleston's most haunted location. It is haunted by numerous ghosts, but three of them make their presence known the most. The first ghost has been named The Lady in White. No one knows who she is or why she haunts this particular theater, but she makes herself known regularly. Was she a hotel worker or an actress that can't leave the theater behind? Your guess is as good as mine."

I lead the group onto the stage before I start my next story. "The second ghost is Junius Booth. Junius Brutus Booth performed here with his theater group when the building was a hotel. Junius was the father of Edwin and John Wilkes Booth who were both actors and, as many of you already know, John Wilkes Booth was the one who assassinated President Abraham Lincoln. Junius was rumored to be a hot head as well, and at one time almost killed the hotel manager when he became angry for an unknown reason. Junius was nowhere near the theater at the time of his death, but those who have seen his ghost are convinced that it is him. His love for performing brought him back to the theater after death and he has been known to breathe down patrons' necks and sometimes even touch them. He has also been seen many times acting on the stage."

The group wanders around the theater for a few minutes before we walk back outside. I draw their attention to the balcony on the second floor. "The last ghost that is known to haunt the Dock Street Theatre is Nettie. Nettie was a twenty-five-year-old girl from the country that came to Charleston looking for a new life. She was a beautiful girl, but she was too old to be considered for marriage during that time period and wealthy men usually didn't marry below their class. She got a job as a clerk at a local church but she didn't feel like she belonged there. One day she went and spent all of her money on an expensive red dress. Looking for love, she put on her new dress and went to the hotel with the intent to seduce the men there. It didn't take long before the wives of her customers were angry. When the men didn't want to risk losing their wives, she quickly ran out of money. One night, during a terrible thunderstorm, Nettie ran to the balcony after another customer rejected her. She started screaming at Charleston's society from the balcony. When the priest from the local church she worked at previously tried to reason with her, she screamed, 'You cannot save me,' and then was struck by lightning and killed instantly."

I let the story sink in for a minute before I continue. "Nettie is still seen in her red dress. However, she has lost her beauty and those who have seen her describe her appearance to be zombie-like. Her appearance scares most that catch a glimpse of her, but some employees of the theater say that they have gotten used to her appearance because they see her almost every day."

As the group dissipates, I saunter over to the girls. "Sorry we didn't see any ghosts, Livi."

"It's all good, that was a super interesting tour, with some really creepy stories," Livi says.

"How about you Genevieve, was it okay? Not too scary?" I ask.

She smiles. "Nope not too scary. Livi's right, it was actually really interesting."

I smirk. "It sounds like you're surprised that I can do my job well."

"No, it's not that at all! You do a great job; I just thought this one was good." She looks flustered.

"And the other tours weren't good?" I tease.

"She wasn't paying attention to the other two tours," Livi says and Genevieve smacks her arm.

"Well, what were you paying attention to?" I ask Genevieve.

Genevieve turns a bright shade of red and looks like she is struggling to come up with a response, as usual Livi has no such struggle and smiles at me.

"I think you can figure that one out yourself." Laughing at herself, she links her arm with Genevieve's. "Come on you two, let's get some ice cream."

We walk to an ice cream shop near the tour office and sit outside trying to eat our ice cream before it melts and still have a conversation. Livi keeps us laughing while we are talking. She is finishing up a story about when Violet, Livi, and Genevieve decided to try and jump out of the tree house with an umbrella, thinking it would make them float down to the ground slowly like Mary Poppins. I laugh and ask them both how many siblings they have?

"Just me and my mom," Livi says. "Well, I guess I have a couple of half siblings somewhere if you count siblings from my dirt bag of a father."

"Not a very good relationship with your dad, I take it?" I ask.

"Nope, he is a waste of skin. Left Mom and me high and dry when I was three and never looked back. He tries to call me, I refuse to talk to him, but Mom does. That's how I know I have some half siblings." Livi shrugs. "I think it is safe to say I have some daddy issues."

She winks. We all laugh.

Genevieve clears her throat before talking. "I have two sisters. Violet and Konnie. We always have a lot of fun together. I really enjoy spending time with my family, especially when we're on the boat or when I am working on blueprints with my dad."

"Speaking of the boat, we haven't gone out since school started," Livi says. "We should totally ask Mr. T. if he will take us out again soon."

"I do miss the boat; we were going out almost every weekend this summer," Genevieve points out. "I'll ask Dad."

Genevieve's face lights up when she talks about her dad. "Does Livi join in on all of the family excursions?" I ask.

"Livi and Darla are pretty much family," Genevieve says. "How about you? Do you have any siblings?"

I pause for a second, not really sure how to answer the question.

"I had a little brother," I finally say.

"Had?" Livi asks.

"Yeah, my family was in a bad car accident when I was nine. I was the only one that survived. I was in the hospital for quite a while before I was able to go live with my Grandma in Mississippi."

Livi as usual has no problem blurting out what comes to mind. "That is sooooo horrible. Who all was in the car? Were you in a coma?"

"Nope, not in a coma, just broke a lot of bones and needed a lot of fixing," I say. "Mom, Dad, and my little brother Jeremy were in the car with me. But my grandparents on my dad's side were also killed in the same accident. Different car."

Genevieve looks horrified. "I'm so sorry, Steve," she says and touches my hand. "I can't even imagine how hard that must have been for you."

I am surprised by the jolt I feel just from Genevieve touching my hand. "Thanks," I say. "It was a long time ago."

"Do you have any other family?" Livi asks.

I shake my head. "Not really. My dad had a sister, but they had a falling out before I was born. She didn't even come to the funerals. I've never met her and have no idea where she lives." I shrug my shoulders. "It was just Gran and I growing up. Mom was an only child and my grandpa had died before she was born, so we never knew him."

"She sounds like an amazing lady," Genevieve says. "I can't imagine not growing up with the craziness of family all around."

"I don't know, sometimes being an only child is pretty nice," Livi pipes in.

I can't help myself, I start talking about Gran and I can't stop. I tell them all about what it was like growing up with my spunky grandma and how she always took me on fun adventures. The girls are listening intently to me talk, which I think might be abnormal for Livi. I notice Genevieve has ice cream leaving a sticky trail down her arm with a gooey pool on the table by her elbow.

I laugh and say, "Here, let me help you with that."

She looks startled, like she hadn't even noticed the ice cream snaking down her arm. "Oh my gosh." She laughs.

I grab napkins and try to help her clean up the ice cream. She is a sticky mess, but I think it just makes her look even cuter.

This is new for me.

"Gen, it's ten. We should probably start driving home," Livi points out.

Genevieve looks panicked. "What?"

I pull my phone out of my pocket and look at the time. Sure enough, it is a few minutes after ten. I walk the girls to Livi's Mustang and this time I remember to ask for Genevieve's number. I watch them drive away for a minute before I start to walk back to my dorm. I am going to be late for curfew too, but I don't even care.

All I can think about is Genevieve.

Chapter 11

Genevieve

When Steve asked me for my number, my worry about being late disappeared and I realized that I actually enjoyed this tour, scary stories and all. I will for sure be going on more tours in the future, but now that we are in Livi's car driving home, my panic about how mad my parents are going to be comes back in full force.

"My parents are going to be so pissed! We were supposed to be home by ten," I say.

"I know, that's why I said we should probably get going," Livi rolls her eyes.

My heart starts beating double-time. I never get in trouble, that was Violet's role in the family. It is strange that my parents haven't called or sent a text. Poor Livi has to deal with my worry the whole ride home until she drops me off in front of my house.

I jump out of the car and wave goodbye to Livi as I run up the front walk and into the house. Konnie is in the living room watching TV and doesn't pay any attention as I walk upstairs to our parent's room. Their door is shut and I knock softly. Mom opens the door, and it takes a minute for her to focus on my face.

"What do you need, Sweetie?" she asks.

"I just wanted to let you know that I am home, Mom."

Surprise passes over her face for an instant and then is gone. "Great, thank you for letting me know. Did you have a good time?"

"Yeah, it was a lot of fun," I answer, but I don't think she is fully listening to me. I say goodnight and go into my room. Mom didn't even realize I was gone, let alone home an hour later than I was supposed to be, and my dad didn't even come to their bedroom door to see how my night went.

Something is definitely wrong.

— • —

The next morning, Dad is already gone for work when I wake up and my worry comes back. It isn't normal for him to leave this early. School goes by quickly and I am so excited when I get a text from Steve. It's just a funny meme, but it still puts a permanent smile on my face for the day.

When Livi drops us off at the house after school I notice that Dad's car is in the driveway. *Dad is home super early today,* I think to myself as I look at the time on my phone. I put my backpack down by the front door. My parents aren't downstairs so I walk upstairs to their room and listen at the door. I can hear Mom and Dad's frantic whispers, but can't quite make out what they are saying. As I creep closer, and by closer, I mean I have my ear pressed against the door, I can barely make out my mom's whispering voice.

"Tony, you're starting to scare me. What is going on?"

"I think the blackmail is real, it's not a prank," Dad replies in a strained whisper.

"I still don't understand what someone would be able to blackmail you with."

"I told you I can't talk about it. It's classified information; I could get in even bigger trouble if I said anything to anyone."

Mom sounds like she might be close to tears. "If you think it is a real threat, don't you think we should call the police or something?"

"And tell them what, Charlotte? I'm being blackmailed for something I can't tell you about, oh, and I also can't tell you what they are threatening me with, because both of them are classified information."

"I'm just trying to help, Tony."

Dad sighs heavily. "I know Charlotte. For now, I'll talk to some of the people that have clearance to the information and try to figure out what I should do."

Before I can hear any actual important information, I am startled by a voice behind me.

"What are you doing?" Konnie asks and I let out a startled shriek.

Frantically, I try to push Konnie into my room before our parents catch us outside their door. No such luck, the door to my parent's room opens.

Mom sticks her head out of the door with a worried expression on her face. "What are you girls doing?" she asks in a strained voice. "How was school?"

"Is everything okay, Mom?" I ask.

"Your father isn't feeling very well," Mom says as she rubs her forehead, like she does when she is getting a headache. "He's probably just going to go to bed."

"Geez. He must be feeling really sick if he is going to bed this early," Konnie pipes in.

Mom looks distracted. "Yes, you girls need to get your schoolwork done. Let your father rest for a while."

I watch Konnie and my mom head downstairs. Mom left in a hurry and didn't latch the door closed behind her. I peek through the crack and see my dad frantically sorting through papers lying all over his bed. I have never seen such a distressed look on his face. *He isn't sick. Someone is trying to blackmail Dad, and why is Mom lying about it?*

Dinner is just as strange. Dad never comes down from his room and Mom is so distracted that she forgets to boil the lasagna noodles before she bakes the lasagna. I am pretty sure we might break some teeth while eating it. Konnie seems completely oblivious to the strained atmosphere around her. Mom is staring at the wall, while trying to crunch through the rock-hard lasagna.

"Is it okay if I go to Livi's house tomorrow after school?" I ask.

Mom continues to crunch her lasagna without responding.

I ask a couple more times before I loudly say, "Did you hear me, Mom?"

She looks at me with a vacant look in her eyes. "What did you say, Sweetie?"

I repeat myself and it seems to take a couple of delayed seconds for her to grasp what I'm saying.

"That should be fine," she says and then goes back to trying to eat the inedible lasagna.

I excuse myself and sneak a pop tart from the pantry. I head up to my room to call Violet. She doesn't answer and I don't feel like leaving a voicemail saying that I think our parents might have been abducted by aliens and their replacements needed some more classes on how to interact with the human species. So I hang up and send a text telling her to call me when she gets a chance instead.

I finish proof-reading an essay for English, make the needed changes and try to go to bed. I have no idea what to do with the information I overheard and I can't fall asleep. Dad is the happiest, friendliest person I have ever met. I can't imagine him having anything that he could be hiding. Giving up on sleep I quietly make my way down to the kitchen for a glass of water. I stop on my way past Dad's office door. I know he charges his phone in the office.

Before I can convince myself that this is a horrible idea I slip into the office and shut the door behind me. Dad's phone is plugged in on his desk, just like I thought it would be. I know the pass code to his phone, that doesn't make it okay for me to go snooping around through it. Torn between finding out what is going on and wondering if this will mean I am a horrible daughter, I put in the code and open his list of text messages. I scroll down until I see a text from a number that isn't in his contacts and open the text stream.

> I know what happened during Desert Storm.

I feel like someone punched me in the stomach. *What happened during Desert Storm?* There are no replies from Dad, but there is a second text message from the same number.

> I know what happened during Desert Storm.

> You will give us the blueprints for the Extinction Torpedo or the whole country will know.

Someone is blackmailing Dad for a weapon. The Extinction Torpedo can't be its real name; I know that they usually give their projects nicknames, so for this person to know the nickname is unsettling. If its nickname indicates anything, I am fairly certain this is not a weapon that should get into the hands of someone with bad intentions.

Thinking my easy-going, happy-go-lucky, always-finding-the-bright-side-in-any-situation Dad could have done anything horrible enough for someone to hold something like this over his head is too much for me to wrap my head around. He is the glass-is-half-full kind of person, always able to see the good in people or the good in any situation. It actually drives us all crazy sometimes.

Like the time when we rented an RV for a family trip and it broke down in the middle of nowhere. No cell service. Not a town for miles and miles.

I thought Mom was going to strangle Dad when he said, "What a beautiful day for a hike."

What could Dad have possibly done that would make them think that he would even consider giving them the plans to this weapon? I hear movement upstairs and frantically exit out of Dad's texts and place the phone back in its spot. On silent feet I leave the office, closing the door behind me and make it into the kitchen for a glass of water a few seconds before Dad walks in. He startles when he sees me drinking my glass of water in the dark kitchen.

"Is your headache feeling better?" I ask.

He looks confused for a minute. "Uh yeah, I'm fine, just thirsty."

"Great minds think alike." I smile. "We missed you at dinner."

"I had a lot of work to get done."

He doesn't even look at me or smile. I put my glass in the sink and say goodnight before I make it back to the safety of my room. Mom and Dad can't even get their stories straight, Mom said he missed dinner because of his headache and Dad says he had too much work to get done. The big question is why are they both lying? I'm sure that they don't want to worry Konnie and me, but it is too late for that.

Back in bed, I stare up at the ceiling begging for sleep to come. When it finally does, I don't get any relief as my brain tries to figure out what Dad is hiding, creating horrible scenarios in nightmare form. I startle awake multiple times throughout the night before my alarm for school goes off.

This has got to be a sick prank. Right? This can't actually be happening.

Chapter 12

Steve

Second hour is just ending and I am packing up all of my supplies when I feel my phone vibrating in my pocket. Pulling it out of my pocket, I am surprised to see it is Genevieve calling. It is the middle of the day, she should be in school too, and it doesn't really seem like Genevieve. I shove the rest of my things into my backpack and rush into the hall to answer.

"Hey Genevieve."

"Um, hey Steve."

She sounds off, I am not sure if she is just nervous or something is wrong.

"You okay?" I ask.

"Um, not really." She pauses. "Can you meet me somewhere this afternoon? I really need to talk to someone."

Not sure what is going on, but I am definitely down for meeting up with Genevieve. And if I am being totally honest, my day got a thousand times better when I looked at my phone and saw that it was Genevieve calling.

"Sure. Where do you want to meet?"

"Does Cleo's Bakery in North Charleston work? It is kinda in the middle for both of us."

"Sure. I'll be there."

"Thank you," she says quietly before disconnecting the call.

A teacher that I don't know walks past me and reminds me that there is no cell phone use during school hours; I need to wait until lunch or after school to talk on the phone. I tell him sorry, it won't happen again before hurrying to third hour.

I get to class and sit down just before the tardy bell rings. I just now realize that I need a pass to go to North Charleston. I have never needed to get a pass before; I hope I can get one easily. It will be nice to be able to drive my Jeep again. It has pretty much just been sitting since I got here.

I try to focus on class, but my mind keeps wandering. I wonder what is going on with Genevieve. This really seems out of character for her, then again, I don't know her very well. We have texted a few times since the last ghost tour, but this was the first time we have talked on the phone. Wondering about what is worrying Genevieve makes me think about my worries. Last night when I was talking to Gran she sounded off. I can't even place what was different; she just sounded tired or sad maybe? I know she wants me to think she loves living at her new place so I really worry that she won't tell me anything even if something is bothering her. Little does she know that her not wanting to worry me makes me worry anyway.

After class, I practically run back to my dorm. On my way in I stop at the dorm parent's office and ask for a pass to leave campus. He asks where I am headed and I tell him the name of the bakery in North Charleston. He doesn't even think about it before saying no. My stomach drops. *No? Now what?*

I leave the office and walk to my room dropping my backpack on the floor. I am going to stand Genevieve up the first time she asks me to do something. I am sure she has already left by now; we are supposed to meet in twenty minutes. I will still be late if I leave right now.

The logical side of my brain is screaming at me, trying to remind myself that this is my last chance at graduating high school on time, but the panic of scaring Genevieve off by standing her up wins out. I grab the keys to my Jeep.

Still torn between meeting Genevieve when I said I would and not getting into trouble, I stand there holding my keys. I look around my dorm room, I finally got all the boxes unpacked, but I left a huge mess on the side of the room that would be my roommate's if I had one. I shouldn't have to worry about it until next semester at the earliest.

I look at the keys in my hand and walk out the door, down the hall, past my dorm parent's office and back outside. I sit in my Jeep for a minute before making my final decision. I knew what I was going to do all along; I don't know why I wasted so much time thinking I might stay on campus. *I am in so much trouble,* I think to myself as I put the Jeep in reverse. Not only am I at risk of getting in big trouble at school, but I hardly know Genevieve and I am already willing to risk my last chance at school to meet her at a bakery for an unknown reason.

I think I may be in more trouble than I even fully realize.

I always say I don't go looking for trouble, it just always finds me, but this time I am pretty sure I am holding up a neon sign.

I look up the address of Cleo's Bakery and get directions. My phone says that I am going to be there about fifteen minutes late. I shoot Genevieve a text letting her know I am going to be late, pull out of the parking lot and don't look back.

Chapter 13

Genevieve

Looking around the room, I don't see Steve anywhere yet. I got the text that he would be late, so I don't know why I am looking for him anyway. I have so many butterflies in my stomach, I feel like I could almost take flight.

Needing something to do with my nervous energy, I walk up to the counter and order a chocolate salted caramel frappe. Livi always teases me when we come to Cleo's Bakery. I never order anything different, it is always the same. I am a bundle of nerves anyway, no need to add a high dose of caffeine and make me a jittery bundle of nerves. Plus, I know what I like, why try something different and risk not liking it? I feel a little bit like a fish out of water without Livi and her obnoxious buffer here to fill in any awkward moments. I find a seat at a table in the back corner of the bakery.

What am I doing? I think to myself. *Why did I call Steve for help?* I hardly know him. I bite my lower lip. This morning when I woke up, I was filled with a huge sense of dread. Violet still hadn't called me back and I know I can't tell Livi about what I overheard my parents talking about. Livi would never purposely let something slip that I don't want her to repeat, but she does sometimes speak before she thinks. Oh, who am I kidding, Livi never thinks before she speaks. As much as I want to talk to her about this, I can't. But what on Earth made me think it would be okay to talk to Steve about it? I even called him during school hours, when I asked if I could leave class to go to the bathroom. I was paranoid I was going to get caught and my phone confiscated, but I did it anyway.

Definitely not my normal behavior.

Let's be honest, I haven't really been my usual self since I went on that first ghost tour. I really hope I am not making a huge mistake confiding in Steve.

I see Steve walk in the front door and pause to look around the room. I notice that he catches the eye of several of the other girls in the bakery. I am trying to decide if I should get up, or just call his name or how exactly to get his attention. I end up not having to do anything as his eyes find mine. He walks toward me and sits down at the table. I tell him he should go order something, he gets up, orders and comes right back.

"All right Genevieve, what's going on? Are you okay?" he asks, worry lacing his voice.

I look into his bright blue eyes, I am pretty sure I could get lost in those eyes.

Realizing that the silence has gone on for too long and it is starting to feel awkward, I blurt out, "My dad is being blackmailed."

Steve looks stunned. Whatever he thought I was going to say, it wasn't that. He clears his throat. "What?"

"When I got home late from the tour on Thursday, normally I would be in huge trouble, but my parents didn't even notice that I was late." I sigh. "Then when I got home from school on Friday my dad was already home from work and I could hear my parents talking in their room. He told my mom that some-one is blackmailing him."

"What are they blackmailing him for?"

"I found a text on his phone asking for the plans for a weapon."

"What are they threatening him with?"

"Something that happened during Desert Storm."

Steve's eyes widen. "What happened during Desert Storm?"

"I have no idea. I just can't wrap my head around the fact that they could have anything on my dad, he is honestly the kindest person I know. He doesn't even go five over the speed limit, for crying out loud."

Steve smiles before turning serious again. "Have you talked to anyone about it?"

"My parents won't talk about it; they just keep making up reasons for their strange behavior. I can't get a hold of my big sister, Violet, and I don't want to worry my little sister, Konnie."

"Did you say anything to Livi?" Steve asks.

"No, I wish I could talk to Livi about it, but Livi lets things slip even when she doesn't mean to."

Steve chuckles. "I can see that happening with Livi. I'm not sure what to do, but I'll try to help you figure out what's going on."

To my horror, I can feel tears rising to the surface. I really don't want to cry in front of Steve, he probably already thinks I am a basket case with how I acted on the first tour and now this.

"I'm sorry, I don't even know why I am crying." I sniff and swipe at my tears.

I don't know why I am so emotional. Everything I am doing is out of character. I barely know Steve and now I am telling him things that I haven't even talked to my sisters or Livi about. I glance at Steve and the compassionate look on his face makes the tears come faster.

"I'm sorry I bothered you, I'm sure you have things you need to do," I mumble.

Steve scoots his chair over next to mine and rests his arm across my shoulders and says, "Don't apologize. I'm glad you called."

Every one of my nerves is tingling. Steve's arm wrapped around me has me feeling like I am on fire, yet at the same time his touch is so comforting. I can't help it; I lean into him and start to cry even harder. He sits there and lets me cry while he rubs my shoulder for a while. When the tears finally stop, I wipe my damp cheeks and reality hits me.

I just ugly cried all over Steve and his shirt and he doesn't even really know me.

Pretty sure I just ended this relationship before it even started. I can feel my cheeks getting hot and I know that I am beet red.

"Sorry about that," I say and then take a sip of my drink. *Now what?* I think. "Um, so how are you liking your classes?" I ask.

"They're okay. How about you? You mentioned you've been stressed with school."

"Yeah, I'm pretty sure I gave myself too heavy of a workload this year. I wanted to graduate with as many dual credits as I can, but I think I overdid it."

"Well, I for sure don't have that problem." Steve laughs. "At this rate I will be lucky if I graduate at all."

"What do you mean?"

"I get distracted easily. I try to do my homework, but when something else that looks fun comes along I tend to do that instead."

I smile. "Yeah, I definitely don't have that problem; everyone is always telling me I need to make sure I have some fun."

"Well, let's make a deal. You remind me to keep up with my schoolwork and I'll make sure you have some fun." Steve grins at me.

"Deal." I can't help but giggle. "I can probably help you with your homework if you need me to."

"It sounds like you have enough of your own work to do. They have tutors at the school, but I promise I will ask you for help if I am going to fail. I can't mess up this time."

"What do you mean 'this time'?"

He sighs and runs his hand over his face. "So, I got expelled from my high school in Brookhaven and then tried to do online school. Two online schools actually."

"How come?" *How come what? How come he got expelled or tried two different online schools?* I think to myself. Thankfully he doesn't make me elaborate.

"I got expelled for punching my principal and I flunked out of both online schools. I had to do home school over the summer with Gran to be able to start my senior year."

I am stunned. Did he just say he punched his principal? If I had a type, I didn't think it would be someone who goes around punching authority figures and flunking out of school. The look on my face must give me away.

"I promise I'm not a violent person," he clarifies. "He was always a big jerk, and never liked me for some reason, but when he started saying mean things about Gran, I punched him without even thinking about it."

A giggle escapes. "You punched your principal because he wasn't talking nice about your grandma?" I can't decide if that is the most adorable thing I have ever heard or the craziest.

Steve's grin comes back. "Well, yeah, I guess I did."

We both start laughing. "So what happened with the online schools?" I ask.

"Remember how I told you that I get distracted easily? Yeah, online school and being easily distractible can be a problem."

"I can see that. How come your grandma didn't want to home school you this year?"

This makes Steve smile. "I'm pretty sure she thought if she had to be my teacher for the whole year she might strangle me. I may not be the easiest student."

I smile and realize that it is almost five-thirty already. "Oh man! I didn't realize what time it is. I told my mom I needed to borrow the car to go to the library. I'm supposed to be home for dinner."

Steve stands up. "Are you going to be late? How long of a drive is it?"

"Yeah, I am going to be a little bit late; it takes about a half hour to get home. Luckily it won't be that weird for me to be late coming from the library." I can feel my cheeks heating up again.

"Why is that?" he asks.

"Sometimes when I am at the library surrounded by all of the books, I kinda lose track of time."

Livi makes fun of me regularly about my love of books. I can get so caught up in a book that I will forget to eat or drink anything. She jokes that we better lock the books up when I move out on my own or I might starve to death. But Steve doesn't tease me.

"Gran loves books too. I don't have the patience to sit and read one, but Gran would always read me books growing up. She would let my play with my Legos while she read and I loved hearing the stories. I still like to listen to audio books and Gran regularly tells me of a new book I need to listen to."

Could this guy be any more attractive? I think not. Before I can even think of how to respond Steve is wrapping his arms around me. I have always felt awkward when others give me long hugs, usually I want to hug and then move on with what we are doing, but I think I could stay in this hug forever. I fit perfectly in his arms and he smells like bergamot and sage, a surprisingly intoxicating combination.

"It's going to be okay," he says as he lets go.

I wish I could just stay in this little bubble forever. No worrying about school or blackmail. Steve walks me to my mom's car before he gets in his Jeep and we both drive away. I spend the drive home reliving the hug. I can still smell his woody citrus scent; I wonder what cologne he wears. As I pull into the driveway, I get a text on my phone. It's from Steve.

Hope ur feeling a little bit better.

Thank you for listening.

Don't worry, we'll figure this out.

Everything will b ok.

I can't help but smile. I get out of the car and head into the house. I really hope he is right.

October

Chapter 14

Steve

For the millionth time, I wonder what I was thinking when I told Genevieve I would help her figure out what is going on with her dad. I don't have the tiniest of clues how to handle anything to do with blackmail.

It was stupid to leave campus without a pass as well; I can't get into trouble at Charleston Academy. I could have been sent home, I hope I wouldn't get kicked out for a first offense, but you never know. I guess if you count sleeping through first hour as a first offense, I have already racked up two. I still can't believe I didn't get caught leaving without a pass. The only thing that makes sense is that my dorm parent is used to me leaving almost every afternoon after class to go to work, or to walk into Charleston with friends.

It was stupid to leave, but I don't regret it.

Since that outing to Cleo's Bakery, I have talked to Genevieve on the phone almost every night. She is not only smart, but she is funny and all around amazing once she opens up. I can tell she loves her family and friends with all that she is and even though she always credits Livi for having the spunk, Genevieve is feisty and will not back down when it comes to something she is passionate about. I have listened to a couple of books she has recommended and I never thought I would say something like this, but I really enjoy discussing the books with her after I have finished listening to them.

I decide to call Gran before I go to class. It has been a few days since I have talked to her and she is usually up this early, but when she answers she sounds like I woke her up.

"Sorry Gran. I didn't mean to wake you, just wanted to check in before I go to class since I have to work right after school."

"No worries, Stevie Boy, how is school going?"

She sounds horrible. Not just tired or sad, she actually sounds sick. Her voice is raspy and not as upbeat as usual.

"Gran, you sound horrible. Are you sick?" I ask.

"Well, that isn't a very nice thing to say to an old woman. I'm fine, just a little bit under the weather. Nothing to worry about. Enough about me, how is everything going for you?"

We chat for a little bit and she does sound better by the time we hang up, but something about the way Gran sounds and the way she is acting is off. I don't think it is just her being 'a little bit under the weather.' Between thinking about how I can help Genevieve and worrying that Grandma is deathly ill, I really struggle focusing in class and when the last bell of the day rings, I am more than ready to head back to my dorm room to drop off my backpack and head to work. Maybe telling ghost stories will take my mind off Genevieve and Gran.

No such luck.

As I walk down the hall toward my room, I hear my dorm parent call after me. I turn around and see him walking toward me.

"Just wanted to let you know, you have a new roommate. He's already unpacking."

Well, it would have been nice to have a heads up. I still have a bunch of my stuff on the empty side of the room. I mean why not, nobody was using it.

"Thank you," I say as I head down the hall.

I am really hoping that this guy is at least somewhat normal. I have never had to share a room with anyone before; this is going to be weird. I pause for a minute before opening the door. *Please don't stink, or have any super creepy habits like watching me while I sleep,* I think as I open the door and walk into the room.

He is unloading some clothes into the dresser on his side of the room and turns when he sees me. He is built. Like, super built. I am rooming with the Hulk. Okay, maybe not that big, but the guy makes me look a little bit small and I am not a small guy. He has longer blonde hair and looks like he could have just walked off the beach from a surf session. Livi is going to go nuts over this guy.

I try to smile my most welcoming smile. "Hey. I'm Steve Adler, I guess we're roomies."

I hold my hand out to him to shake and he grabs it enthusiastically, almost shaking my whole body. He grins and says, "Hey! I'm Mark Lykaios. Nice to meet you!"

"I'm a little bit surprised that I got a new roommate in the middle of the semester," I point out.

"Yeah, my uncle pulled some strings for me."

"Sounds like a good uncle to have."

"Yeah, Uncle Sebastian has a lot of influence, he can make a lot of things happen that aren't 'supposed' to happen."

"Remind me not to get on his bad side," I joke.

Mark laughs, but he looks like there is something he isn't saying. Makes me even more leery of this new arrangement. He seems like a nice enough guy; I should probably give him a chance before I make any snap judgments, I remind myself.

As he continues to unpack, he rolls up his sleeves and I can see tattoos on both arms. Yep, Livi is going to flip. I thought I had a relaxed guardian, but I don't think Gran would be up for me getting any tattoos quite yet.

At least maybe now Livi might give Gen and I some breathing room when we are together. Don't get me wrong, Livi is fun and hilarious, but she does have a little bit of a problem with personal boundaries. Having someone to entertain her when I am with them might be a definite perk.

"So where are you from?" I ask.

"New York."

"Like New York the state or New York the city?"

"Both." He laughs. "I live with my uncle in New York City, which is in New York State, but my mom lives in a small town several hours away, also in New York State."

"Gotcha. So what brings you to Charleston Academy?"

"Needed a change of scenery."

Well, that was vague.

"Do you have a girlfriend back home?"

"Nope. Work back home keeps me pretty busy, don't have time for relationships."

It's looking more and more like I might have a distraction for Livi on my hands. "Where do you work? Or I guess I should ask where you worked? Since you're here now."

"I help my uncle with the family business."

"Oh, that's cool, what's the business?"

He looks a little bit irritated when he glances at me. "A little bit of this and that. It is kind of hard to explain."

Oooookay. Message received. He doesn't want to talk about home.

"I'm assuming you're a senior since we're roommates?"

"Yep. Can't wait to be done with high school." He looks over at me. "How about you? You have a girlfriend?"

"Kinda." I sigh. "We hang out and talk all the time, but we haven't made anything official."

Thankfully, we get interrupted by a knock on the door. It is Troy and his usual following. I introduce all of them to Mark and notice as all the girls' eyes light up when they see him. They invite us to walk into town with them. I realize that I really don't want to go out tonight, surprising myself. I tell them I have to go to work but maybe next time, and Mark tells them that he needs to finish unpacking.

— • —

It feels strange to come back to the room after work and see all of Mark's stuff on the other side of what I have gotten used to as my own space. I shower and get comfortable before I call Genevieve. It is our new nightly routine; unless one of us has something going on we always talk to each other each night before we go to bed.

"Hey! How was your day?" she says when she answers the phone.

"Good, just got done with work, so I didn't really get any homework done. But other than that, things are good. Oh, and I got a roommate"

"A roommate? In the middle of the semester?"

"I thought the same thing. Yeah, his name is Mark; I think he might be Livi's type."

Mark raises his eyebrows at me and asks who Livi is. I say I will tell him later.

"If he truly is Livi's type you might have your hands full." Genevieve laughs at her own joke. "How was work? Did anyone scream on your tours tonight?"

I chuckle. "Nope, the stories made a couple of the people pretty nervous, but you still take the cake for loudest blood curdling scream on a tour."

"A trophy I would totally be okay giving to someone else."

I laugh. "How was your day?"

"Good, I'm going to have to get off the phone soon actually. I told Dad I would work on our blueprints together tonight. I am hoping that maybe he'll tell me what is going on."

"Well, have fun with that. Let me know if you find out anything."

"Will do, thanks Steve. Hope it doesn't take you too long to catch up on your homework."

"Thanks Gen, talk to you tomorrow?"

"Of course," she says before disconnecting the call.

I find it funny that I have met another person who is just as anti-saying-goodbye as Gran is. I thought Gran was one of a kind in that department. I surprise myself again when I realize that I really didn't want to get off the phone. I have never been one to talk on the phone for long periods of time, but I feel like I could talk on the phone with Genevieve for hours and not be ready to hang up.

Mark asks me a bunch of questions about Charleston, my job, classes at Charleston Academy, Livi and Genevieve before we go to bed. Despite his never-ending questions he only answers my questions with vague answers that could mean multiple things. He is funny, easy going, and seems like he might be a fun roommate.

At least I hope so.

Chapter 15

Genevieve

"What are your plans for your birthday?" Livi asks.

We are painting our nails and catching up. My bed looks like a tornado of nail polish bottles and snacks came through and left all its debris behind. Between school, talking on the phone with Steve, and trying not to be paranoid about my parents' odd behavior, it has been a little while since Livi and I just got to hang out. I haven't even really thought about my birthday either.

"I don't have any plans," I say.

"It's still pretty warm; it would be fun to go out on the boat one last time before it gets too cold to swim."

It is warmer than usual for October; the temperatures are still staying in the eighties. It would be fun to have a birthday out on the lake.

"That does sound fun; I'll talk to Dad about it."

Mom made a big deal out of Violet's eighteenth birthday. It was formal dress and had a four-course meal. I am pretty sure she invited the whole town to the party, at least it seemed like she did. It was so big, it didn't really even feel like it was about Violet. Mom had all her friends there and Violet's friends were there too, but she never looked like she was having a lot of fun. It was beautiful and extravagant, but I really hope that I can convince Mom to let me have a relaxing eighteenth birthday instead.

"So have you been talking to Steve a lot?" Livi asks.

"Almost every night for the last little while." I blush.

Livi lets out a high-pitched squeal. "Really?! Tell me everything!"

I laugh at her enthusiasm. "There isn't a whole lot to tell. We just text throughout the day and usually talk at night. He did tell me he got a roommate though."

"Really? Is he cute?"

"I don't know, I haven't seen him and I'm not about to ask Steve if his roommate is cute."

"You should invite them both to whatever you decide to do for your birthday."

"I haven't told my parents about Steve yet." Livi's jaw drops and I can't help but giggle. "What?" I ask.

"I'm just surprised. You've always been so open with your parents about everything, I can't believe that you haven't said anything to them."

"They've just been so stressed; I haven't gotten around to it."

"What have they been stressed about?" Livi asks.

I walked right into that one.

I want to confide in Livi about the blackmailing so much, and it feels weird keeping something from her. I normally tell Livi and Violet everything, but this just feels different and it isn't really my secret to share. I already feel a little bit guilty telling Steve about it, and I still haven't gotten a chance to tell Violet— she never answers the phone anymore. Almost like she can feel my frustration clear in New York, I am saved from having to answer Livi by a Facetime call from Violet.

Talking to Livi and Violet at the same time is almost like life is back to normal, nothing has changed. Except Violet is on a screen instead of painting her nails with us.

"I'm sorry I can't come home for your birthday, Genevieve, I can't miss that much school." Violet looks mischievous. "How crazy is Mom going for your party?"

"I'm hoping that she'll let me have a relaxing birthday instead of a big party."

Violet scoffs. "Good luck with that."

"So Vi, what do you think about Steve?" Livi asks changing the subject.

Violet looks confused. "Who's Steve?"

Livi turns to look at me with her mouth hanging open again. "You haven't told Vi about Steve?"

I grab a handful of popcorn and shove it into my mouth to avoid answering. "Um, HELLO! Who is Steve?" Violet asks again.

"I want to know who Steve is too," Konnie says from the doorway startling all three of us. She laughs as we all flinch at her sudden appearance. "Can I join in?"

I scoot over on the bed, making room for Konnie as Livi launches into the story of the first ghost tour. Her version is definitely more dramatic than mine. Violet, Konnie and Livi are all in hysterics. I have to admit that Livi's version is pretty funny, even if exaggerated a bit.

Konnie has a smirk on her face. "Do you have a picture of this guy? I want to see if he's cute."

I groan. "He's definitely cute, but I don't have a picture." I can feel my face starting to heat up. Dang my red hair and freckles and the drastic blush that always gives away my embarrassment.

"Even I have to agree, he's hot." Livi fans her face dramatically, sending Violet and Konnie into another fit of giggles.

"How come you didn't tell me you have a boyfriend, Gen?" Violet asks.

"I don't have a boyfriend, we're just friends."

"Right." Livi rolls her eyes. "You talk every night and you forget how to speak when you are around him, but he's just a friend."

"I can speak just fine around him, when we went to Cleo's Bakery I didn't have any trouble talking."

"Wait, what! You went to Cleo's with Steve and didn't tell me about it?" Livi whines.

Oh yeah. I forgot I hadn't shared that bit of information with Livi. Time to change the subject.

"Why haven't you been answering the phone Vi? Maybe I would have told you about Steve if you would have called me back." *And the fact that our dad is being blackmailed,* I think, *but you are too busy to return a phone call.*

"Sorry Gen, school is hard. I may have been at the top of the game in Moncks Corner, but the dancers here are on a whole other level." Violet sighs. "I've had to put in extra practices just to keep up with everyone."

"I've seen you dance Vi, you'll get there," I say.

I desperately want to talk to Violet about the blackmailing and I am worried I won't be able to talk to her again for a while, but I don't want to bring it up in front of Livi and Konnie. I haven't wanted to text her about it either; this feels like a conversation that should not be had via text. Plus, Violet seems really stressed with school, maybe I shouldn't give her more to worry about.

After our nails are painted and all three of them are done grilling me about Steve, Livi leaves to go home and Konnie goes to bed. I wander around the house looking for my parents before I find them in the kitchen. Mom is steeping some tea and it smells delicious. They both look up when I walk into the room.

"The tea smells great, Mom," I say. "I was hoping I could talk to you guys about my birthday?"

"Of course, Sweetie. Do you want a cup of tea?" Mom asks.

"With honey, please," I respond.

"What were you thinking?" Dad asks.

"Well, I was talking to Livi and we were thinking it might be fun to take the boat out. Maybe we could do a barbecue after?"

"I think I can handle that. It isn't every day that my Genna Bear turns eighteen." Dad winks at me.

"Thanks, Dad."

I look at both of them. They look so tired and old. They have never looked old to me before.

"Are you guys okay? I've been a little bit worried about you both lately." I look down at the table. My hands feel clammy and the room feels super hot. How can I ask about the blackmailing? I don't want them to know I was eavesdropping, but I need to know. "I may have overheard you say something about blackmail the other day."

Mom looks up quickly and spills some tea onto the counter. She looks over at Dad, but Dad just stares at me with a blank look on his face, like he didn't understand what I said.

I think I broke Dad.

The sound of the decorative clock on the wall marks the seconds as they pass. Tick, tick, tick. The silence is getting extremely uncomfortable before Dad finally snaps out of it and reaches over to pat my hand.

"Nothing to worry about. Who are you thinking you want to invite out on the boat with us?" He asks, expertly changing the subject.

I get that he doesn't want to worry me, but why won't he tell me anything? Is he hiding something?

"*If* we go out on the boat." Mom shoots Dad a look. "I thought we might have a big birthday party for your eighteenth birthday. You had fun at Violet's party, right?" Mom asks.

Exactly what I was afraid of. "I would really rather have a relaxing birthday, Mom. Violet won't be able to be here because of school so I was thinking just you guys, Konnie, Livi and Darla to help me celebrate." I shift, suddenly getting nervous. "And I was hoping that maybe you would be okay if I invite a new friend? It's a guy."

Both of my parents look surprised and Mom hands me my tea. I take a sip as I look back and forth between the two of them.

"Is this a Livi guy friend or a you guy friend?" Mom asks.

"He's friends with both of us, but mostly me I guess."

"I didn't know you had guy friends," Dad teases.

"Well, he's a new friend, like I said. I was thinking of inviting him and maybe he could bring a friend so he feels more comfortable?"

Dad is smiling, but Mom looks more alarmed than happy.

"Is this a boyfriend, Genevieve?" Mom asks.

"I don't think so?" I say with a question in my voice.

I don't know. I mean, I know I really like Steve and I am pretty sure he likes me, but we have never actually gone out on a date or anything. Just the ghost tours, ice cream, and talking on the phone. I don't think we can count the hysterically sobbing at Cleo's Bakery a date.

"How do you not know if you have a boyfriend?" Mom asks.

I shrug. "I mean we talk on the phone a lot and I really like him, but we've never talked about it. Or even gone out on a date."

"Is he in some of your classes at school? Anyone we know?" Dad asks.

Uh oh. I am just now realizing that this could be dangerous territory.

"Ummm, no. Livi and I met him in Charleston. He's been our tour guide on the ghost tours that we've been going on."

"What!" Mom screeches.

Dad looks a little bit concerned but says, "Let's hear her out, Charlotte."

"You've been hanging out with college boys without telling us?" Mom asks. She doesn't sound very happy.

"No, Steve is a senior at Charleston Academy and we mostly just talk on the phone. I don't see what the big deal is."

Mom looks like she is about to explode, but Dad reaches over and grabs her hand before she can say anything.

"We'll talk about it and let you know, Genna Bear," Dad says.

Mom glares at him and I leave to let them talk. I wasn't sure what to expect, but I didn't think Mom would be quite so upset about Steve. Violet has had more than one boyfriend and she never seemed to mind. I really hope that they don't tell me I can't talk to Steve anymore.

What did I just get myself into?

I can't help myself, I have to know if Mom is going to ban me from talking to Steve, so I pretend to head back upstairs before tiptoeing back to where I can hear my parents talking.

Yet another out of character thing for me to add to my growing list of things I would never have done before, but for some reason can't stop myself from doing now.

Mom is easy to hear, her voice loud and animated. Dad's voice is calm and quiet, but I can still make out what he is saying.

"I think we should tell her she can't talk to this boy anymore. I've heard some stories about some of the wild kids at Charleston Academy," Mom says.

"Char, I understand your frustration, but we can't judge him just by the school he goes to. I've also heard that Charleston Academy has one of the best academic programs in South Carolina."

"Why would she hide him from us if there wasn't something we wouldn't like?"

"I don't know, but I think demanding that she stop talking to him would just make her want to talk to him even more." Dad pauses for a moment before continuing. "Having him come to the birthday party would give us a good opportunity to meet him and see how we feel about Genevieve spending time with him."

"And since when has Genevieve not wanted a big eighteenth birthday party?" Mom asks, sounding hurt, and I wince at the tone of her voice.

"I don't think Genevieve has ever wanted a big eighteenth birthday party. She's more reserved and I think a big get-together where she is in the spotlight would make her really uncomfortable."

"But I was so excited to throw a big celebration. It might be her last birthday at home."

Dad sighs. "I know Char, but it is Genevieve's birthday, not yours. I think we should probably celebrate it how she wants to celebrate it."

"I guess so," Mom says grudgingly. "But I'm still going to make a big fancy cake."

Dad chuckles. "I've no doubt it will be magnificent."

"Have you heard anything else about the blackmailing?"

I hold my breath waiting for his response.

"Don't worry about that, Char. I'm taking care of it."

"How in the world did Genevieve find out about it?"

"I'm not sure; we apparently need to be more cautious when talking about it. I don't want to worry you or the girls."

"I'm already worried, Tony. And it sounds like Genevieve is too."

Dad sighs. "I'm still trying to figure it all out. Right now, the only thing I want you and Genevieve worrying about is making her eighteenth birthday special."

The sound of chairs scraping against the floor as my parents get up from the table has me scrambling up the stairs to my room. I barely have enough time to close the door and pull out some homework to make it look like I have been up here the whole time, before I hear a soft knock on the door and Dad peeks his head into my room.

"Hey Genna Bear, Mom and I talked and we would love to meet Steve and go out on the boat for your birthday."

Even though I already heard the information, I can't keep the excitement out of my voice. "Really, Dad? Thank you so much!"

Jumping off my bed I give Dad a hug. I hold on tight, hoping that everything will be okay.

"Why is Peter Pan always flying?" Dad asks.

"Oh Dad," I laugh. "I don't know, why?"

"He neverlands."

I smile and give him another squeeze and he kisses the top of my head. "Goodnight, Genna Bear, I love you."

"Love you too, Dad."

He closes the door behind him and I can hear him check on Konnie and make his rounds through the house making sure everything is locked up, before I hear him close his own bedroom door behind him.

Warring emotions battle in my mind, excitement for Steve to come on the boat with us, worry about my parents meeting Steve, and dread about the blackmail. I send a silent plea out for my parents to like Steve, his blue eyes the last thing I think about before finally falling asleep.

Chapter 16

Steve

"Do you and your new roommate want to go boating with my family on Saturday? We're celebrating my birthday. Livi will be there too." Genevieve sounds nervous on the other end of the phone.

"That sounds fun. I'll talk to Mark and check my work schedule."

"My dad wants to meet you."

I have never been nervous meeting anyone's parents before, but for some reason Genevieve's dad wanting to meet me has me feeling like I might throw up the burger I just got done eating.

I look over at Mark; we are on break at work, eating a quick dinner between tours. Mark and I have been spending a lot of time together. Not only is he my roommate, but I talked to Mr. Langston and helped Mark get a job touring with me. I have been training him all week. The company has been getting ready for their October tours, which are bigger and scarier for the Halloween month. On top of training Mark, we have both been learning the new additions to the Halloween tours.

"Should I be worried?" I ask.

Genevieve laughs. "About meeting my dad? No. Meeting my mom on the other hand should maybe scare you a little bit."

"Note to self, win over Genevieve's mom."

Genevieve's laughter is contagious. It takes a couple of minutes before we can both compose ourselves enough to continue the conversation.

"I hope you and Livi will come up for one of the Halloween tours."

I know Livi will be excited, but Genevieve already doesn't like to get scared. I am sure an 'extra' scary tour won't be too appealing to her. I really just want to see her more.

Genevieve sounds wary. "On a scale from one to ten, how scary are the normal tours versus the Halloween tours?"

"Normal tours like a five or six and the Halloween tours maybe an eight?"

"I don't know, Steve."

"What if you stay right by me and I'll make sure to warn you so that it isn't as scary?"

"I'll think about it."

At least it wasn't a no. We say goodbye and I hang up the phone. I pull up the schedule to check and make sure neither Mark or I are scheduled to work on Saturday and then sit back down on the bench next to Mark.

"Genevieve just invited us to go out on the boat with them for her birthday." I grab another fry and stick it in my mouth.

"That sounds like it could be fun. I've been curious about the non-girlfriend that you're always talking to."

I shake my head and send a text to Genevieve letting her know we will be there. I decide that I am not going to even bother trying to ask my dorm parents for a pass to go, I will just ask Mr. Langston. I hope he will give me a pass; my odds are definitely better asking him.

"She says that her dad wants to meet me," I say.

"Uh oh," Mark laughs. "That sounds intimidating."

"Yeah, not sure why I feel so nervous about it."

Mark smirks at me. "Maybe it's because you actually want him to like you. Does Genevieve have a big family?"

"She has two sisters and her parents."

"Have you met her sisters yet?" Mark asks.

"I haven't met any of her family yet, just Livi, who is her best friend. But she told me that Livi and her mom are pretty much family."

"Do you know what her parents do for a living?"

"Not really, I think her dad is in the Navy. Maybe she said something about her mom being a realtor?" I say as I try to remember if Genevieve has told me anything else. I purposely leave out the blackmail part and wonder if Genevieve has learned anything else. She hasn't brought it up for a while. Mark seems really interested in Genevieve and her family, which seems a little bit odd.

"How come?" I ask.

"Just curious how nice this boat we're going to be on will be," Mark says.

I laugh. "I think you'll like Livi, she's quite the character."

"Can't wait." Mark looks at his phone. "Next tour is in five minutes, we better get going."

We both gather up our trash from dinner and throw it away. I follow Mark to the group and let him start the tour. It is his first tour without my help; I am only here if he forgets something. As I follow the group down the street to the Dock Street Theatre I smile, despite my nerves at meeting Genevieve's family. I can't wait to see her again.

Mark is giving a surprisingly good tour. Even I am getting a little freaked out and I already know all the stories. Some of the stories are pretty messed up, but even during all my training going on the tours, I never really got scared. Standing at the back of the group, listening to Mark tell the stories about the Lady in White and Junius Booth, my skin starts to tingle and goose bumps form on my arms.

The temperature of the room seems to drop a few degrees, which makes the hot breath on the back of my neck even more startling as all the tiny hairs on the back of my neck stand straight up. I spin around, only to find nothing behind me.

I turn back around to listen to Mark finish his story when a hand grabs my shoulder.

I barely manage to stifle my yelp as I whirl around to find yet again an empty booth behind me.

I can't even count how many tours I have been on now, and there have been some crazy things happen, but they have never happened to me. I am starting to understand why Genevieve doesn't like to get scared; my heart is beating so fast I am starting to feel light-headed. Or maybe that is because I am holding my breath? I let my breath out and have never been so happy to leave a building before as I follow Mark and the group back outside.

Are we actually going to see Nettie this time to top it off? I wonder as we listen to Mark tell the tragic story of Nettie. *I mean, she is supposedly the most seen ghost in Charleston.*

Livi is going to freak out when I tell her about this, maybe I shouldn't say anything though, I don't want to make Genevieve more reluctant to come to Charleston for the Halloween tours.

After the tour we make it back to the tour office, turn in our badges, and start walking back to campus. Mark is going on and on about the girls in the front of the group and how scared they looked. He seems to really enjoy the tours and scaring the crap out of people. I am glad I was able to get him a job with the tour company. Anyone wanting to get scared on a tour will not be disappointed with Mark as their tour guide.

"Were you okay back there?" Mark asks. "You looked pretty spooked in the theater."

"Yeah, that may be the most eventful tour I have been on yet. It felt like someone was breathing down my neck and then grabbed my shoulder."

"What? That's crazy, Bro. It had to have been Junius right? Isn't that what he usually does?"

"Yeah, but it's never happened to me before. Freaked me out." I shudder.

Mark just laughs and claps me on the back. "You have no idea. Ghosts may be the least scary thing in this world."

Well that was cryptic, I think as I watch Mark open our dorm room door and disappear into the room.

Chapter 17

Genevieve

Sometimes riding in the car with Livi can be terrifying. She is currently weaving in and out of traffic with the top down and the music blasting. How she hasn't gotten more speeding tickets is beyond me. I feel my phone vibrate and loosen my death grip on the arm rest to check it.

> Headed to work. Excited to see u tomorrow! TTYL

> Excited to see you too!

> Have fun at work.

Smiling I shove my phone back in my pocket just in time for Livi to screech to a halt in my driveway. I am so excited, but so nervous for Steve and his new roommate to come to my party tomorrow.

"Steve just texted, sounds like they're still planning on coming tomorrow," I tell Livi.

"How come you don't sound excited?"

"I'm excited. I'm just super nervous. Mom and Dad didn't react so great when I told them about Steve."

"Well, they're letting him come on the boat, so it must not have been that bad," Livi points out.

"Trust me, it was bad. Mom looked like she was going to explode. I don't even understand why she was so upset."

"Well, don't worry too much about it. You get to see Steve tomorrow and I get to meet his roommate. I can't wait, tomorrow can't come soon enough."

I can't help but roll my eyes. *Is eye rolling contagious?* I wonder. Usually it is Livi doing all of the eye rolling; she definitely has the eye roll perfected. I hop out and wave at Livi as she speeds down the street.

Konnie is staying after school to do a project today and Mom and Dad aren't home yet. Now would be the perfect time to call Violet, if she will actually answer the phone. I pull out my phone and call; she surprises me by answering after the first ring.

"Hey Gen. What's up?"

I didn't quite think through how I was going to bring the topic of blackmail up. In true Genevieve fashion, I panic and just blurt out the first thing that comes to mind.

"Dad is being blackmailed."

There is complete silence on the other end of the phone for what seems like hours.

Violet starts to speak, stops to clear her throat and then starts again. "I'm sorry; I thought you said Dad is being blackmailed."

"That is what I said, Vi. And I've been trying to call you and tell you about it forever."

"That doesn't make any sense Genevieve, you must be confused. What would anyone have to hold against Dad? He doesn't even go five miles over the speed limit."

I want to smile, thinking about how I used the same example when I was talking to Steve, but I can't. "I don't know, but I saw a text about it on Dad's phone. Both Mom and Dad have been acting really weird too. I got home super late one night and they didn't even notice."

"Yeah, that is weird. What did the text say?"

I tell Vi what little information I know.

"Have you told anyone else about it?"

"Just Steve. I didn't want to worry Konnie and I was afraid to tell Livi."

"Probably a good call," Violet agrees. "And you're sure you didn't misunderstand something?"

I tell Violet everything I heard, which to be fair wasn't much, but even when I brought it up to them in the kitchen, they never denied it. Dad just told me not to worry about it.

"But Violet, even if I misheard something Mom and Dad were saying, I didn't misread the text message I saw."

Violet sighs. "This is so bizarre. Dad is seriously the least likely person in the universe to have scary skeletons in his closet."

"We don't really know a whole lot about when he was growing up. He doesn't like to talk about it. And he doesn't talk about Desert Storm at all," I point out.

"Maybe. Let me know if you find out anything else, but I don't think you should worry too much Gen. I'm sure Dad will figure it out."

"I hope so."

"I'm super sad I won't be there for your birthday tomorrow; don't have too much fun without me."

"Never." I smile. "Who can have any fun without Violet here?"

"How in the heck did you convince Mom to give you a low-key birthday? Remember how crazy she went on my eighteenth birthday?"

"I don't think anyone can forget your eighteenth birthday party. It was more like a wedding than a birthday party." I laugh. "Dad is the one who convinced her."

"A birthday out on the boat sounds awesome. I could really use a boat day right now."

"I wish you could meet Steve."

"I'm excited to meet him during Christmas break," Violet says.

"Wait, what? Aren't you coming home for Thanksgiving?"

Violet sighs again, I don't think I have ever heard her sound this tired. "I really wish I could, but a couple of the seniors are staying here for Thanksgiving and said they would help me practice during the break."

"You can't just practice when you get back?"

"There are only a couple of weeks between Thanksgiving break and finals and I really need to work hard. I really wish I could come home Gen, I promise."

"I understand," I say. "I'm just going to miss you. It's already weird not having you at school and my birthday, but Thanksgiving too?"

"I'll for sure be home for Christmas. I have to run though."

"Okay, call me when you can."

I disconnect the call and think about how different this year has been without Violet. I can't help but think that if she was here, she would have already found out what is going on with Dad. For someone who really doesn't like change, this year has been full of change for me. Not having Violet here is hard enough, but having our first Thanksgiving without her? I just can't imagine it. *Why does everything have to change all at once?* I wonder as I walk into the house.

I drop my backpack by the table before heading to Dad's office to borrow some of his permanent markers for my Social Studies project that is due this week. They aren't in the top drawer where they usually are, so I start to rifle through the other drawers. Frustrated that I can't find the markers anywhere, I shut the drawer harder than I mean to and notice a yellow corner of a manila envelope become dislodged from underneath a pile of Dad's things.

I carefully slide the manila envelope out, there isn't anything written on the front. I peek at the door to make sure Konnie hasn't come home yet before I open the envelope and slide the contents out into my hand. On top of a stack of pages is piece of regular printer paper with something typed on it. Lifting the paper up I suck in a breath as I read the words centered on the paper.

YOU'RE OUT OF TIME.
If you won't take us seriously,
it is time for us to up the stakes.

My heart starts to beat erratically as I slide the paper off the stack and see a picture of a much younger Dad with a group of men in military gear. I recognize several of the men, one of them being Miguel, his best friend that he served with during Desert Storm.

The second picture is Mom working in her real estate office.

My heart starts to race and I can feel my palms getting slick with sweat as I look at the next picture of Livi and me walking in Charleston on one of the ghost tours we went on.

There is a picture of Konnie mowing the lawn.

And last, a picture of Violet dancing at Juilliard.

My blood turns to ice. Whoever this is, they are watching my whole family. Somehow they even have pictures of Violet in New York and Livi and I while we were in Charleston. They aren't just watching my dad, or even just our house. They are actually following all of us.

And they just put targets on the backs of everyone Dad loves.

Chapter 18

Steve

I am anxious when we pull into the driveway of the address Genevieve texted me, which is new for me. I am not usually someone who has to deal with being nervous. It is a nice house with a giant pink tree house in the front yard. It looks like every kid's dream tree house, minus the pink part. Mark and I walk up to the door and when I just stand there staring at it, Mark reaches over me to ring the doorbell.

My stomach feels like it is doing aerobics inside of me. The mixture of nerves and excitement has me feeling a little bit woozy. I can't wait to see Genevieve again, but I have never been so nervous to meet someone's family in my life. I really want them to like me.

A tall, thin man with glasses and a huge smile answers the door. He doesn't look anything like Genevieve with his dark brown hair and tan skin.

"You boys must be Steve and Mark," he says as he holds out his hand to Mark. "I'm Tony and this is my wife Charlotte." He motions to the woman next to him.

We both shake his hand and introduce ourselves. Genevieve may not look like her dad, but she is a carbon copy of her mother. I feel like I am looking at a future version of Genevieve and I am not going to lie, it is kinda creepy. Especially since I don't think Charlotte has even smiled at us yet. I am pretty sure if looks could kill, I would be dead. I thought it was the dads that boys were supposed to be afraid of, but Genevieve did warn me.

Lesson learned.

Mark doesn't even seem fazed by her obvious hostility. I sigh in relief when Tony asks if Mark and I will help him load the coolers into the truck. We follow him back outside and help load several coolers and other various supplies into the back before we help him hook the boat trailer up to the truck. It is a big pontoon boat with three engines. It looks like it should be a fun day.

"So where are you boys from?" Tony asks.

"I'm from Brookhaven, Mississippi," I say.

"What part of Mississippi is Brookhaven in?"

"It's a small town about an hour south of Jackson."

"Nothing wrong with small towns, we love Moncks Corner and it definitely isn't a bustling metropolis," Tony says and then laughs at his own joke. I can't help but smile. "How about you Mark, where are you from?"

"New York."

Mark's short answer doesn't seem to faze Tony in the least. "How fun, our oldest daughter is going to school in New York."

"I see you've already met my dad," I hear Genevieve say from behind me.

I turn around to see Genevieve, Livi, and a young female version of Tony. Genevieve introduces her younger sister Konnie who is the same height as Genevieve even though she is a couple of years younger. She is tall and gangly and has Tony's dark brown hair, glasses, and big smile.

"Nice to meet you, Konnie. Everyone, this is Mark," I say motioning toward Mark.

Genevieve smiles at Mark and says, "I've heard so much about you."

"Hopefully all good things," Mark says with one of his famous grins that always makes the girls on the tours fawn over him.

I've never been intimidated by another guy when I am around girls, but for some reason I start to worry that Genevieve will be more attracted to Mark than me. Thankfully, I don't have to worry about it for long as Charlotte, and who I assume is Livi's mom Darla, walk out of the house and Tony tells everyone it's time to go. Livi asks if she and Genevieve can ride in the Jeep with Mark and me and Tony say he doesn't see why not. I am glad it is Tony getting the death glares from Charlotte instead of me now.

Mark tells Genevieve that the birthday girl gets to sit in the front seat and climbs into the back with Livi. I hop in the Jeep and follow Tony to the lake. As usual, Livi keeps up a constant flow of chatter during the drive and while we are unloading the boat. Genevieve is being really quiet. I try to remind myself that she didn't talk to me the whole first tour, which backfires and makes me wonder if she isn't talking because she thinks Mark is better looking.

I don't think I have ever felt this self-conscious before.

Mark and I are about the same height, he is a little bit taller. He definitely has bigger muscles than I do, but I am pretty built myself. I look down at my arms, definitely not scrawny. At least I can grow facial hair, something Mark struggles with. *Good grief. STOP! What am I doing?* I think to myself. Was I really just comparing myself to Mark?

We all climb into the boat and I sit on one side of Genevieve, with Livi on the other side. While Tony is driving the boat out farther into the lake the atmosphere gets more comfortable as everyone chats with each other. I really like Genevieve's family a lot. They are super nice and just fun to be around—even Charlotte, after she relaxes a little bit.

Darla and Charlotte seem to be really close friends as well; I find it interesting that the moms and the daughters are both best friends. They seem to be almost the exact opposites of their daughters, which makes me laugh as I think about it. Darla is reserved and quiet while Charlotte is outgoing and opinionated.

Mark is asking Tony all sorts of questions about what he does in the Navy, it seems pretty interesting. It makes me wonder if Genevieve has learned anything new about the blackmailing. We haven't talked about it for a little while. I have no idea what they would be blackmailing Tony with, he seems like a pretty follow-the-rules type of guy, super corny dad jokes and all. But listening to him talk to Mark, just the fact that he works at the Naval Weapons Station has me willing to bet that whatever weapon he is being blackmailed for is not something you would want to get into the wrong hands.

Which is scary to think about.

Tony brings the boat to a stop out in the middle of the lake and asks who wants to go for a ride on the giant tube being pulled behind the boat.

"The birthday girl gets to go first," Livi says, jumping up and pulling Genevieve up with her.

Genevieve laughs and says, "Yes, and it has nothing to do with the fact that you'll be on the tube with me?"

Livi shrugs her shoulders and puts on a life jacket. She hands life jackets to Mark and me as well. "Well, are you two coming?" she asks.

We put on our life jackets and the four of us jump into the water. Mark and I end up in the middle of the tube with the girls on each side, Genevieve next to me and Livi next to Mark. The longer we stay on the tube the faster Tony goes, he makes a sharp turn and we go airborne as we hit the wake we just made. Genevieve laughs and screams as she and Mark are thrown from the tube into the cold water. Livi and I sit on the tube waiting for them to swim back.

Mark says something to Genevieve and she laughs as they both swim toward us. I can tell Livi is a little bit annoyed. I am sure she isn't used to Genevieve getting the attention. Livi is gorgeous and exactly the type of girl that Mark is usually drawn to. I mean, to be honest most guys would be drawn to Livi, but Genevieve is beautiful and the fact that she doesn't seem to know that she is makes her even more attractive. I don't know why I have gotten so insecure today, I haven't known Mark for long, but I don't think he is the type of guy to go after a girl he knows his roommate likes.

Genevieve and Mark get back to the tube and I help Genevieve climb back on and suggest that the girls be in the middle this time so they are less likely to be thrown off. The rest of the day on the lake goes by without any incident and by the time we load up to go back to Genevieve's house, I am feeling a lot more confident about Genevieve and her family liking me. It is nice being with a family again. Growing up with Gran was great, but watching Genevieve with her parents and sister makes me miss my own family even more.

When we pull up to the house, Mark and I help Tony unload everything and we all head into the backyard where Tony starts up the grill. The smell of the burgers and brats cooking has my mouth watering. Charlotte has gone all out on the sides too, I am pretty sure that there is enough food to feed triple the amount of people here, but it all looks delicious. Watching Genevieve with her family makes me like her even more; she laughs more and looks completely at ease. Total opposite from when we are on the ghost tours.

When we have all eaten so much I am not sure how I am going to move, Charlotte comes out with the most elaborate cake I have ever seen. It is huge, three tiers, and covered in an intricate floral pattern. After we sing happy birthday, Genevieve closes her eyes for a long time before she blows out her candles.

I can't help but wonder what she wished for.

I don't know how she can eat more, but Genevieve cuts herself a giant piece of cake and between forkfuls tells Mark and me that this is her favorite cake ever. Chocolate Raspberry. I grab a slice and even though I am too full to move, I can't stop eating the delicious cake.

"This may be my new favorite cake too," I tell Genevieve.

Tony pats his belly and says, "I thought the dryer was shrinking my clothes. Turns out it was the refrigerator all along."

We all laugh; it is even funnier because Tony is as far from overweight as they come. After everyone has eaten their cake, Charlotte starts bringing out gifts. I run out to my Jeep to grab the card I got for Genevieve.

"Happy birthday, Genevieve," I say as I hand her the envelope.

She looks surprised, but opens it and pulls out a gift card to a bookshop in Charleston she has talked about on our nightly phone calls. I know how much she loves books, but I wasn't sure what to get her, I figured being able to walk around one of her favorite places and pick out a new book would be a good one. I hope I am right.

The smile on her face when she sees what it is makes my anxiety over whether she will like the gift worth it. "Thank you, Steve! Are you going to go with me so I can show you the shop?"

"Sounds good to me." I smile at her.

Tony looks uncomfortable. "I'm not sure I want Genevieve to go to Charleston for a little bit."

Genevieve looks surprised and Livi looks confused. They have been coming on the ghost tours all fall. I can't decide if it is that blackmail that has Tony worried or if he is worried about the girls being alone with Mark and me.

"We'll make sure the girls are safe when they're in Charleston," I say, hoping that he is worried about the girls because of the blackmail and not us. "We'll even make sure they aren't walking alone to and from the car."

Tony looks thoughtful before agreeing that he is okay with that scenario.

"Open our gift next," Charlotte says, and hands Genevieve a beautifully wrapped box.

Genevieve tears the wrapping paper off the box and pulls out a stack of papers. Her face is scrunched in confusion as she reads the papers before she squeals with excitement.

"Really, Dad?! Thank you both!" she says as she gives both of her parents quick hugs.

"What is it?" Konnie asks.

"Dad is taking me to tour Rice University during spring break!" Genevieve tells her excitedly.

I try to think if I know where Rice University is. Luckily, I don't have to wonder for long.

"Isn't that the one in Texas you applied to?" Livi asks.

"Yes! They have one of the best architecture programs and I wanted to see it before I make my decision of where I want to go. That is, if I get accepted."

"Of course you'll get accepted," Livi says matter-of-factly.

"Sounds like a boring spring break to me," Konnie says. Genevieve sticks out her tongue at Konnie.

Texas?

I knew Genevieve was planning on going to college, but for some reason I just assumed that she would stay on the East Coast. I didn't even know she was thinking of going to Texas and the thought of her moving away hurts more than I thought it would. I really don't want her to move, I feel bad, but I really hope she applied to a school closer to home and that she doesn't get into Rice University—which is kind of messed up that I don't want her to get into a school that she is so obviously excited about.

Am I even planning on staying in the Charleston area after I graduate? I had always planned on going back to Mississippi after graduation, but now I am confused about everything.

As the celebration winds down Mark points out that we need to leave soon if we are going to get back in time for curfew. Mr. Langston didn't even think twice before writing us passes to go to Moncks Corner and I really don't want to make him regret it, so I need to make sure we are back on time.

I finally get a chance to pull Genevieve away from the group as we are getting ready to leave. When we're alone, she stops and looks around.

"I found pictures of my family with a threat from the blackmailers," she whispers.

"What?" My heart starts to race.

"It said something about being out of time and it had a bunch of pictures of all of us. There was even one of Livi and me on one of the ghost tours."

Okay, that is seriously creepy.

106

It makes more sense now why Tony didn't want the girls to go to Charleston. I'm not sure what to say or do, but the thought of Genevieve being in danger speeds up my pulse even more.

"What should we do?" I ask.

"I tried to ask my parents about it the other day and Dad said there wasn't anything to worry about, but I'm not sure if I should believe him."

"Yeah, that sounds like something you should worry about."

"I don't know what to do, Steve. There has got to be a reason Dad isn't going to the police, which makes me wonder what they have on him. I still can't even picture my dad doing anything that he would need to hide from the police, but I also don't want to get him into any trouble."

"Yeah, that's a hard spot to be in. Your dad has never even hinted about anything that happened during Desert Storm?"

"I know he has nightmares, but I always just thought it was being in the war that caused them. Now I'm questioning if Dad is as good of a person as I've always thought he was, or if he is hiding things from us. What if he is a bad person and he has just fooled us all?"

"He seems like a genuine person, but I have only known him for a day. Just because someone makes a mistake doesn't mean they are a bad person."

Genevieve sighs. "It depends on how big and bad the mistake was."

Voices from the backyard silence us and we start to walk to the Jeep. I don't know how to help Genevieve, but I don't want tonight to end like this. I don't want her worrying about things she can't control on her birthday. I grab her hand and stop walking as we get to the Jeep. I really don't want to let go of her hand. She looks up at me and smiles.

"Thank you for inviting me today," I say.

"I'm glad you got to go with us."

"Me too, it was a lot of fun. Your family is really great."

"I sure think so. Mom told me to tell you that you and Mark are both welcome at our house for Thanksgiving if you aren't going home."

"Thank you! That sounds great, if we're in town we'll be here."

Genevieve is still wearing her swimming suit with a T-shirt and shorts thrown on over it. Her hair is a mess from the lake water and drying in the humid heat, but I don't think I have ever seen anyone so beautiful.

She is looking at me with those forest green eyes that seem like they hold all the secrets of the world when you look into them and I can't help myself, I lean down and kiss her.

I have kissed more girls than I probably should have before, but nothing could have prepared me for the way I feel when our lips touch.

Time stops and my head goes blank.

My stomach feels like I just went over the top of the tallest drop on a roller coaster and I realize I am holding my breath. I pull back to look at Genevieve and breathe in her sweet tropical scent.

I pull her to me again, this time with a hunger that I didn't even know I had, claiming her lips with mine, feeling an intensity like I have never felt before in a kiss.

"You guys want us to come back later?" I hear Livi ask, and the moment is shattered.

We pull apart and Genevieve whispers, "Best birthday present ever."

I give Genevieve a hug and tell her I hope to see her soon before climbing into the Jeep with Mark. We are quiet on the drive home, my head spinning from the kiss and over thinking every minute of the day. It is exhilarating and terrifying as I realize that I have found something in Genevieve that I never thought I would find.

I have a real connection to her, and for someone who has trouble forming true connections with anyone, it is quickly becoming something that I don't think I can live without.

And that scares me.

Chapter 19

Genevieve

How did I get conned into this? Everyone knows I hate being scared, so why in the world is everything we do scary? Ghost tours, now scary movies and haunted boat rides at Cypress Gardens.

I blame it on Livi. She knows that I will want to be anywhere Steve is, so she brings up all the things that she knows I wouldn't want to do when we are with him. When he says it sounds fun, I kinda just go along with it because when he talks about it, it does sound fun.

Until I get home and my brain has a second to catch up to what I agreed with.

I have made it my full eighteen years without going on the October haunted boat rides at Cypress Gardens and now somehow I have agreed to go this weekend. I have to admit that since my birthday party the four of us have gone to a couple of movies and out to get ice cream a couple of times, but the majority of what we do together is designed to scare people. At least the haunted boat ride will be at one of my favorite places.

I love Cypress Gardens and the peaceful quiet that is always surrounding me while I am there. I love bright pretty blue water as much as anyone else, but there is something about the stillness of the black water swamp that touches my soul.

Unless it is raining, the water is perfectly still and smooth as glass. You can see a mirror image of what is above the water. Black water may sound like it isn't beautiful, but it is. It doesn't look murky; it looks like something that shouldn't be possible. Like an obsidian mirror that is only interrupted by an animal or a fallen log. It's weird not being able to see what's underneath the water. It leaves you feeling like there is a mysterious world under there that no one is meant to see, just wonder and dream about. The lily pads and their beautiful flowers provide a break in the black that just adds to its otherworldly beauty.

Then there are the cypress trees. Their tall straight trunks that reach up to the sky with hardly any branches until the top almost look like they should be in a haunted forest. But there is something about the cypress trees that draws me to them. They are majestic.

Walking around the black water swamp, seeing the alligators, hearing the other wildlife, the boat rides on the peaceful still water. Everything about the swamp calms me. Although no amount of money could actually get me into the water myself. I can't even count the number of alligators I have seen poking their heads out of the water.

I think that is one of the reasons that the haunted boat tours scare me so much. I have heard they have scuba divers in the black water that do things to make the boat ride scary. I don't want something jumping out of that black water at me! But I think I am more terrified of seeing one of the scuba divers getting mauled by an alligator. Why on earth anyone would volunteer for that job is beyond me. They apparently have a death wish. Most of my friends and family have been on the haunted boat tours, some go every year and so far no one has seen an attack. So apparently I shouldn't be as worried about it as I am, but that doesn't make me feel any better.

Cypress Gardens and Mepkin Abbey have always been my safe havens. Somewhere I can go to feel calm and think without the distractions of everyday life when I need to get away from the world.

I don't want one of them ruined by a stupid haunted boat ride. What if I get so scared that the haunted boat ride is all that I can think about every time I go to Cypress Gardens from now on? Not to mention that Steve had brought up wanting to see Cypress Gardens and this is not the way I want him to see one of my favorite places.

Ugh. I sigh and bring my attention back to the mirror. I am attempting to do my makeup, but I am nowhere as skilled in this department as Livi is. Maybe I should call her and ask if she will help me.

Nope.

I would never hear the end of it and she would expect me to be completely dolled up with makeup every day from here on out if I show any sign of interest. I stick to my basics that I know I can handle: a light sheen of powdered foundation, some black eye liner, mascara and just a slight dusting of some eye shadow that Mom got me for my twelfth birthday. I look like me and that is what is important.

I pull on my favorite pair of jeans and throw on a cute flowery top that I rarely wear, but love. I should definitely wear it more.

On the way out of my room I grab one of my hoodies in case it gets chilly. We have been having a muggy hot week, so I probably won't need it, but I would rather have it and not need it than need it and not have it.

Taking the stairs two at a time I slide into the kitchen on my socks, I don't care how old I get, I am pretty sure sliding through the house on the hard floors with socks will always be a daily occurrence for me.

The smile on my face disappears when I overhear Dad having a heated phone conversation. I can only hear his side of the conversation, but it is obvious it is about the blackmail.

"I don't really think you did it, Miguel, I just can't figure out where they are getting the information from," Dad says in a strained voice.

I know Miguel served with Dad during Desert Storm and they have been best friends ever since then. He listens to whatever Miguel is saying on the other end before responding again. "It has to be someone who was there but isn't currently active duty. There aren't that many of us still serving and all of us who are, have high enough clearance to just get the blueprints themselves. There would be no need to involve me."

Another long pause, I wish I could hear what Miguel is saying. Dad sighs. "I'm running out of time. They sent another text today that just said 'tick tock.' I have to protect my family, Miguel, and if this gets out, it won't only ruin my life but it will ruin the lives of everyone who was with us that day."

It sounds like Dad really did do something horrible. I just can't wrap my head around my sweet, funny Dad doing something that could ruin multiple lives.

Maybe he isn't really who we all think he is.

Dad sounds defeated. "I can't give these people access to a weapon that can cause so much harm. If anyone with bad intentions gains access to this weapon, my family won't be safe anyway."

I wait for him to disconnect the phone call before I peek my head around the corner and as soon as I see him, my doubts about his moral character disappear.

Dad is standing at the window looking out at the dense woods behind our house.

He looks haunted.

I have been so worried about seeing ghosts on all of the tours, but looking at Dad I think I have been living with one. He may not be an actual ghost, but he looks like he could be. And who knows, maybe the ghosts of his past are lingering, haunting us all.

I know that he has had problems with sleeping in the past because of his time in Desert Storm, but I really don't know much about it. He never talks about it and Mom always brushes it off and changes the subject when we ask her about it. I often wonder if she even knows about the trauma that Dad suffered while he was there.

But looking at him now, he looks tortured, in so much pain that it hurts me to look at him. I always thought that it was only in his dreams that he had problems, not while he was awake. He has always been the fun, goofy Dad that can make everyone smile, or see the good in any bad situation.

To see him like this shakes me.

Has he been hiding his pain from us all this time? Or does he have a dark side that he has kept buried all these years?

Who am I kidding, my dad is still the same man who tucked me in at night and scared away the monsters under my bed. He is a good man now, even if he did something horrible in his past. I start to feel a little creepy staring at him, staring out the window.

I clear my throat. "Hey Dad. You okay?"

He startles and looks at me. "Hey Genna Bear. Yeah, I'm fine." He sighs and turns toward me. "Where are you off to this evening?"

"I guess we are going to a scary movie," I grumble.

"You seem to be going on a lot of haunted attractions lately, which is not your usual style."

I groan. "Don't remind me! They even somehow convinced me to go on the haunted boat rides in Cypress Gardens this weekend too."

His eyebrows rise up to his hairline. "I tried to get you to go on those boat rides with me every year for years. Who is the magical creature that convinced you to go?"

Blush creeps up my neck until I am pretty sure my entire face is beet red.

Dad chuckles. "Never mind, I'm pretty sure a tall handsome boarding school boy might have something to do with it."

"Daaaaaaaad," I whine and try to hide my blushing face.

"Genevieve, listen to me." He sounds so serious I forget my embarrassment and turn to look at him. "Do not EVER be embarrassed or hide what makes you happy. I love you no matter what and I just want to be a part of your happiness."

Wrapping my arms around him I squeeze and say, "You will always be a part of my happiness, Dad."

He sighs and kisses the top of my head. "I hope so. I really hope so."

Before I can react, Livi bursts through the front door.

"Who is ready to get scared?" she singsongs as she marches into the house.

"Not me!" I yell back.

Dad chuckles and squeezes me a little tighter before he pulls away. "Have fun, Genna Bear."

When we get to Charleston, I send Steve a text and he meets us at the car just like he told Dad he would. Even though I talk to him daily and I have seen him pretty regularly since my birthday, I still get butterflies in my stomach every time I see him. The closer we get to the theater the more I dread watching a scary movie. The last one Livi convinced me to watch gave me nightmares for weeks. I bite my lower lip and fold my arms.

Steve slows down and looks at me. "Are you okay?"

"I really don't want to watch a scary movie, but I know Livi really wants to go."

We all stop in front of the theater, even the poster for the movie is terrifying. Steve squeezes my hand. "Are you guys okay if I take Genevieve to the bookstore instead of the movie?"

"A bookstore. Seriously?" Livi whines.

"I wouldn't mind seeing this bookstore Genevieve loves so much," Mark says.

Steve laughs. "Do you even own a book, Mark? You guys go ahead and go to the movie and we'll meet up with you guys after."

Livi looks happy to have Mark to herself, but Mark doesn't look as pleased.

"It'll give Genevieve a chance to use her gift card I gave her for her birthday," Steve says. "As long as you are both okay with it."

Livi says she is fine with it and starts tugging Mark into the theater before he has a chance to respond. I am relieved that I don't have to sit through the movie and the alone time with Steve is a definite plus. We wander down the street toward the bookstore in comfortable silence. When we get to the bookstore, I can hardly contain my excitement. I have loved this bookstore for as long as I can remember. One of Dad's friends, Charlie, which he served in the Navy with, used to own it before he died. Now his wife, Sarah, owns it, but we don't come and visit as much as we used to.

Steve opens the door for me and we walk in. I stop and inhale. There is nothing else that compares to the calming smell of being surrounded by books, old and new.

Sarah spots us right away. "Genevieve! It's been too long!" She wraps me in a hug.

"I know. Trust me, I would spend every waking moment in this store if I could."

Sarah's musical laugh makes me smile. "I'm sure you'd get bored eventually. Who do you have with you?"

"This is Steve. I've been telling him about your store and he got me a gift card from here for my birthday."

"Nice to meet you, Steve," Sarah says as she shakes Steve's hand. "You two browse and see if you find anything that interests you."

We spend the next hour looking at books and I find too many that I want to take home with me. I take them to the checkout counter and have Sarah help me decide which ones I should keep and which ones I should leave.

As we are leaving the store, Sarah calls out, "Oh Genevieve, wait a minute. I found a box with your dad's name on it while I was going through some of Charlie's things. Let me send it home with you."

We wait while Sarah grabs the box. She comes back with an old beat-up shoebox and hands it to me. I thank her and we head back out onto the street.

We still have a little bit before Mark and Livi's movie is over so we walk over to a bench looking out onto the ocean and sit down.

"What do you think is in the box?" Steve asks.

"I don't know. Charlie and Dad were good friends; they served together during Desert Storm." My breath catches and I snap my head up to look at Steve. I never even thought to see if I could get any information about what happened during Desert Storm from Sarah. Maybe Charlie told her something. "Do you think it would be horrible of me to see what's inside?"

"I don't think so. Maybe we can find a clue about what happened."

I sit for a minute warring with myself. I'm not sure if this crosses any boundaries or not. Mom lets me look through her keepsake boxes, but I already have permission to do that.

I suck in a quick breath and lift the lid.

The first thing I see is a stack of pictures. One of Charlie and Dad, smiling happily at the camera. Another of Dad, Charlie, and Miguel. My heart skips a beat when I see the next picture. It is the same picture that I found in the manila envelope in Dad's office.

"What is it?" Steve asks.

"This is one of the pictures that was in Dad's office."

"One of the pictures from the blackmailer?"

"Yeah." I start to dig through the box faster.

"If it's the same picture then all the people in the photo have to be a part of what happened right?"

"I don't know. Probably."

"Do you know any of the other men?"

I look at the picture carefully. I recognize Dad, Miguel, and Charlie for sure. A couple of the faces I am pretty sure are Dad's shipmates who died during Desert Storm, and another one I remember going to a funeral with Dad for, but I am not sure I ever met him. The other two men I don't know.

"I think they've all passed away except for Miguel and maybe these two. I have no idea who they are though."

Steve takes the picture out of my hands and scrutinizes it while I continue to dig through the box. Under the pictures is a stack of news articles, they all seem to be about the same cruise ship. I check the dates of the articles. They are all in January of 1991.

"Steve, can you look up on your phone when Desert Storm was?"

Steve scrolls through his phone for a minute. "It looks like the Gulf War was from August 2, 1990 to February 28, 1991, but Desert Storm itself only lasted from January 17 to February 24, 1991. Granted, I don't know how accurate the information I am getting is."

"All of these articles would have been during Desert Storm then."

"What are the articles about?"

"Every single one is about a cruise ship that sunk. It says that it was carrying refugees; it was full of women and children who all died when it sunk. There weren't any survivors."

"That's horrible."

"I know, right? Why would my dad have so many articles about this?"

"Does your dad ever talk about Desert Storm?"

"No not at all, he doesn't really even talk to Mom about his past or his current work in the Navy. I think a lot of it is stuff he isn't allowed to talk about."

"Makes sense, I mean the blackmailers want the designs for some sort of crazy weapon, seems like he works on stuff that he wouldn't be able to talk about. Have you ever asked your dad about his past?"

"Yeah, he just gives the bare minimum of information and then changes the subject."

"I'm sure he doesn't want to talk about stuff like that with his teenage daughter."

"You're probably right, but I don't think he talks to Mom either."

"Maybe he is hiding something, or maybe he just doesn't want to remember his past." Steve thinks for a minute. "Does it say how the ship sunk?"

"Not in this article, it just says that it was under investigation." I skim through more of the articles trying to find a cause. "This last article says that they were using a decommissioned cruise ship and it wasn't seaworthy. It doesn't seem like anyone thought something specific happened to sink it, just a terrible tragedy."

"It has to have something to do with what happened during Desert Storm, don't you think?"

"What are you guys looking at?" Livi's voice from behind us makes up both jump and I start to put everything back into the box quickly.

"Sarah from the bookstore had a box for Genevieve's dad. She found it with her husband's things and sent it home with Genevieve," Steve says saving me from having to answer.

"Anything interesting?" Mark asks.

"Not particularly, just some news articles and some pictures of Tony with his shipmates."

"Can I look at them?" Mark asks.

"I should probably make sure my dad is okay with anyone looking at them first. I shouldn't have been looking at them without his permission."

"We better get the girls back to their car soon anyway. All of us need to get back in time for our curfews," Steve points out.

I follow Steve, Livi, and Mark back to the car with my mind frantically trying to put the pieces together. There is no way my dad could have anything to do with a whole cruise ship of women and children dying. *Right?*

We make it back to Livi's Mustang and Steve gives me a kiss before letting go of my hand and opening the door for me. No matter how many times he kisses me, every time it is like every single one of my nerves goes on high alert, all of my senses collide and I feel like I am floating.

You would think that just talking about blackmail and my dad maybe not being who I think he is would make a kiss less effective, but no, definitely still effective. I can't help but smile and feel giddy. Before we leave, I give him one last hug and breathe in his woody citrus scent before giving him one last quick peck.

"We'll talk later," he whispers as I slide into the car and he shuts the door.

"You look pretty happy over there," Livi says.

"I'm pretty sure that kiss was worth getting scared for. Almost. I'm glad Steve took me to the bookstore instead of the movie though."

Livi bursts into laughter. "Genevieve, you are ridiculous."

"Am not. What about you? You look pretty cozy with Mark."

"I really like Mark and he is super hot, but I'm not sure he's that into me."

"Who wouldn't be into you Livi? I am sure he is just taking his time."

"Maybe," Livi says with a frown on her face.

"It's super fun when we all go out together, I wouldn't mind having more double dates."

"Was that a double date?" Livi asks. "We spent most of the time in different places."

"And you didn't want some time alone with Mark?"

Livi smirks. "Touché. You've got me there. Speaking of our dates, are you and Steve official yet?"

I sigh. "I don't really know what we are. In my mind we're a couple, but we have never really talked about it."

"Well, whatever you guys are, you sure look cute together."

I smile at Livi, but wonder why we haven't talked about it. I have never had a boyfriend before, so I don't really know how it works. It seems a little grade school to just ask Steve, "Do you want to be my boyfriend?" I don't have doubts about my feelings for Steve, but maybe he has doubts about his feelings for me? Or maybe there is another girl at Charleston Academy?

My happy mood from the kiss quickly sours as I spiral into my inner doubt and turmoil. *What happens if he doesn't want to be with me? And what happens when I leave for college in the fall?* I wonder. For the first time my forever dream of going to school to become an architect dims a little bit.

Is there a way to have both?

Chapter 20

Steve

I can see why Genevieve loves Cypress Gardens so much. As we walk toward the dock where the boats are lined up, the black water beyond is eerily beautiful. When I think about black water, beauty is definitely not the first thing that comes to mind, but there is something magical about the black water swamp.

It is both completely still, yet teeming with life.

The water looks like glass, but you can hear the plops of animals entering and exiting the water and the constant hum of the cicadas and songs of the different frogs and toads. I can't see them, but I know that there are alligators under the water. I always loved watching for those two eyes and snout popping up out of the water when I was a kid fishing with Dad. It is one of the few vivid memories I have with him.

The water really is black, but it doesn't look murky and gross, it looks like I am looking down into a giant pot of black tea, transparent yet nearly impossible to see beneath the surface. As I look up and out across the swamp, with the last remaining dusky light of day the reflections of the tall cypress trees are mirrored clearly on the surface of the water. There is something almost otherworldly about this place.

I turn to ask Gen about the swamp, but she isn't behind me anymore. I search all the faces around me. I can't see Gen, Livi or Mark. *Where did they go?*

Finally spotting them back up the trail a bit, I start to wander toward them. Livi's fists are clenched and she has a scowl on her face.

"Come on, Genevieve. You're being ridiculous," Livi says in an irritated voice.

"I'll just wait here for you guys and watch," Genevieve says as she wraps her arms around herself and bites her lower lip, both signs I have learned mean she is nervous about something.

Usually Livi gets a little irritated with Genevieve when she is nervous about something, but Livi's brows are furrowed and she has a deep frown on her face. She looks like she wants to slap Genevieve, which I definitely have never seen before. Sure, they get into little tiffs when we are together, but I have never actually seen them in a full-on argument or fight. *What happened while I was down by the water?* I wonder.

Mark puts his hand on Genevieve's shoulder and leans toward her. "I really don't mind waiting with you, this isn't really my thing either."

And it all makes sense now as Livi shoots daggers out of her eyes at Genevieve. What in the heck is Mark doing? This is starting to get annoying. When he talks to me he seems interested in Livi, but every time we get together with them he seems to want to stick with Genevieve and me. Or is it just Genevieve?

"Sorry I lost you guys for a minute," I say, stepping between Genevieve and Mark. A tight fit, but he takes the hint and steps back. "Why don't you and Livi go get in line and Gen and I will catch up?"

Livi turns and starts stomping down the trail toward the boat docks and thankfully Mark follows. I watch them become distant figures as they disappear toward the inky black water. I turn to Genevieve. She has a sheen of tears in her eyes and looks like she is barely keeping it together. Her eyes don't stray from the direction that Livi and Mark went. A light breeze rifles my hair, it feels good in the muggy heat, but Genevieve tightens her arms around herself. I gently lift her chin so she is looking at me.

"You okay?"

She just nods.

"You want to tell me what that was all about?"

I watch as a single tear escapes and leaves a wet, winding trail down her cheek. She doesn't even bother to try to brush it away, so I reach up and slowly swipe it away for her with my thumb.

"I don't even know." Her lower lip trembles. "All I said was that I was scared and didn't think I wanted to go on the boat, Mark said he would wait with me and Livi got mad."

I pull her closer to me and wrap my arm around her shoulders. She melts into me.

"I think Mark was just trying to be nice, but Livi freaked out," she says.

"If I'm being honest, it kinda pissed me off too."

That pulls a little smile out of her. Wiping her eyes she says, "What exactly are you saying?"

"I'm saying that I'm not too excited about other guys giving you a lot of attention. Or any attention if I am being one hundred percent honest."

After saying it out loud I realize just how much I mean it.

I don't want to be with anyone except Genevieve.

She is the first thing I think about when I wake up and the last before I go to bed. I have never been the instigator of any of my past relationships; they have all placed the labels, not me. I have never wanted to in the past because I was the one who always had to undo the label when the relationship had run its course.

I look down and Genevieve meets my gaze with her own curious eyes. This is harder than I thought it would be. I mean, what if she says she doesn't want a serious relationship. I can't blame her; I never have wanted one before either.

I clear my throat. "What do you think? Want to be my girlfriend?"

Oh, for crying out loud, could I sound more idiotic? Probably not. Am I back in fifth grade again?

She breaks my mental berating when she says, "I was thinking about asking you the same thing, I just didn't know how."

"You were going to ask me to be your girlfriend?" I tease and watch as blush creeps into her cheeks.

"Stop. You know what I meant."

"So it's official?"

"It's official," she says and smiles at me before looking back toward the path leading to the boat docks.

"How come you don't want to go on the boat ride? Are you just worried about getting scared?"

"You know I don't like to get scared, but that isn't the only reason. This is probably going to sound stupid, but Cypress Gardens is one of the places I come when I need to relax and I really don't want to get scared here. What if that's all I can remember next time I come here to escape?"

"That doesn't sound stupid, Genevieve. How about you show me some of your favorite places while Livi and Mark go on the haunted trails and boat ride?"

"Are you sure? I really don't mind waiting for you guys if you want to go," she says as she tugs on her bottom lip with her teeth.

"Positive. I would much rather hang out with you."

I grab her hand and tug her toward the boat dock. We find Mark and a still fuming Livi and tell them to go without us before Genevieve leads me to The Butterfly House. Walking through the double sets of doors we follow the path through the large greenhouse. I was expecting a bunch of butterflies, but not only are there a bunch of different butterflies, there are birds and all sorts of plants and flowers. They even have a small pond inside the greenhouse.

I notice Genevieve watching me as I take in our surroundings. She looks pleased at my reaction and I wonder if she has been nervous I wouldn't like Cypress Gardens as much as she does.

"This is pretty cool," I say as we continue along the path.

"I love The Butterfly House, but just wait until I take you to my favorite spot."

"I can't wait. Have you heard anything new about what's going on with your dad?"

"No. I tried to mention it again when I gave him that box from Sarah, but he just told me not to worry about it."

"Maybe he has it figured out?"

She bites her bottom lip again before continuing. "I don't think so. The pictures that I found in his office insinuate that they are following all of us, and then one of the same pictures shows up in the box that Sarah gave me? It is too coincidental. Something about that cruise ship has to be linked to what is going on. Right?"

I can feel the fear creeping in. I even get goose bumps on my arms. "If your dad had something to do with a whole cruise ship of people being killed, that would not be good, Genevieve. That would definitely be something that he would want to hide and not tell the police about."

"I know, I guess I was just hoping Dad was telling me the truth, that I don't have anything to worry about. But he seems to be getting more stressed each day. I think it might be getting worse."

I squeeze her hand. "Maybe he does have it under control, I'm sure it would be stressful even if he has found a way to take care of the situation."

"I overheard him talking to his best friend; he told him that he is running out of time." She sighs. "It sounded like he thinks one of the people they served with might have something to do with the blackmail."

"Is there anything I can do?" I ask.

"Distract me."

I chuckle. "Oh, that I can do." I pull her toward me and claim her lips with my own.

Finally, I get her to laugh. She steals another quick kiss before tugging me out of The Butterfly House and down a gravel path. It is getting pretty dark now and I wonder if we should go too much farther when she stops at a bench and sits down. There is a good view of the swamp from here and we can see some of the haunted attractions across the reflective water.

"This is my favorite spot here. Normally it's super quiet and peaceful."

"You mean when people aren't screaming in terror as they scare themselves on purpose?"

She giggles. "Yep, exactly what I mean."

We sit in silence; our fingers laced together listening to the swamp come alive as the animals and insects begin to start their nightly activity. The cicada's song is occasionally disturbed by the screams of those participating in the haunted areas of the swamp.

Too soon it is time to meet back up with Livi and Mark so we walk back toward the commotion. When Livi sees us she runs toward us and tells Genevieve about the scariest parts, excitement lacing her voice. Genevieve's grip on my hand loosens as she relaxes knowing that Livi is back to her usual enthusiastic self. She turns and gives me one of her heart-stopping smiles and I squeeze her hand before we head back to the Jeep to take the girls home.

After we drop the girls off and are driving back to Charleston Academy, I can't hold it in any longer. The more I think about it, the more it makes my blood boil.

"You really need to back off of Genevieve, Mark."

He looks confused. "What do you mean?"

"You don't think that maybe it should have been me to offer to stay with my girlfriend in the first place?"

"I'm sorry dude; I really wasn't trying to cause any problems."

I realize I am clenching my teeth and try to relax my jaw. "Well, it's really starting to piss me off and it is causing tension between Genevieve and Livi too."

"I honestly didn't realize that I was causing any problems, Steve, I'll make sure to pay more attention next time we're with the girls."

"Thank you."

"You said girlfriend earlier. Does that mean you guys are officially a couple now?"

"Yep," I say in a clipped tone, indicating I am done talking.

We finish the drive in silence. Mark seems genuine, but there is no way that he didn't realize the tension he was causing. I have always felt like I could trust Mark, but I have an uneasy feeling that I can't quite place, as I realize I really don't know much about the person I share a room with.

November

Chapter 21

Genevieve

Someone is watching me.

I don't know who, or how I know they are watching me, but I can feel their eyes on me. My skin feels like it is crawling and my heart speeds up to a frantic fluttering inside my chest. I stand up quickly, almost knocking over the dining room chair I was sitting on, and walk to the same picture window that Dad was staring out of days ago. I peer through the glass into the darkness.

I can't see anything, but the feeling intensifies.

I close the blinds and gather up my schoolwork before heading upstairs to my room, tossing my books onto my bed before falling back onto the bed myself. I haven't seen Steve since we went to Cypress Gardens a couple of weeks ago.

I officially have a boyfriend.

It is weird to think about, and even weirder that I have seen him less now that we are a couple than I did before. The last week of October he was busy with all the Halloween tours and this last week I have been busy studying for my upcoming finals. I still can't believe that it is already November and the first trimester will be ending. I am ready for these classes to be over with, but my next trimester classes will be just as difficult, so I guess it doesn't really matter.

I roll over and open my chemistry book back up. We get one note card for the final so I am trying to cram as much information on there as I can. Hopefully I can read the tiny letters when I need to. The ding of a text notification distracts me; it is from a number I don't have saved in my phone.

> Hey Gen. It's Mark. Just thought you should know that Steve has been going to A LOT of parties lately.

I stare at the text. What exactly am I supposed to do with that information? Before I can respond he sends another one.

> If I was in your position I would want to know.

Ooookaaay. It is probably pretty normal for there to be parties at a boarding school. *I think?* But he has been too busy to do anything with me. How come he has time to go to parties? Logically, I know that driving to Moncks Corner adds on a lot of drive time and he also has to get a pass to leave, and be back by curfew. I probably shouldn't even worry about it, but now that it has been brought to my attention, I can't help but feel a little bit hurt. Even though I have been studying like crazy, Livi and I could have probably driven to Charleston if he had time to hang out.

Trying to get my focus back on the chemistry final, I continue my tiny note taking, but it is hard to concentrate. I slam my book shut and call Steve. When he answers the background noise is really loud.

"Hey Gen. Give me a minute to go someplace quieter," he says as soon as he answers.

He is at a party right now. I try to keep the rational part of my brain in charge, but the emotional side wins out. My pulse is racing and I feel like I am ready to explode by the time he tells me he is somewhere he can talk.

"Where are you?" I ask shortly.

He takes a minute to respond, probably confused by my tone of voice. We have never gotten into anything even resembling an argument before.

"I'm at a get-together at one of the dorms. Is everything okay?

"No, everything is not okay." Oh great, now I can feel the tears trying to surface.

"What's wrong Gen? Did something happen?"

"I don't know, you tell me. You're the one who hasn't had any time to do anything, but apparently you have plenty of time to go to parties."

"Genevieve, what are you talking about? I'm so confused right now."

"Mark sent me a text letting me know that you have been going to a lot of parties. We haven't been able to talk some nights because you were so busy, it definitely doesn't feel great knowing that you don't have time to talk to me, but you have time to go to parties."

"I'm not sure why Mark would have sent you that text, but I swear to you that I've been busy trying to get my grades up. I've gone out a couple of times with some friends, but I realized that I couldn't get good grades and go out every night when school first started." I can hear him take a deep breath over the phone. "And you know how many tours I was doing that last week before Halloween."

Now I feel crazy.

I know I overreacted, but I still feel upset. I don't even know how to navigate this, so changing the subject seems like the best option at the moment.

"I take my last final on Thursday. It'll be nice to be done with these classes."

"Yeah, that will be nice; I know you've had a lot of homework." He pauses. I am not sure what to say, luckily he breaks the silence. "I don't have to work this weekend, would you want to go to Magnolia Plantation with me? I've been wanting to check it out."

"Sure, that sounds fun." I can hear the coldness in my own voice, but I am not sure how to relax.

"Mark has to work so it will just be me."

"K, I won't mention it to Livi."

"Are we good, Gen?"

"Yeah, we're good," I say before disconnecting the call.

I do feel better, but I just don't understand why Mark would send me that random text if there wasn't something going on that I should worry about.

Life was so much simpler before Steve showed up.

Chapter 22

Steve

I feel like punching Mark right in his smug face.

I get riled up every time I think of the text he sent Genevieve. *How did he even get her number in the first place?* It seems like he is purposely trying to stir up problems, which is so confusing because he seems so genuine and nice when you interact with him. He is always willing to help me out when I need anything. He seemed completely oblivious about the problems he caused at Cypress Gardens, so maybe he is just clueless. *I hope he is just clueless and doesn't have hidden feelings for Genevieve or something.*

I don't have the time or the mental energy for those type of thoughts, so for now I am going to give Mark the benefit of the doubt and hope nothing weird happens again. I am going to be late picking Genevieve up. Thankfully, Mr. Langston gave me a pass to take her to Magnolia Plantation; I have a couple of grades that still aren't the greatest, so I am sure my dorm parent would have said no. I pull into Genevieve's driveway where she is waiting outside for me, she climbs into the Jeep and says hi, but after that we sit in uncomfortable silence on the drive back toward Charleston.

As we drive thick, dark clouds move in blocking the sun, making the gloomy sky match our moods.

I am relieved when we pull into the Magnolia Plantation parking lot and we are able to get out of the Jeep. As we walk through the parking lot toward the ticket booth, I get brave enough to grab Genevieve's hand. She doesn't pull away; she laces her fingers with mine. Even though she still hasn't said anything, this has got to be a good sign, right? I mean, she wouldn't hold my hand if she was still pissed off. At least I don't think she would. We make it to the ticket booth and I buy tickets for us to have a tour of the plantation house and explore the gardens.

Looking at the schedule, I notice that the next tour of the house starts in fifteen minutes and ask Genevieve if she wants to do the tour first, before we head into the gardens. She says that will be fine and we make our way over to one of the benches to wait for the tour to start.

I can't handle this awkwardness between us. "Are you still mad at me?" I ask.

She shakes her head no, but still doesn't say anything. *Why are girls so confusing? If she isn't mad, then what is the problem?*

"Do you not want me to go to the parties at school?" I ask her.

She finally looks at me. "It's not that. I want you to have fun. It was just weird that Mark felt the need to text me about the parties. It just made it seem like there was something else going on."

"I agree. It was super weird, but Genevieve," I wait until her eyes meet mine before continuing, "I promise you have nothing to worry about."

Before she has a chance to respond, the heavy grey clouds burst open and rain begins to pour down on us and pound the ground mercilessly. Genevieve shrieks and we run laughing onto the porch of the plantation house, hoping the rain will let up by the end of our tour. We make our way through the house as our tour guide tells us facts about the Drayton family and the house they lived in. When the tour is over, we step back out onto the porch to see that the rain hasn't let up, it may even be raining harder than it was when we went into the house. The parking lot is almost completely empty, indicating that everyone who was here decided to go home.

I turn to Genevieve. "Do you want to come back another day to see the gardens?"

"You bought tickets for the gardens and we're already sopping wet, we might as well walk around for a bit," she says with a smile. "Magnolia Gardens is always beautiful, but we'll have to come back in the spring when everything is blooming. The gardens are truly spectacular then."

With that, she walks down the stairs into the pouring rain and starts walking toward the gardens. I think we have them completely to ourselves, we haven't seen anyone as we walk the trails. I can't believe the amount of time it must have taken to create all the different areas—even crazier that they have been open to the public since the 1870s. On the tour they told us that some of the gardens are even older than that, the oldest being more than 325 years old. They are full of wild, uncontrolled beauty making them like nothing I have ever seen before.

Although we haven't seen any other people, we spot several alligators and turtles as we walk the trails. We stop by a large tree hanging over the Ashley River. Genevieve looks out over the water, the rain is still constant and she is drenched. Her long hair is dripping and bedraggled, but she looks peaceful as she watches the water flow past us.

"Tell me something you haven't ever told anyone else," she says without taking her eyes off the river.

I don't even have to think about it. "I feel guilty for moving away from Gran and I worry about her every day. She's my best friend and I didn't realize until moving here that even though I have a lot of friends, I don't really feel close to any of them. No one truly sees me."

She turns to look at me. Her serious green eyes look even darker as the rain runs down her face. "I see you," she says quietly as she leans up to brush her lips against mine.

The rain, the cold, the gardens, everything disappears as Genevieve becomes my whole world. Standing next to the Ashley River in the middle of a rainstorm, all my worries and problems evaporate as Genevieve's lips move against mine. When we finally come up for air, I rest my forehead on hers and wipe some of the rain away from her face.

"How about you?" I ask. "What's something that you've never told anyone else?"

"I don't actually know what I want to do after high school. I know that I love architecture, but I have no idea what I want to do with it. Everyone expects me to know every detail of my life, but I don't have a clue what I actually want. Except to be wherever you are."

"Well, don't worry, I'm not going anywhere and I still don't know what I want to be when I grow up." We both burst into laughter as we start walking back toward the car.

"How is your dad doing?" I ask.

"I'm worried about him; he seems to be pulling away from everyone and he is hardly home for family dinner anymore. Family dinner has always been important to him."

Not knowing what to say, I wrap my arm around her waist as we walk. We couldn't be more soaked if we had actually jumped into the river. Our shoes make strange squishing noises with each step.

Even though today didn't turn out like I had planned, I think that it might be one of the best days I have experienced so far in life.

Chapter 23

Genevieve

The wind whips through my hair as we drive down the road. Livi is crazy for still wanting to drive with the top down. It is starting to get too cold for that. I pull a hair tie off my wrist and try to tame my wild, blowing hair into a ponytail for the drive to Charleston.

We are meeting the guys for dinner and a party afterward. I guess we will go to the party after dinner if Steve and Mark were able to get us permission to go onto campus. They have to have passes to drive off of campus and apparently we have to have passes to go onto campus. I am glad we are doing something other than going on another tour. We have been on all of the tours multiple times now; at this point I think I could probably give most of the tours myself. That is, if I wanted to stand up in front of a group of people and tell ghost stories.

No thanks.

The good thing about going on the tours so much is that they don't really scare me anymore. I already know all the stories and I have been to all of the places, so they just don't seem that scary. The only tour I still don't like to go on is the Haunted Jail Tour. The Old City Jail just feels sinister. No matter how many times I go in that building.

Just walking into the jail gives me the creeps.

Livi has been quiet during the drive and I realize she seems agitated, constantly shifting her position in her seat and when Livi isn't talking it is a sure sign something is wrong.

"Is everything okay, Livi?" I ask.

"I'm fine."

"You don't look or sound fine, what's up?"

"I am just irritated that Mark never wants to do anything with me unless we are with you and Steve. He always has some excuse."

I don't really know how to respond. It is strange that Mark wouldn't want to spend time with Livi when Steve or I can't go. I thought Mark and Livi were doing great, they aren't a couple or anything yet, but they talk a lot and they always seem like they are having fun together when we go out as a group.

I haven't told Livi or Steve, but Mark has been sending me weird text messages pretty regularly now. I haven't responded to any of them. They seem innocent usually just saying hi or asking what Livi and I are up to, but it seems weird that he is texting me. Livi is so sensitive about Mark right now I have been afraid to tell her about them and I have been nervous to tell Steve about them too. I don't want to hide anything from either of them, but I also don't want to cause problems within the group.

The whole situation with Mark is really frustrating, especially since his attention toward me is unwanted. I hope if I don't respond he will stop texting without me having to talk to him about it. We have a lot of fun when we do things together as a group and I really don't want to change the dynamic. I am pretty sure if I told Steve that Mark has been texting me he would be mad, thinking that Mark was trying to stir up more trouble. Steve has to share a room with Mark and they seem to be getting along great lately, I just really don't want to start any drama.

Livi pulls into the parking lot and parks. My stomach flutters when I see Steve waiting for us in front of the restaurant. He spots us and grins; I can't help but smile back. Livi, Steve and I get a table and start looking at the menus.

"Where's Mark?" Livi asks.

"His last tour was running a little bit late, he said he would meet us here. He should be here soon." Steve rests his arm across my shoulders. "I got you both passes to come onto campus for the party tonight."

"Yes!" Livi squeals. "I've always wanted to see the mysterious Charleston Academy's campus."

"I'm not sure it's mysterious." Steve laughs.

"Haunted for sure, though," Mark says as he slides into the booth next to Livi.

Livi grins. "Oooh. Haunted. That sounds promising. Have you seen any ghosts on campus?"

I look wide eyed at Steve and he laughs. "No, I haven't seen any ghosts on campus."

The dejected look on Livi's face has us all rolling with laughter when the waitress comes to take our order. The food is delicious and the company is even better, it doesn't feel like any time has passed before it is time to head to the party.

Anxiety fills me.

I am not sure I want to see one of the parties that Mark felt the need to point out to me. I usually feel uncomfortable in new situations, and I'm not sure seeing Steve being so comfortable in a situation that I am so obviously uncomfortable in will ease my fears about all these parties Mark thinks I should be worried about. I thought I was over this. Apparently not.

I follow everyone to Livi's car and we all climb in and drive the short distance to Charleston Academy's campus. Mark gives Livi directions on where to park. I take in the old brick buildings. The campus is beautiful, with the buildings nestled near the water surrounded by immaculate landscaping. Steve grabs my hand as we walk toward a building labeled Magnolia Hall, I can hear the muffled thumping of music coming from inside. Mark opens the door and ushers Livi inside before Steve and I follow. The music is loud, and despite the air conditioning and ceiling fans the room is hot and suffocating. I already want to leave. Several people call out to Steve and he waves at them as we pass.

"Is this your girlfriend I've heard so much about?" a tall guy with a petite blond hanging on his arm asks Steve.

Steve smiles at him. "Yeah. This is Genevieve. Genevieve, this is Troy. We have most of our classes together."

"Well, I haven't heard anything about her," the blonde says as she sends a glare my way. The obvious hostility rolling off her doesn't help my anxiety of being here, or my worry about Steve going to the parties. I look around for Mark and Livi, realizing that Livi is like my security blanket in new situations.

"And this is Kinsley. Don't worry, her bark is worse than her bite," Troy says before laughing at his own joke.

Kinsley rolls her eyes and disappears into the crowd. I try to put a convincing smile on my face. "It's nice to meet you."

Steve and Troy talk for a few minutes as I try to follow along with the conversation. *Where on Earth did Livi and Mark go?*

Finally, Steve leans down. "Do you want to get out of here?"

I nod and follow him out into the fresh air. Taking in a deep breath, I can feel my nerves start to calm as we walk to a bench in an elaborately landscaped area between the dormitories. Steve sits down and pats the bench next to him, sliding me closer as I sit down.

"Not quite your scene, huh?" he asks.

"Was it that obvious?"

"Not at all, the sheer panic on your face the whole time was hardly noticeable."

I groan and peek at Steve who is giving me a teasing smirk and bumps me with his shoulder before wrapping his arm around me and giving my shoulder a squeeze.

"I'm sorry, Steve. I know you wanted to go to the party."

"Don't worry about it. I wanted to tell you about some information I found online about the cruise ship anyway."

I perk up when he mentions the cruise ship. "What did you find?"

"Apparently there are witnesses that say they heard loud explosions and the ship was engulfed in flames as it sunk."

"That doesn't sound like the ship wasn't sea-worthy and sunk on its own like the other article said."

"I don't think so either."

"What do you think happened?"

"I'm not sure, but it sounds like it might not be the tragic accident that the papers were making it out to be. I think it might have been sunk on purpose."

"I hope not. That is horrible!"

I am trying to process this new information and make sense of it when Livi comes storming out of the party.

"Uh oh, Livi's on a rampage again," Steve says as she spots us and stalks toward us.

I figured we would be here for as long as we could before heading home, but Livi motions to me to follow her and walks past us toward the car with a scowl on her face.

I follow Livi to the Mustang, trying to keep up as Mark and Steve trail behind us. I ask Livi what is going on, but instead of responding she gets into the car and shuts the door.

Baffled, I turn to Steve. "I'm sorry, I don't know what's going on, but I'll call you later."

He looks upset that we aren't staying to hang out and I don't blame him, I want to stay too. I give him a quick kiss and climb into the car; my door isn't even completely shut before Livi starts to pull out of the parking space and speeds out of the parking lot.

I can tell Livi is mad and I don't know if I should ask her what is going on or just let her calm down before we talk. She has a death grip on the steering wheel and she has such a pronounced scowl that I think it might leave permanent wrinkles behind when she finally relaxes her face. Thankfully, I don't have to decide if I should ask her what is going on or not.

"Mark is more interested in your relationship with Steve than anything to do with me," Livi says in a clipped voice.

I am still trying to come up with something to say when Livi starts to cry and says, "The whole time during the party he was just telling me all of the reasons that you shouldn't be with Steve anymore."

"What?" This doesn't even make sense. "Why does he think I shouldn't be with Steve anymore?"

"Oh, trust me, he had plenty of reasons. None of them are legit," she says as she angrily wipes at the tears streaming down her face.

Why would Mark do this? He is ruining the dynamic of the group. There is no way Livi will want to do anything with us while she is this upset at Mark. Come to think of it, I don't think I have ever seen Livi cry over a guy before, she is usually the one doing the heartbreaking.

We spend the rest of the drive in tense silence before Livi drops me off at my house and squeals her tires as she drives away. I really don't have any idea on how to navigate this situation, Livi is mad at me for something that I didn't even do. I know she is mad at Mark, not me, but somehow I am getting lumped into her fury toward him.

I walk into the house and up to my bedroom before calling Steve. Maybe he can help me figure out what we should do, but he doesn't answer and I lay on my bed with silent tears flowing down my cheeks before I fall asleep.

Chapter 24

Steve

Genevieve is trying to call and I can't answer. I want to find out what is going on with Livi, but I am on hold with the assisted living facility Gran lives at. After Genevieve and Livi left, I noticed that I had missed a call from them during the party and I have been waiting for at least ten minutes for the person who called me to come to the phone.

"Is this Mr. Adler?" Says a young, feminine voice with a deep southern drawl.

"Yes."

"Your grandmother is Juliette Paige correct?"

"Yes, is she okay?" I ask, worry starting to creep into my voice.

"She is fine honey, we just needed to inform you that she caught a cold last week that has turned into pneumonia, because of her age and how low her oxygen levels were the doctor suggested that she be hospitalized. From what I understand the doctor thinks that once she gets on some oxygen and antibiotics she'll make a full recovery."

Needing to be hospitalized doesn't seem fine to me, I think as I try to process the information. She gives me the name of the hospital before we disconnect the call. I try calling Gran's cell and the hospital, but no one can tell me what is going on and Gran isn't answering the phone. I am about ready to get in the Jeep and start driving home when Gran finally calls back.

"Hey, Stevie Boy," she says in a hoarse voice.

"Gran, are you okay? I'm going to start heading that way."

"No, you're not. You need to stay at school. I'm already starting to feel better from the medicine they've given me."

"I'm sure it will be okay if I miss a little bit more class and take a longer Thanksgiving break, Gran."

"You shouldn't come home for Thanksgiving, it looks like I'm going to be in the hospital and we won't be able to celebrate anyway."

I let out a frustrated sigh. "Gran, that's even more reason why I should come home. I haven't been able to get someone to cover me for work yet, but I'll keep working on it."

"Listen to me," she says in her no-nonsense voice. "Don't stress about trying to get time off work. I don't want you stuck in a hospital room for Thanksgiving."

No matter what I say Gran is not changing her mind, but after we get off the phone I call work anyway. There is no way I will have enough time to drive home unless I can find someone to cover my shifts. I have Thanksgiving Day off, but both Mark and I work the day before and the day after so I can't even ask him to cover for me. I can't drive home and back in one day. The secretary says that there is no one else to cover our shifts; they are all going out of town for the holiday.

I call Genevieve back and she answers the phone with a sleepy hello.

"Did I wake you up? I'm sorry, I just got some news that has me stressed out, but we can talk tomorrow."

"You did, but it's fine I need to talk to you too. What's going on?"

I can hear the strain in her voice, I am sure it has to do with whatever was going on with Livi when they left. "Gran's in the hospital with pneumonia. She says she is fine, but I don't think she would tell me if she wasn't. She told me not to come home for Thanksgiving. Not that it matters, because I can't take enough time off work to drive home anyway," I say in frustration.

"I'm so sorry, Steve. Is there anything I can do?"

"I don't think there is anything that either of us can do. It just sucks. Is everything okay with Livi?"

"No, she's super mad again," Genevieve says, her voice getting shaky. Now that I am listening to her talk, I can tell she has been crying. "Livi said that all night Mark was telling her all of the reasons that we should break up, she says that he doesn't care about her at all, just *our* relationship."

"Are you kidding me? Why was he saying we should break up?"

"I don't know, Livi didn't give me any specific details, but there is something else I need to tell you." She pauses for a second before continuing. "Mark has been texting me pretty regularly. I didn't want to say anything because I didn't want to start any drama. They've all been totally normal texts and I haven't responded to any of them, but it made me feel a little weird that he was texting me."

What is Mark's problem? I try to keep the irritation out of my voice. "What is he saying in the texts?"

"Nothing really, usually just things like 'hey' or 'what are you and Livi up to tonight?' I'm just frustrated that Livi is mad at me and I didn't do anything."

"I am sorry Gen; I'll talk to Mark and see if I can figure out what is going on."

"Are you sure that will go over well?" she asks.

"Well, I'm going to have to talk to him anyway, so I guess it doesn't really matter."

"I know Mom invited both of you over for Thanksgiving, but Darla and Livi come to our house for Thanksgiving every year, so I'm not sure how that's going to work out."

"I don't really want to be by Mark right now either, but I'll let you know what happens after I talk with him."

I hang up the phone as Mark walks into the room after his shower.

"What the heck, Mark? Why were you telling Livi that Genevieve and I should break up tonight?" I ask angrily.

"I don't know what you are talking about, man. Livi must have misunderstood what I was saying."

"Well, what exactly were you saying?"

"I have fun hanging out with everyone, but Livi is a bit much for me. I was trying to make it sound like we should hang out with you guys to babysit you two. It had nothing to do with you and Genevieve. I just wanted an excuse to not have to be with Livi by myself."

"And what about all of the text messages you've been sending Genevieve?"

"Just random texts when I'm bored, I send texts to you and Livi too when I'm bored. You can even look through my phone if you want to."

He unlocks his phone and hands it to me. I see Livi, Genevieve, and me all on the list of recent text messages. As much as I want to trust him, I click on his text stream with Genevieve. Sure enough they seem pretty innocent, asking her how her day was or what she and Livi are up to. There are the text messages he sent about me going to parties that brings another wave of anger, but I can't help but smile to see that Genevieve hasn't responded to a single one of his texts. Now if only Mark would take a hint.

Mark seems like he is telling the truth, and Livi can be a little intimidating sometimes. I probably wouldn't want to be stuck alone with her either. I can't make Mark have feelings for Livi, but how can we smooth things over with Livi without her feelings getting hurt?

"Genevieve is worried about us coming over on Thanksgiving now because Livi and her mom will be there."

"I'll smooth things over with Livi, tell Genevieve Thanksgiving will be fine. I definitely don't want to miss out on any of Charlotte's cooking."

I laugh. "Right? Me neither."

I finish scrolling through his texts to Genevieve and sure enough, it looks like he is just being friendly. It honestly could be taken both ways, because on one hand he could just be bored texting a friend and on the other hand why is he texting my girlfriend so much? Especially when she isn't responding.

"Thanks for showing me; maybe you should just stop texting Genevieve completely for now. We really don't need to rile Livi up any more than she already is."

"Okay, no worries. No more texting Genevieve, got it."

Mark seems fine with everything, but there is still something bugging me about his interest in Genevieve. I send a text to Genevieve letting her know that we are planning on being there for Thanksgiving and Mark says he will patch things up with Livi before then. I am emotionally exhausted and don't even change out of my work shirt before falling into a restless sleep.

Chapter 25

Genevieve

I am normally an anxious person, but my anxiety today is on a whole new level. Not only is Thanksgiving going to be completely different this year with Violet in New York and Mark and Steve here, but things with Livi have been strained. Mark is really starting to get on my nerves. I really hope he can fix things with Livi and today isn't a disaster.

Livi's voice floats up the stairs, she and Darla are apparently here already. Normally I would be excited they were here early, but today I am dreading finding out if Livi is still mad or not. Livi comes bounding up the stairs and bursts into my room. Looks like Livi is her usual happy self.

"You seem like you are in a good mood today," I point out.

"It's Thanksgiving, why wouldn't I be? We get to stuff ourselves full of your mom's delicious food that my mom pretends to help make."

I laugh. "She does help. She hands Mom stuff when she asks for it."

Livi rolls her eyes. "That's not helping. Anyways, Mark called me last night and we figured everything out."

"So you're excited to see Mark today?"

"So excited, today is going to be epic!" Livi says as she gives my jeans and T-shirt a once over. "Is that what you are wearing today?"

Luckily, I am saved from a Livi wardrobe makeover by the ding of the doorbell downstairs.

"They're here!" Livi squeals as she grabs my hand and drags me down the stairs.

Livi throws the door open and ushers Steve and Mark into the front room, where Konnie is waiting. Thanksgiving tradition in the Clark household is the kids and Dad play board games while Mom and Darla get everything ready. She hates any of us trying to help her in the kitchen, saying she just trips over us if we are in there. Grandma used to be in the kitchen with Mom and Darla preparing the Thanksgiving feast, but now it is just the two of them.

I have never played board games with Steve before, he gets really competitive and the competition between Livi and Steve to win each game is pretty entertaining. I could just sit and watch them fight over who is playing the games right without joining in, and still be amused.

I glance around the room and realize that Dad isn't here. Usually he will play the games with us, or sometimes he will be reading his book while we play, but he is usually always in the room with us each year.

We haven't even worked on my dream house blueprints for weeks. I'm not sure if that is because Dad has been preoccupied with the blackmail, or if it is because I have been so caught up with Steve. How can I be so happy and excited about Steve and so worried and scared about Dad and his blackmail at the same time? I am distracted by Livi diving over the board game for the dice in Steve's hands.

"It's my turn; don't even think about trying to skip me," she screeches.

Steve looks startled as Livi steals the dice out of his hands and I can't help but burst into laughter. He looks at me and mouths the word 'help' toward me, which makes me laugh even harder.

Konnie tries to grab the dice from Livi, and Livi slaps her hand away. "It's actually my turn," Konnie grumbles.

"Shouldn't you be at the kiddie table, Konnie?" Livi teases.

I sigh. The tension between Livi and Konnie is starting to get annoying. Would it kill Livi to let Konnie hang out with us sometimes? We hung out with Violet all the time when she was here.

"Livi, be nice," I chide.

"Dinner is ready kids," Darla says sticking her head into the room.

The game is forgotten as we all head toward the dining room. As usual Mom has the table decorated beautifully and the food looks amazing. We all find our name cards on the table and sit down. Dad has materialized and is sitting in his usual spot at the head of the table ready to carve the turkey. Once our plates are full, the room is almost instantly quiet with only the sound of forks scraping plates and people chewing the mouthwatering food. It would be someone with misophonia's worst nightmare.

There isn't much conversation going on while we all eat, but I can't help but notice the silence from Dad's end of the table. He isn't his usual, cheerful self. He isn't talking, but he also isn't eating very much. It looks like he is mostly pushing his food around his plate and not actually eating anything.

He hasn't even told one of his stupid dad jokes today.

Now that I think about it, I don't think I have heard one of his stupid dad jokes for several weeks, which is abnormal. Taking a good look at him, he looks like he has lost weight. His cheek bones protrude out from his sallow skin, he doesn't just look stressed anymore, he looks unhealthy. His shoulders are hunched and his eyes seem to dart to a different location of the room every few seconds. *How did I not notice how horrible Dad looks?* I wonder.

Guilt washes over me as I realize that I have been so preoccupied with Steve and the drama with Livi and Mark that I haven't even noticed the changes in Dad until now. Dad's blackmailing has always been in the back of my mind, but Mom has been back to her normal bubbly self and when I talk to Violet about it she doesn't seem too worried. So I guess I figured Dad would figure it out.

Looking at him now, I am not so sure.

My thoughts are interrupted by Mom's phone getting a FaceTime call. Normally there would be no phones allowed at the table on Thanksgiving, but this year Mom makes an exception and we pass the phone around so everyone can say hi to Violet. When it is my turn, Livi leans in and we both tell Violet how much we miss her.

"I'm sad I'm not there today. Make sure to eat a piece of pie for me!" Violet says.

"I think we can handle that," Livi teases before digging back into her dinner. I introduce Violet to Steve and Mark. After introducing Steve, she winks dramatically at me which makes me blush as I quickly pass the phone to Darla.

When everyone is stuffed and the dishes have been cleared, everyone gravitates to the living room to watch a movie while our food digests. Dad has disappeared again so I peek into his office looking for him. The office is empty. As I turn to go look for Dad upstairs, I hear his text message tone go off in the office. I know I shouldn't, but I can't help myself, I walk into the office and close the door behind me. His phone is sitting on his desk and it lights up again with a text notification. I can't open the texts or he will know I have read them, so I tap the screen and hope I can see enough from the preview on the home screen.

There is a Moncks Corner address and a date and time. Three days from now at 10:00 a.m. That is all I can see in the first preview, the second one says, "Come alone."

I think the number the texts are from is the same number that I saw when I looked at the blackmail texts. I can't be certain though. I put the phone back on Dad's desk, jot down the address on a scrap piece of paper, shove it into my pocket and leave the office with thoughts bombarding me. *Dad is meeting the blackmailer somewhere? Dad wouldn't give them a weapon, would he?*

Uncertainty creeps back into my mind.

Maybe I don't know Dad as well as I think I do. *Should I call the police?* There has got to be a reason why Dad hasn't called them himself. *Should I trust Dad to handle this on his own?* If someone would have asked me that question a couple of months ago I wouldn't have hesitated to say yes, but as much as I want to trust Dad completely like I always have, doubt continues to creep in.

I don't feel like I can sit still and watch a movie right now, so I ask Steve if he wants to go on a walk with me. He follows me outside, the chilly breeze makes me shiver and I realize I don't have one of my hoodies with me. Instead of going back inside to grab one I decide to take Steve up into the tree house instead. We climb the ladder and push open the trap door. It has been a while since I have been in the tree house; there is a thin layer of dirt covering everything and the remnants of the willow's yellow leaves that it dropped getting ready for the winter months cover the floor.

Steve looks around the beloved room. "This is a really cool tree house, even if it is pink."

I laugh. "It's light maroon, not pink."

He raises his eyebrows. "Is there a difference?"

"Mom wanted to paint the tree house a bright pink color. It was quite the debate, Konnie was excited about the bright pink, but Dad who had spent hours designing and building the tree house, was not too thrilled painting it the color of bubblegum."

"I can understand why."

"After weeks of arguments between all five of us, the decision was made to paint it light maroon. Don't call it pink in front of Dad; it's still a sore subject."

"My lips are sealed," Steve says as he pretends to zip his lips and throw away the key.

"Did you notice how bad my dad looked today?"

"Yeah, it was kinda hard to miss. He looks like he's wasting away."

"I know, and I have no idea how to help him."

"I honestly don't know how we can help either."

I look at Steve and bite my lip. He smiles. "You always do that when you are nervous about something. What's up?"

"I saw a text on my dad's phone." I pull the crumpled paper out of my pocket. "I think it was from the blackmailer. It had this address with a date and time."

Steve takes the paper out of my hand and looks at it. "Do you think he is giving them what they want?"

"I hope not. I mean, I want my family to be safe, but will we really be safe if he gives them the blueprints for a scary weapon?"

"Probably not."

A thought crosses my mind, and before I can think it through, I blurt it out. "Will you follow him and see what he does?"

Steve looks startled. "You want me to follow your dad?"

"Not follow him I guess, just be at the address three days from now at 10:00 a.m. and see what he does."

Steve is quiet for a minute before he answers. "I'm not sure this is a good idea, but I guess I will do it if you think it will help. Mr. Langston has been great about giving me passes when I ask for them."

I let out my breath that I didn't realize I was holding. "Thank you so much Steve, I really appreciate it."

I lean my head on Steve's shoulder and he laces his fingers with mine. We sit in silence in the tree house until Mom calls us back into the house for dessert.

Steve's eyes grow big and light up when he sees the table full of delectable pies. We fill our plates with small slices of as many of the pies we can fit on our plate and stuff ourselves even more.

There is always more room for pie.

By the time we are finished eating, I don't think I am going to be able to eat again for at least a week. *Until I eat leftover pie for breakfast in the morning,* I think to myself.

We make ourselves comfortable on the couch and Steve FaceTimes his grandma to check on her and tell her Happy Thanksgiving.

"How is my Stevie Boy?" she answers the call.

I mouth 'Stevie Boy' to Livi and we both giggle. They chat for a few minutes before Steve says, "Gran there's someone I want you to meet." He slides closer to me and I lean in so I can see the screen. "This is Genevieve, Genevieve this is Gran."

Gran smiles and says, "It's very nice to meet you Genevieve, you look much too sweet to be hanging around my Stevie Boy. He usually is surrounded by the wild ones."

It is the first time I have seen Steve turn almost as red as I do.

"Gran," he says defensively.

"What? It's true. Remember Evie? She looked like she had a skunk on her head."

I try to hold my laughter in, but it doesn't work and Steve seems even more embarrassed than before.

Livi pokes her head in front of the camera. "Do I fit the description?" she asks.

We all start laughing again when Gran responds with, "Definitely."

"I'm hanging up now, Gran, I'll talk to you later," Steve says and quickly disconnects the call.

"I like your grandma," I say. "I can't wait until I can meet her in person; I think I might be able to get some pretty interesting stories out of her."

"If I have my way, you two may never speak again," he grumbles and I can't help but burst into another fit of laughter.

As the night winds down and I watch as Steve and Mark drive away with Livi and Darla leaving close behind them, I decide that today was still a great Thanksgiving. Of course, I wish that Violet could be here, but it wasn't the depressing event that I thought it would be.

There was just as much fun and laughter as there always has been, even if Dad wasn't his usual happy self and Violet was hundreds of miles away.

Chapter 26

Steve

Spending my Sunday morning stalking my girlfriend's dad was not what I had in mind for this weekend.

The address Genevieve gave me is a gym in Moncks Corner. I got here fifteen minutes early. I don't really know what I am supposed to do; I have never tried to spy on someone before. Probably a good thing.

I should be studying for my finals next week. Finals were definitely a lot less stressful when I didn't care if I got good grades. Between work and trying to make sure I pass my first semester classes, I haven't had much free time. I haven't seen Genevieve since Thanksgiving and it sucks. We talk every night, but I hope we can hang out a lot before my next semester starts. It stinks that I am on a semester schedule and Genevieve is on a trimester schedule, none of our breaks line up.

My stomach knots up when I see Tony walking down the sidewalk to the gym doors. He is carrying a tube that could definitely be holding blueprints. He looks around nervously before going into the gym. *Now what? Do I follow him into the gym?* I really don't want to, what if he sees me or what if the blackmailer sees me. If they have been following the whole family like Genevieve thinks, I am sure they have seen me with Genevieve.

The whole front of the gym is glass, so I see Tony go into the locker room. Before I can decide whether I am going to follow him into the locker room, he comes back out without the tube.

Did Tony just give them designs for the weapon?

I watch Tony walk back out to his car and drive away before I call Genevieve. She answers on the first ring; she must have been waiting for my call.

"Did you see anything?"

"Well, hello to you too."

"I'm sorry. Hi! How are you? What did you see?"

I laugh. "I'm okay. The address was to a gym and I watched your dad walk into the locker room with a tube that looked like it could hold blueprints and when he came out of the locker room the tube was gone and he left."

Genevieve is silent on the other end.

"Did you hear me, Gen? I think your dad gave them the blueprints."

"There has to be another explanation. He wouldn't do that."

I sigh. "I don't want to believe it either, but I watched him walk in with something and leave without it. I think he might have."

"You don't know him like I do, Steve. There is no way he would do something like this."

"It is looking more and more like your dad is definitely trying to hide something and I think people will do a lot of things that they wouldn't normally do when everyone they love is being threatened. Have you found any more information about the cruise ship?"

"No, not yet. Dad has been home a lot this week so I haven't had a chance. Do you really think he just gave them the blueprints?" She sounds close to tears.

"I don't know Genevieve, but that is definitely what it looked like."

"I just can't believe it. Are you sure you saw what you think you saw?"

"Yes. And it's not like I wanted to spend the Sunday before finals spying on your dad, Genevieve. You asked me to do this. Just because what I saw isn't what you wanted me to see doesn't mean it didn't happen."

"I'm sorry I asked for your help. I'll talk to you later," Genevieve says, sounding hurt before she hangs up.

Well, I could have handled that better. Genevieve just got more evidence that her dad might not be as straight-laced as she thinks he is and instead of being understanding I snapped at her. I feel like such a jerk.

A call from an unknown number interrupts my thoughts. Most of the calls from the hospital updating me on Gran are from unknown numbers, so I don't think anything of it when I answer the phone.

"Hello. I am calling from St. Dominic-Jackson Memorial Hospital in Jackson. May I please speak with Mr. Adler?"

A hospital in Jackson? Why would they be calling me?

"This is Steve Adler."

"I'm so sorry Mr. Adler, but we are calling to inform you that your grandmother Juliette Paige was transferred here early this morning. We have been able to stabilize her for now, but it would be best if you could get here as soon as possible."

"What?" Even though I heard the information, I am having trouble processing it. "Can I talk to her?"

"I can transfer you to her room where a nurse can hold up the phone for her. You would be able to talk to her but she has been sedated and placed on a ventilator so she won't be able to respond."

A ventilator? I thought Gran was getting better. I write down all the information I need to get to the hospital and start the long drive to Mississippi instead of heading back to Charleston Academy. As I put the address of the hospital in my phone to get directions, I notice that my phone battery is only at five percent. Searching the Jeep frantically I realize I don't have a charger with me. *Crap. Now what?* I try calling Genevieve to let her know what is going on and she doesn't answer. I'm sure she is mad about our earlier conversation. I disconnect the call without leaving a voice message and call Mark.

"Hey Steve, I just got back to the room. Where are you?"

"I'm headed to Mississippi. Gran got transferred to a different hospital and isn't doing well. My phone is about to die and I forgot to grab a charger, can you please let Genevieve know what is going on? We got into a little bit of an argument and she didn't answer when I called. I'm going to shut my phone off so that I can use it for directions when I get closer to the hospital."

"Yeah. No worries, man. Drive safe."

I wish I could talk to Genevieve myself, apologize and tell her what is happening, but I disconnect the call and shut my cell phone off, hoping that this will keep the battery long enough to get me to the hospital when I get closer. I have been to Jackson a couple of times, but I am not familiar enough with the city to find my way without directions.

I can't even listen to the radio while I drive. The guilt for leaving Gran is crushing me. I shouldn't have left her in Brookhaven by herself. I should have done better at the online schools so that we were both still at home. I should have gone home for Thanksgiving. I wish I never got kicked out of Brookhaven High, how could I have been so stupid? Or maybe I should have convinced

Gran to move to an assisted living facility in Charleston. If she was moving anyway, why not come to Charleston with me? I doubt I can convince her to leave her friends and Brookhaven, but I am for sure going to try to get her to come back to Charleston with me when this is over.

The ten-and-a-half hour drive goes by in a blur. I don't remember most of the drive, but when I see the exit signs for Jackson, I turn my phone back on to get directions. Notifications flood my phone as I turn it on. I have several voicemails and texts, but traffic is heavy and I don't want to risk the battery dying before I make it to the hospital. I will have to check them when I get there. Hopefully, someone at the hospital will have a charger I can borrow until I can buy one.

While following the directions to the hospital, I realize that I left school without getting a pass. I will call Mr. Langston as soon as I can. I am sure he will help me out; he will probably want to know how Gran is doing too. I also left without grabbing any clothes or bathroom supplies. At some point I am going to have to make a run to get some deodorant and a toothbrush.

I pull into the hospital parking lot and find a place to park before sprinting into the brightly lit main lobby. The lady at the front desk tells me to take a seat while she calls someone to escort me to Gran's room. I plop down into one of the abstract-patterned chairs and open Genevieve's texts. I don't even get a chance to read them before my phone shuts off. I groan and put my dead phone back in my pocket.

After just a few minutes of waiting I am surprised when a doctor comes and calls my name. I thought a volunteer would take me to Gran. I follow the doctor down the hall into a small room with a desk and some chairs in it. *Why isn't he taking me to Gran's room?* I wonder as I look at the uncomfortable look-ing chairs and decide to stay standing. I lean against the wall and fold my arms.

He looks at me with sympathy in his eyes and hesitates before speaking. "Mr. Adler, I am so sorry. We tried calling you but couldn't get through. Your grandmother passed away about an hour ago. We did everything we could to try to resuscitate her."

There is a loud ringing in my ears that drowns out the rest of what the doc-tor is trying to say to me. No. This can't be right. I just talked to Gran yesterday and she said she was feeling better. She can't be gone. This has to be some hor-rible case of mistaken identity.

"I think you've made a mistake. My grandma is Juliette Paige. I just talked to her yesterday; someone was supposed to be taking me to her room."

"I'm very sorry, there hasn't been a mistake. She was moved from her room when we couldn't reach you." He hands me a bag. How did I not notice it in his hands before? "Here are the few items that your grandmother had with her when she arrived."

Looking at the bag with Gran's things in it my emotions go on a roller coaster ride, from shock to sadness to pain. I slide down the wall, crumpling to the floor and start to sob. The doctor places a hand on my shoulder for a few seconds before leaving the room to let me grieve in private. Gran is the only family I have left; she can't be gone.

My pain turns to anger and I violently throw my phone at the wall and watch as it shatters on impact. It isn't until later, when I pick up the pieces before leaving the room, I realize that all the phone numbers that I need are in my phone.

The phone that I just broke.

I can't call Genevieve, or Mark or Mr. Langston. Why don't Genevieve's parents let her have social media? It is so frustrating. I wish I could send her a DM with Gran's phone number. I know that she was upset the last time we talked, but I desperately need to hear Genevieve's calming voice right now.

I feel shattered, just like my phone. No matter what I do there is no way I can put all the pieces back together.

I am alone.

December

Chapter 27

Genevieve

It has been several days since I missed Steve's phone call. His phone goes straight to voicemail and he hasn't called me back. I can see that he read the last text I sent him, but he still hasn't responded. Maybe I should try to text again. I don't understand what is going on. Racking my brain, I go over and over our argument. I wasn't as nice as I should have been, I know he was doing me a huge favor and I snapped at him, but I didn't think it would make him this angry with me. We had been talking every night since Thanksgiving up until the night I missed his phone call and everything was great until I hung up on him. The weird part is that he did call, so he can't be that mad, right?

I really wish I hadn't missed that phone call.

"So anything new and exciting going on that I should know about?" Dad asks, pulling me from my inner torture.

Dad and Mom try to do something one on one with all of us girls every now and then. I guess it is their way of trying to make sure we are getting all the parental attention we need. Today Konnie and Mom are getting pedicures and Dad and I decided to drive to Isle of Palms to look for sand dollars.

The trees pass by my window in a blur. "Not really." I don't want to tell him I got in a fight with Steve.

What am I going to say when he asks what we fought about? 'He wasn't a fan of me asking him to follow you Sunday morning and then getting mad at him after he told me what he saw.' Yeah, no thanks.

I have always been able to talk to Dad and I want to go back to our normal relationship, but everything that has happened with the blackmailing has me questioning how well I know him. Deep down I feel like I can trust him completely, but doubt keeps creeping back in.

"You seem quieter than usual. Are you sure everything is okay?" he asks.

"Yeah Dad, I'm fine. Just tired."

Great, now I am lying too. Guess I can't give Dad too much grief for not telling me the truth.

Dad nudges me with his elbow. "What did the ocean say to the beach?"

I sigh. "I have no idea."

"Nothing, it just waved."

"I think your jokes might be getting worse, Dad," I say with a smile.

"Probably, but they can still get a smile out of you. Every time. Come on, Genna Bear. Talk to me, what's wrong?"

"I just haven't been able to get a hold of Steve for a few days; I think I made him mad."

Dad reaches over and pats my leg. "He'll come around. He seems pretty smitten every time I've seen you two together. Why do you think you made him mad?"

Great. Should have kept my mouth shut. "I don't know Dad, we just got irritated with each other and I hung up on him." I look over at Dad in the driver's seat. He has a smile on his face, but the worry and tension around his eyes is unmistakable. "What about you, are you doing okay?"

"I'm fine."

"You don't look fine, Dad. You always seem stressed and you're losing weight. We haven't even worked on the blueprints together."

"Well, you have been busy with school and Steve. I have been under some stress, but everything will be fine."

"Are you still being blackmailed? Maybe we should go to the police."

Dad stiffens and stares silently out of the window. "Genevieve, I told you not to worry about that. I mean it." He pulls into a parking space and parks the truck. "Let's forget about all of our problems and enjoy this beautiful day."

I climb out of the truck and follow Dad down the beach, letting the cool ocean breeze sweep my worries away, for a few hours at least.

Several hours later and with four nice-sized sand dollars in tow, we climb back into the truck. Both of us seem to be in better spirits on the drive home.

"Are you okay if we stop by the store real quick? I told your mom I would pick some things up for dinner tonight."

"Sure Dad, that's fine."

Waiting for Dad out in the parking lot, my mind returns to Steve. I am desperate to know what is happening. Against my better judgment, I pick up my phone and call Mark. He answers on the third ring and I hope that this isn't a horrible idea.

"Hey Mark. Are you with Steve by any chance?" I ask hesitantly.

"No, he isn't here. I thought you would know where he is."

"What do you mean? You don't know where he is? When was the last time you saw him?"

"He just left one night and never came back. I have no idea where he went."

"You mean he hasn't been at school?"

"Nope, he hasn't been here or at work."

My heart skids to a halt before resuming its rhythm in double time. Why would Steve leave school without telling Mark? He has been studying so hard for his finals, it doesn't make any sense that he would just up and disappear right before taking them.

"I don't know where he is either; I'm starting to get really worried." I can hear the quaver in my own voice.

"Don't worry, I'll come over and we can try and figure out what is going on."

Dad climbs back into the truck. "Okay, sounds good. Dad and I are just leaving North Charleston."

"Wait, you're with your dad?" Mark's voice sounds strained.

"Yeah, but we will be home soon."

"Okay, I'll leave now and I won't be too far behind you."

"Sounds good."

Before I have a chance to say bye to Mark and hang up the phone, a dark SUV comes barreling toward us through the intersection we are crossing and slams into Dad's side of the truck.

We spin around a few times before coming to a stop.

I am dazed and trying to process what to do when the SUV slams into Dad's side of the truck again, pushing us toward a small but steep hill leading down to the dense South Carolina woods at the bottom.

Everything is happening too fast and yet it feels like I am watching it in slow motion as Dad's truck is pushed toward the hill.

The tires make contact with the curb and with another shove from the SUV, the truck pushes through the guard rail and tips over the curb.

The sound of metal crunching and glass shattering is all I can hear as the truck rolls down the hill toward the trees.

There is one more loud crunch as the truck hits the line of trees.

I am vaguely aware that the truck has finally stopped moving. We are upside down with Dad's side against the trees. It is hard for me to gather my thoughts and figure out what I should do.

Something slick and wet trickles through my hair. Something drips down onto the roof of the truck sounding like water from a leaky faucet. *Is it raining?*

I reach my hand up and it comes away slick with blood.

No it isn't raining, I watch as drops of blood plop down in a steady rhythm. I stare at the pool of blood forming below me on the headliner of the truck as I hang from my seatbelt.

I look over at Dad who is also hanging from his seatbelt. The truck is so smashed around him and there is blood everywhere.

I start to panic.

Is he dead?

"Dad? Dad!"

No response. My breath starts to come faster and I feel claustrophobic. I need to get out of here and get help. I try to unbuckle my seatbelt, but the weight of my body hanging from it and my shaking hands make it hard.

I startle when the door on my side of the truck is ripped open.

The bright light behind Mark almost makes him look like he has a halo.

I don't know how he is here, but I have never been so happy to see a friendly face in all my life.

"Genevieve, are you okay?" Mark asks in a frantic voice.

"I think so." I tug at my seatbelt with no luck. I start to panic. "I can't get unbuckled."

Mark climbs into the crunched metal that used to be Dad's truck and cuts my seatbelt with a pocketknife.

He pulls me out of the truck before climbing back in to check on Dad.

My whole body is shaking now, but I don't feel anything.

I'm not sure if I am cold or hot.

I can hear Mark in the truck trying to talk to my dad and it snaps me back for a second. I yank on the driver's side door, but the truck is pinned tight against the trees and I can't open it.

Mark climbs back out. "He's breathing, but unconscious. I don't think there is any way to get him out without help."

Oh right. I should call 911. I look around for my phone. "Mark, we need to call 911, I can't find my phone."

"I already called 911 Genevieve; I'll call your phone and see if we can find it that way."

Mark calls my phone and finds it a little way back up the hill as the first responders begin to arrive. He hands my phone to me, which miraculously isn't damaged, just a little dirty.

Mark wraps an arm around my shoulders as we watch emergency personnel try to untangle my dad from the wreck.

A paramedic wraps a blanket around me and asks me to walk to the ambulance to check me out.

I am having trouble focusing on anything.

I can hear Mark tell the paramedic that he is fine, none of the blood is his.

The paramedic tells me that I look okay, but I should get checked out at the hospital just to make sure.

As soon as they pull Dad from the twisted metal, everything happens faster than I can comprehend. They load Dad into an ambulance and Mark loads me into his car. We follow the ambulance to the hospital where they immediately rush Dad away.

A nurse takes Mark and me to a room in the ER and cleans the blood off my face before a doctor checks my injuries. I have a small laceration on my forehead that needs stitches, but other than that I am in good health. After I am all stitched up, someone comes to tell me Dad is going into surgery and they walk me to the surgical waiting room with Mark by my side.

I cling to him like he will somehow make everything better. We sit down and I close my eyes trying to process everything that just happened.

"How did you find us?" I ask Mark quietly.

"I heard the crash on the phone and I was already headed to your house. It wasn't long before I came across the accident."

"That SUV hit us more than once, Mark. Do you think they did it on purpose?"

"Why would anyone want to hit you guys on purpose? They probably just hit you multiple times as they were spinning and rolling too."

I guess that makes sense, I don't want to tell Mark about the fact that Dad is getting blackmailed. I turn to look at Mark and see that he is covered in blood and dried mud. I am sure I look similar. Mark wraps his arm around my shoulder and gives me a squeeze as Mom and Konnie come bursting through the doors. Konnie has tears running down her face and Mom sees me and bursts into tears, running to me and crushing me in a tight embrace.

"Genevieve, are you okay?"

"They said I'm okay, I just needed stitches."

Mom hugs me tight one more time before Konnie squeezes in and wraps her arms around me.

Both of them look terrified.

We sit down and wait for news about Dad.

"What happened?" Mom asks.

"We were driving home and an SUV hit us. We rolled down a hill until we hit some trees at the bottom. Mark got me out of the truck, but Dad was stuck and we had to wait for help to get him out."

What if it had something to do with the blackmail? I think, making my panic rise back to the surface.

What if they are trying to get rid of him now that he gave them what they wanted?

Maybe Steve did see Dad give them the blueprints.

Or maybe he didn't give them what they wanted and this is the consequence.

"It was probably good you didn't move him. Thank you Mark for helping them," Mom says, reaching over and squeezing Mark's knee. "I'm sure your father was terrified, feeling like he needed to get you out of the truck."

I glance at Mark. "Dad was unconscious the whole time, Mom."

"He's going to be okay," Mom says. I think she is telling herself that more than she is telling us.

She grabs my hand and holds on tight.

My already wound tight nerves start to frazzle and I can't hold back the tears. I stand and walk to a window, looking out at the parking lot below. Mark follows me to the window and wraps an arm around me. I start to cry even harder and lean into his comfort. He wraps his other arm around me and starts to rub small comforting circles on my back.

I know I should back up, put some distance between us. Steve and Livi are already irritated with the attention Mark has shown me, but I just can't.

Mark just saved me.

I feel like I have a death grip on a lifeline and Mark is the only thing keeping me from drowning in my own emotions. I tighten my arms around Mark. I don't have enough energy to think about that right now.

"What is going on?" I hear an angry Livi say.

I look up and my eyes lock with Livi's for a moment. She takes in both Mark and I covered in blood and mud holding tightly to each other, before she storms out of the waiting room. I can only imagine what it looks like to Livi, seeing Mark comforting me. Darla, looking confused, tells us she will be right back and follows Livi out of the waiting room.

Feeling defeated, I tell Mark he should go talk to Livi. I don't know if I am upset or glad that Mark tells me he isn't going anywhere.

Dad's boss, Admiral Smith, shows up and waits with us. Mom must have told him about the accident.

Soon someone tells us that Dad is out of surgery and immediate family can go see him.

"Let me know if you all need anything," Admiral Smith tells us as I follow Mom and Konnie to Dad's room, leaving Mark and Admiral Smith in the waiting room.

I try to make sense of what the surgeon is telling Mom. My brain is foggy and I can't seem to grasp the information like I normally can.

I hear something about a badly broken leg and some other internal injuries. I sigh in relief when I hear him say that he expects Dad to make a full recovery.

Dad looks so small and frail lying in his hospital bed attached to an array of machinery. His eyes are closed, but I feel comfort in being able to watch the steady rise and fall of his chest as he breathes.

I send a text to Steve telling him that Dad is in the hospital and Mom calls Violet. Violet wants to come home, but Mom tells her to stay at school, that the doctors say Dad is going to be okay. I don't venture back out of my dad's room until Mom says it is time for us to go home and get some rest.

I check my phone. Steve still has not read the text I sent hours ago. My poor brain can't decide who I should be more worried about, Steve or Dad?

Following Mom out to the waiting room, I am surprised to see Darla, Livi, and Mark still there, although Livi is sitting on the opposite side of the room as Mark and making it a point not to look in his direction.

Mom wants to stay at the hospital with Dad and asks Darla if she will give Konnie and me a ride home. Mark looks awkward, his hands are shoved into his pant pockets and he looks like he isn't sure what he should be doing. He tells Konnie and me to call him if there is anything he can do, as we follow Darla and Livi out to their car.

Livi sits in the front seat with her arms folded tightly and a furrowed brow. She won't look at me or respond to anything I say. I give up trying to talk to her and we ride in silence the rest of the way home.

I don't have the energy, I have way too much to worry about.

Livi and her temper tantrum will have to figure itself out. How is it that I was just in a bad car accident, my dad is hurt and in the hospital and Livi feels like she is the victim in this situation?

And why does Steve think it is okay to just ghost me?

Where is he and what is he doing? My worry quickly turns to hurt and anger. I don't remember ever being this angry at Livi and as of right now, I couldn't care less if Steve ever decides to make an appearance again. I don't need either of them in my life if they are going to cause me any more pain than I am already feeling right now.

I get out of the car and slam the door shut when Darla pulls into our driveway. I stomp angrily into the house and lock the door behind Konnie, without even saying thank you to Darla for the ride home. Konnie looks baffled when I tell her to get in bed and stomp upstairs to my room, shutting my door with a lot more force than I meant to.

I don't make it very far into my room before the hot tears spill down my face. I angrily swipe them away.

My phone starts to ring and for a second I let myself hope that it is Steve, before I remind myself that I wouldn't answer the phone even if it was Steve. It is Mark calling. I answer the phone and collapse onto my bed.

"I was just calling to check on you. Are you doing okay?" Mark asks.

"I don't even know right now," my voice sounds tired.

I listen to Mark tell me everything will be all right before we disconnect the call.

I take a long hot shower, watching the dirt and blood mix together and wash down the drain. The hot steam calms my nerves and I realize too late that I probably wasn't supposed to get my stitches wet yet as I bump them and wince while washing my hair.

Finishing my shower, I slather some antibiotic ointment on my cut, climb into bed, and curl up underneath my blankets.

How is it that in just a few days, somehow Mark is the only person here for me when I need someone the most? I have always been able to count on Livi, and now when I am struggling, she doesn't even consider my side of the story before shutting me out. I thought I could count on Steve, but he has vanished without saying a word.

How come it is the people you love the most that can cause the most pain?

Chapter 28

Steve

Can you survive when your world stops turning?

Apparently.

I know that the actual world didn't stop turning, but mine sure did.

Gran has always been my rock, my safety; she is the one person I know I can always count on.

Was.

She *was* the only person I could count on. Now she is gone, and I don't even know what I am supposed to do.

I park the Jeep and walk into the assisted living facility where Gran lived. It seems like just yesterday I was helping her move into her apartment and I was heading to Charleston. The lady at the front desk takes me to Gran's room and opens the door. It still smells like Gran in here.

Lavender and lilies.

How long does it take for a person's smell to fade? Am I going to wake up one day and her things won't smell like Gran anymore? I fight back tears again as I start loading Gran's things into the boxes I brought with me. She has pictures of us everywhere. Pictures of us at the beach, fishing, riding horses on a trail ride we went on one summer. There are other pictures as well; pictures of her and Grandpa before he passed away, pictures of my family, and some of Gran and Mom. They make me miss her even more as I pack them up.

It doesn't take very long to pack up her apartment and load it into the back of my Jeep. I drove straight to the assisted living facility from Jackson, after staying in a hotel for a few days. At first it was because I needed to make arrangements for Gran's body and then I just didn't want to do anything else.

I am afraid to go home to the empty house waiting for me. The house is still furnished; Gran has been renting it out as an Airbnb while I was at school. We moved all our personal possessions into the attic before I left.

Oh crap, school.

I still haven't called the school; hopefully I don't get into too much trouble for leaving without telling anyone. How many days has it been? Three, maybe four? Time seems to be passing without me noticing. I might have the best chance at staying enrolled in school by explaining what happened to Mr. Langston.

I pull into the driveway and look at the small white house I grew up in.

Gran never took down the tire swing in the giant Magnolia tree in the front yard. I climb up the front steps onto the wraparound porch and look at the rocking chairs that Gran loved to sit in every evening.

Taking a deep breath, I unlock the door and walk into the house. It looks the same, minus all our family pictures that we took off the wall before we left. I turn on Gran's desktop computer and look up Mr. Langston's office number on the school's website. I never thought I would think this, but I am glad that Gran never disconnected her landline as I dial Mr. Langston's number. I really need to get a new cell phone.

"Hello. Xavier Langston speaking."

"Hey Mr. Langston, it's Steve Adler."

"Steve!" The alarm in his voice takes me by surprise. "Where are you? Are you okay? I have been trying to get a hold of both you and Juliette for days."

I take a deep breath, trying to keep the quaver out of my voice. "Gran died."

It is all I can get out before I choke up. Mr. Langston is silent on the other end of the phone for a few minutes before answering.

"Are you doing okay? Where are you?"

"I am at home. I just got here. I drove straight to the hospital when they called, but I didn't make it in time."

"Oh Steve, I'm so sorry. What can I do to help?"

"Well for starters, I didn't get a pass or tell anyone at school or work that I was leaving."

"I can take care of all of that for you. I'll let everyone know, but when you feel up to it you will need to email your other teachers and work out how they want you to take your finals."

Oh yeah, finals—I forgot about those. I don't even know how I am going to be able to focus on my finals right now. I tell Mr. Langston that I don't have a cell phone right now and he tells me to make sure to let him know of any funeral arrangements before we hang up.

I send emails to all my teachers and then call the number listed for my dorm parent's office. I tell them what is going on and leave a message for Mark to call me on my grandma's landline.

With social media and DM's now you don't even think about gathering email addresses, but I really wish I had gotten Genevieve or Livi's email information. Maybe they booked one of the ghost tours online and the tour company has some information. I call the tour office; hope burning in my chest as one of the front desk employees, Marsha, answers the phone.

"Hey Marsha! This is Steve, I'm not back yet, but I was really hoping you could look up some information for me."

"Sure, what do you need?"

"Is there an email or phone number listed for Genevieve Clark or her friend Livi? They've been on multiple tours with me."

She is silent for a few minutes and I can hear typing on her end. "I'm not sure that I'm supposed to give this information out, but I'm hoping since you work here and could get the information yourself it is okay."

"I promise I won't tell anyone you gave it to me if it gets brought up."

"They must have never made a reservation online because there aren't any email addresses listed, but there is a phone number for Livi."

I sigh in relief as I write down the information, hang up the phone, and dial Livi's number. It goes straight to voicemail, so I leave a message and try to look up any of Genevieve's family's numbers online. I can't find any listed and there are some sites that say if I pay they can get phone numbers, but I have no idea how to tell if they are legit or not.

I remember that Charlotte was doing something with real estate, but I never asked what real estate company and looking up her name isn't bringing anything up. Probably because she is just starting out, she may not even be a licensed realtor yet for all I know.

The next few days go by in a blur; Gran had left pretty detailed instructions with her two best friends Maggie and Claire for what she wanted for her funeral. She didn't want a big funeral, just a small memorial for her friends and her only family left, me, to get together and celebrate her life. I decided to buy two plots in the local cemetery for both Grandpa and Gran. Grandpa's ashes have always been on the fireplace, but now that Gran is gone too I feel like they should stay together.

I never realized how expensive everything is until now. Most of the business owners in Brookhaven knew Gran and are willing to let me pay for things like burial plots and headstones after the life insurance money comes in, some even gave me large discounts as their way of paying their respects.

Mr. Langston comes to Brookhaven for the memorial and I am surprised when Maggie and Claire gave him big hugs and tell him that he has been away for far too long. I knew Mr. Langston and Gran knew each other from school, but I guess I just always assumed that it was from college, not high school. It is strange to think that Mr. Langston and Gran grew up in Brookhaven together.

After the memorial, we get to the cemetery a little bit early and I walk to my parents' and little brother's gravesites. Gran had them buried here so that we could visit whenever we wanted to instead of having them buried in Atlanta, where my family was living at the time of their deaths.

The three headstones bring back painful memories.

It hurts even more that I can remember my parents and Jeremy, but I can't really picture their faces in my mind anymore. I can recognize them in pictures, so I know what they look like, but I can't picture them.

I also can't remember the sounds of their voices and I try to catch my breath as I realize that at some point, I will forget the sound of Gran's voice too.

The burial service goes by quickly. Gran didn't want an elaborate ceremony so it is just close friends and the local priest who says a few words. Lilies were Gran's favorite flower, so I brought a bunch of large white lilies to place on her casket.

Their bright, white petals are a stark contrast against the dark cherry wood, and seeing it somehow makes everything feel real. Gran is really gone.

Jake and several of my old classmates are here and I can see Evie and Jake standing a little bit away from the burial site waiting for me to finish talking to all the well-wishers. I don't have the energy to deal with Evie today, I wish she hadn't come. Mr. Langston walks up and squeezes my shoulder.

"I talked with the principal and your teachers for next semester and got everything worked out for you to start the new semester online while you are taking care of everything here."

I must look like I have no idea what I am doing—because, in reality, I don't.

"I know Juliette told me you struggled with school online, so if you need any help, please call me. Any help at all, with school or anything else you may need."

I nod. "How did you know Gran, Mr. Langston? I know you went to school together, but were you guys good friends?"

A sad smile crossed Mr. Langston's face. "Juliette was the one that got away. My one true regret in life was not going to college with her like we had planned. She will always hold a special place in my heart."

Wait. Mr. Langston and Gran dated? That is too weird to even think about.

"Grandpa died even before my mom was born, how come you never tried to reach out to Gran?"

"We would talk occasionally, but she always seemed to have so much going on. I really should have tried harder."

The pain in Mr. Langston's eyes is almost too much to look at. "Can you do me a favor when you get back to school and make sure that my roommate Mark got my messages?"

Mr. Langston nods and gives me a hug before climbing into his car and driving out of the cemetery. I try to sneak to my Jeep without being seen, but Jake notices and walks over.

"I'm sorry about your grandma, Steve," Jake says.

"Thanks, man." I don't know what else to say.

"Are you up for some company?"

I shrug, why not? At least I got away without having to talk to Evie. Jake climbs into the Jeep and I drive back home.

It doesn't feel like home anymore. Not only does it not have any of our personal things on the wall so that it would be ready to rent out, but it just feels empty without Gran here. Jake and I play Xbox for a little bit before he says he has to go meet up with our old group of friends.

"Why don't you come out with us tonight? Take your mind off things," he asks.

Normally, that is exactly what I would do. Brush my feelings off and go have fun. Have fun with a bunch of people who call me their friend, but in reality don't know me at all. The thought of trying to put on a happy face for all my old friends seems like too much tonight.

"Maybe another day. I think I am just going to get some rest, it has been a long day," I tell Jake.

"You've got my number."

I nod before I remember my broken phone. "Actually, I don't. My cell isn't working."

Jake scribbles his number down on one of Gran's floral notepads and leaves. I don't think I have ever felt this tired before.

It is like every cell in my body is screaming for me to go to sleep.

It's not just my body either; I am so tired of remembering. Everything reminds me of something Gran said or did and I am emotionally and physically exhausted.

I don't even bother taking a shower or changing out of my suit. I lay down on the couch and let sleep take me somewhere less painful.

Chapter 29

Genevieve

I am glad that my second trimester classes are ridiculously hard. It makes it easier to think about something other than Dad in the hospital and Steve, wherever he is. Livi still won't talk to me. I take a couple more bites of food before dumping my tray and walking to the library.

After a couple of days eating lunch alone in the lunchroom, I decided that I might as well spend lunch working on my homework or reading if I wasn't going to be talking to anyone.

It would be really nice if Konnie had the same lunch as me, but she doesn't, so the library has become my safe haven during lunchtime. Being surrounded by books, books that can take me out of my own world for a little bit, is the closest I get to feeling calm these days.

Not having Livi or Steve to talk to has been horrible. I thought that Livi would cool down and let me explain my side of the story, but it hasn't happened yet and until now I didn't realize how much I had come to rely on those nightly calls with Steve. Even though I am still so angry that he up and left without saying anything, I still miss him.

I miss him so much it feels like an actual physical ache.

Like a piece of me is missing and I can't find it no matter how hard I look.

Worrying about Dad and not being able to talk to Livi about it is just making everything hurt worse.

My nightly calls with Steve have been replaced with calls from Mark. At first, I was leery about talking to Mark every night, but Mark is so supportive. He calls every night to ask how Dad is doing, how I am feeling and let me know if he has heard anything from Steve. So far neither of us has heard a peep.

How does someone just disappear?

I can feel my face getting hot as I think about everything. How can Livi abandon me when I need her the most? I just wish she would at least listen to me, but she won't even let me talk to her. She won't answer the phone or return any of my texts. The bell rings and I angrily shove my things into my backpack and walk into the bustling halls. I can see Livi walking up ahead of me; maybe if I am right in front of her she will listen.

I catch up and tap her shoulder. "Hey Liv, can we talk?"

The hateful look in her eyes startles me and I take a step back. "Are you still talking to Mark?" she asks.

"Yes," I say quietly, not wanting to lie, but before I can explain anything Livi turns away from me and walks down the hall.

Is she really going to give up on our lifelong relationship over a boy? A boy that I don't even have any interest in dating? Trying to keep the tears from falling, I almost sprint to my next class and sit down at my desk. I pull my phone out of my pocket.

I don't know what I was expecting, maybe to miraculously find a text from Steve waiting for me? I pull up my text stream with Steve; he still has never read the text I sent about my dad. I take a deep breath trying to hold back my emotions. I text Mark.

> Livi still won't talk to me.

How is it that I went from having a great support system, to Mark being my only friend?

> I'm sorry Gen! You want to do pizza and a movie at your house tonight?

> Sounds good to me. Bring enough for Konnie, Mom is still at the hospital most nights.

> See you tonight.

I smile. At least I still have Mark; he has made this whole ordeal bearable. I go through the motions and make it through the last class of the day. When the bell rings, I find Konnie and we walk to the bus together. We haven't had to ride the bus since Livi got her driver's license; it takes so much longer to get home from school now. Not to mention that for some reason the bus always smells like Fritos and feet. How is it that it always smells like Fritos when there is no food allowed on the bus? We get home and I bury myself in homework to keep my brain from wandering again.

"Hey Genevieve, can we talk for a minute?" Konnie asks from the doorway.

I slide my pile of textbooks and notebooks over and pull out a chair for her to sit down in.

"Is everything okay? I mean I know that Dad is in the hospital, but things seemed a little bit weird before then too."

I really don't want Konnie to have to worry about the blackmailing too. I'm not sure what to say. "We'll be fine. Steve and I got into a little fight and I haven't been able to get a hold of him since. I haven't really been myself since he left."

"What do you mean since he left?"

"He left school; Mark doesn't know where he is either."

"And he didn't say anything to either of you before leaving?"

I shake my head. "Weird, right? At first I was really worried, now I can't decide if I am mad or worried."

"Probably both," Konnie says as she gives me a side hug.

Mark shows up right on time, interrupting our conversation with pizza and Dr. Pepper. We pick a new comedy and I realize that it is the first time I have laughed in a while.

Looking at Mark and Konnie as they laugh so hard Konnie spits Dr. Pepper out of her nose, I realize that even though things may not be how I want them to be, everything is going to be okay. I wish Livi and Steve were here with us, but I still have people who care about me.

"How are you holding up?" Mark asks after the movie ends.

Konnie is snoring softly next to me. I turn to look at Mark who is sitting on my other side.

"I'm okay. I'm worried about Dad, worried about Steve and I'm really angry at both Livi and Steve."

"Understandable."

"You know you don't really talk much. I mean you talk, but you don't actually give anyone any real information." I twist so that I am sitting criss-cross applesauce facing him on the couch. "I mean we talk every night and I don't even know if you have siblings."

Mark laughs and his signature smirk appears on his face. He really is handsome, but I can't let my thoughts go there.

"What do you want to know?" he asks.

"Everything."

He laughs again. "Well, I'm not sure I can fit everything into one conversation, but I do have a sibling. I don't see her much, Clara is three years younger than I am and lives with my mom."

"So do you live with your dad then?"

"No, Dad hasn't been in the picture since shortly after Clara was born, but I actually went to live with my Uncle Sebastian when I was seven."

I'm not sure what I was expecting, but his answer surprises me. "How come you went to live with your uncle?"

"He asked my mom to send me to him and she did." Something about the question I asked makes Mark close back up again. "It's getting late; I better get back to campus before curfew."

Mark gets up off the couch and helps me clean up before I walk him to the door. He gives me a hug before he drives away in his sleek silvery grey car. I never really paid attention to his car before, it looks expensive. I watch as his taillights disappear. Even though I try to tell myself I am okay with my new situation, I can't help but hope that in the future everyone will all be laughing, eating pizza, and watching movies together again.

With Mark gone and Konnie in bed I try to sleep, but once again sleep evades me.

Konnie and I are home alone and there is no way Dad could catch me snooping right now. If I am not going to get any sleep, I might as well try and figure out the link between Dad and the mysterious cruise ship that sunk.

I tiptoe quietly past Konnie's room, not wanting to wake her and close Dad's office door behind me before I flip on the lights. The draft table in the corner sends a shock of sadness through me. Will we ever finish the blueprints for my dream house? Will Dad be around to help me build it when I am older?

If he is hiding something horrible from his past and it gets out, all our lives might be drastically different than we had all imagined. If whatever information the blackmailer has gets out, will Dad go to prison? What will that mean for the rest of us? All of this is just so confusing.

Looking around the room, I decide to start with the gun safe that he keeps the blueprints in. I don't know the code for the safe, so I try all the birthdays in the family—none of which work. I'm at a loss. I look around Dad's desk for a notebook or any papers that would have the code to the gun safe on it, but don't find anything so I move on to the file cabinets. I flip through files with bills, health documents, school report cards, and information for Konnie, Violet, and me. I slam the drawer shut harder than I mean to and try to open the next drawer, but it doesn't budge. I try one more time, but the drawer doesn't move at all. Leaning down to inspect it, I notice a lock.

Finally, something promising.

I run to the garage and unscrew the jar full of keys Dad has hanging above his work bench. I always thought they were random keys that weren't in use anymore, but this seems like a good place to hide a key you didn't want anyone to notice. With the jar of keys in tow I head back to the office and dump them out on the floor in front of the file cabinet. There are more keys than I realized.

I start the slow and tedious process of trying to fit each key into the lock. It has become so monotonous that when one of the keys turns the lock it takes me a minute to realize that I just unlocked the drawer.

Anxiety spreads through me as I pull open the drawer and peer inside. There are no files in this drawer. The box Sarah sent home with me is in the drawer sitting on top of another shoe box. Lifting the lid on the box from Sarah, I rifle through the papers and pictures. It looks like all the same things I saw when I went through the box with Steve. I don't think Dad added anything. I place it on the floor next to me before opening the shoebox beneath it.

The box is old and starting to fall apart. There are more articles about the cruise ship and more pictures of Dad with his shipmates. Nothing in the pictures gives me any more clues. I find obituaries for most of the men in the pictures. I think that leaves only two of the men in the group picture besides Miguel that are still living. Remembering the phone call I overheard between Dad and Miguel, I realize that it must be one of these men who is feeding the blackmailer the information, or may be the blackmailer themselves.

I am pretty sure Miguel wouldn't be involved and I don't know if Charlie ever told Sarah anything. It dawns on me that I don't know how Charlie died. I guess I was so young that I didn't even think to ask what happened, or maybe Mom and Dad were just good at changing the subject. I read through his obituary and it doesn't tell me either, just that he died unexpectedly.

I move the obituary out of the box and pick up the envelope underneath it. I slide the letter out of the envelope and notice that it is a letter from Charlie before I start to read.

Tony,

I have tried to put our past behind us, but I can't. I still have nightmares every night about what happened.

We killed all those people.

I know we didn't mean to, our intel was wrong, but we sunk a cruise ship filled with women and children.

Even if it was supposed to be a shipment of weapons, not refugees, we are still the ones who launched the torpedoes toward that ship, sending them all to their deaths.

We have been told over and over again that it wasn't our faults, if we had known we would never have sunk that ship, but I am tortured with the knowledge that I am partially responsible.

Their screams as the burning ship sunk into the water haunt me even when I am awake and when I try to sleep I see them.

I don't know what is worse, the fact that it was covered up and we didn't have to face any consequences or the fact that we are free, but because of the cover up we can't even talk to anyone about it.

I know I could get into so much trouble for even writing this letter, but by the time you read this it won't matter for me. If I can't find any peace on the other side, I hope that the nightmares will stop at least. Be glad you weren't one of us that actually sent those cursed torpedoes toward that ship.

I can't ever forgive myself.

Please check in on Sarah now and again for me.

Charlie

My hands are shaking and my breath gets caught in my throat. I re-read the letter several more times before I put it back in the envelope. Robotically, I place all the contents back into the box, the boxes into the drawer, and lock it up. Dropping the key into the jar of keys, I pick up the jar and put it away in the garage before I slowly walk back up the stairs to my room.

I guess I know what Dad is getting blackmailed with now, and why he can't go to the police. If it was covered up, he can get into just as much trouble talking about it as he would if the information is leaked. I don't expect him to answer, but I try to call Steve anyway.

I need him to tell me everything will be okay, but his phone doesn't even ring, it goes straight to voicemail. I hang up without leaving a message.

The ship my dad was on killed all those women and children on the cruise ship. What am I supposed to do with that information?

Chapter 30

Steve

"I'm sorry, sir; we can't give you any of that information without the permission of the account holder."

I try not to lose my temper. "How exactly am I supposed to get permission from someone who has died?" I ask in a tense voice. "Look, man, I just need a new phone, can we at least do that?"

The guy behind the counter at the cell phone store looks even more uncomfortable.

"Unfortunately, there was no insurance purchased on your phone and you have another six months before you are due for an upgrade," he says.

Great. I don't have the money to buy a new phone right now. I used most of the money I had access to for Gran's memorial expenses and I am still waiting for everything else to go through. I can't access any of Gran's accounts until the lawyer does whatever it is he is doing.

"Can we at least try to get the contacts off of my phone?"

He looks at the pieces of my shattered phone with a doubtful expression on his face. "We can try," he says and picks up the broken phone.

I wait at the counter for a few minutes before he returns. "I'm sorry, we can't get any information off this. Did you have your stuff backed up to the cloud?"

He hands the piece back to me. I sigh. "My pictures are in the cloud, but not my contacts."

After remembering about the cloud, I logged in to find all my recent pictures including that last picture I took with Gran before I left for Charleston, but no contacts. I get the papers I need to fill out to gain access to the cell phone account and drive home. I call and leave another message for Mark with the dorm parent before dialing Mr. Langston's office.

"Have you been able to talk to Mark?" I ask, before even saying hello.

I know it's rude, but I am having a bad day and it would be really great to be able to finally hear Genevieve's voice again.

"I'm sorry, Steve. I have left messages at your dorm room, but I haven't been able to talk to Mark in person yet. He never seems to be at the dorm. I will try to catch him at work this week."

"Thank you," I say before hanging up.

Would it be okay for me to call Genevieve's school and leave a message? The school would probably think I was some creep and not even give her the message. Once again, I wish Genevieve had any sort of social media account. I never spent much time on my accounts before, but now every night I am glued to Gran's computer.

I tried to look up Violet, who apparently still doesn't have an account even though she is in college. I have sent messages to both Mark and Livi and the last time I checked it still says that neither of them has seen the messages. Livi hasn't even posted anything new these last few weeks, which is weird because she posted almost daily before.

I am pretty sure that anyone watching me would think I have lost it. I spend my nights looking through all the pictures in my cloud of Genevieve and Gran and now I have resorted to looking back through all of Livi's posts. Genevieve is in a lot of them.

Maybe I am losing it.

I just need to go through all of Gran's stuff and get back to school and away from all these haunted memories.

I pull into the driveway and head inside to start going through everything. *Time to get this done and get out of here,* I think to myself as I lug the heavy boxes from the attic down into the dining room. After the attic is empty, I sit down in the dining room, surrounded by the boxes of Gran and my life. This is too much. I don't know how to decide what to keep and what to get rid of. The sound of the doorbell startles me; I stand up and brush the dust off my pants before answering the door.

Jake is standing on the front porch. "Hey Steve, a few of us are going bowling. Want to come with?" he asks.

I turn around and look at the intimidating pile of boxes in the dining room. I pretty much want to be anywhere than here right now.

"Sure," I say before putting on my shoes and walking out the door.

We pull into the bowling alley parking lot and walk in. The whole group is there, laughing and snacking on fried cheese sticks and french fries. It is exactly the same as before I left. Everyone is there including Evie.

I groan inside, it is going to be impossible to avoid her tonight. As if she knows I am thinking about her she looks up and locks eyes with me. She gives me a knowing smile and I look away, but not quickly enough. Jake and I walk over to the group and sit down. Evie comes and sits right next to me.

"It's been a while, Steve," she says. "How come you haven't been returning any of my texts?"

"Yep, it's been a while. I don't have a phone right now. Mine broke."

"That doesn't explain all the texts I sent when you left for Charleston," she whines.

"I've been pretty busy."

I look around for Jake hoping he will come save me. *Where in the heck did he run off to?*

"How is Charleston?" Evie asks.

"Charleston is great. I can't wait to go back."

Evie pouts. I try not to roll my eyes. How did I ever find her attractive?

"So what's so great in Charleston?" she asks.

"The city is really cool, I really like my job there, the school is pretty awesome, and my girlfriend is pretty great too."

Evie's eyes turn cold. "You have a new girlfriend?"

"He says he has a girlfriend, but I've never seen a picture, so I won't believe it until I do," Jake says plopping down next to me.

Finally. "Where did you go?" I ask him.

"To get some cheese sticks, want some?" he asks, holding his tray of cheese sticks out for me to grab one. I grab one and take a bite, burning my tongue on the melting cheese.

"Well, I can show you some pictures of Genevieve on the computer next time you're over. I think it may be a while before I can replace my phone," I say as I suck air into my mouth trying to cool off my burning tongue.

Evie looks irritated and walks over to talk with some of the other girls. The rest of the night goes pretty smoothly. It is fun to catch up with the friends that I grew up with. It is almost like I never left. I am feeling a lot better when I get home, until I walk in the front door. I walk past the boxes in the dining room and go to my old room. It was fun bowling with the old gang, but all I really want to do is call and talk to Genevieve.

Chapter 31

Genevieve

I should really clean the blades on my ceiling fan, I think as I watch it spin around and around. The dim light leaking into my room from the hallway makes it possible to see the dust particles floating down. I lean over and look at the time on my phone; it's 2:34 a.m. I have never had trouble sleeping before and now it is a common occurrence. It is weird that I can't sleep, because all I want to do is lay in bed when I am not doing my homework. I am pretty sure I have every rise and fall of the texture on my room walls memorized.

Mom is always at the hospital and Konnie and I spend most of our time alone at the house after school. Life has become a monotonous cycle of school, homework, trying to sleep, and trying to forget the information I have learned about Dad.

Violet got home a couple of days ago for Christmas break; I don't even want to bring the blackmailing up to her at all anymore. I don't want to tarnish either of my sister's feelings toward the father we have loved so much all our lives.

Especially not during Christmas.

It doesn't even feel like Christmas though, normally Mom and Dad go all out with the Christmas decorations. Not this year, it is Christmas morning and we still don't even have a tree. Mom didn't even get the Christmas bins out and pretend like Christmas would be the same.

I get up and walk downstairs. I don't know what I was expecting. I think deep down I thought there was no way Mom would let Christmas pass without doing anything. I was hoping to come down to find the tree lit up with presents underneath, but all I see is the empty rooms.

Empty.

That seems to be the vibe of my whole life right now. I feel empty, like I don't have anything left to give. I sit down on the couch and stare out the window until I can see the sun peeking out from the horizon.

Violet comes down the stairs and startles when she notices me sitting in the dim room.

"Holy crap, Genevieve, you scared me!"

"Sorry," I say without looking away from the window.

She sighs and sits down next to me. "You okay, Gen?"

"I'm fine."

"I tried to talk to Livi yesterday and explain what happened."

"Oh yeah? How did that go?" I ask in a monotone voice.

"She didn't want to listen. I'm hoping that she at least heard some of what I said. After she has a chance to really think about it, I think she will calm down."

"Maybe."

"Ugh, Genevieve will you please look at me?" Violet pleads.

I turn to look at her, but can't hold her gaze for very long before turning back to the window.

"Have you heard anything from Steve?" she asks.

I shake my head no.

"Are you still talking to Mark a lot?"

I nod. "Yeah, he is the only person willing to talk to me."

"Hey, I am talking to you," Violet whines.

"You don't count, you're my sister. Plus, you hardly talk to me anyway."

She ignores my comment. "Am I going to get to meet him while I am here?"

"I think he is planning on coming over sometime this afternoon."

"Are you sure you're okay, Gen? I'm worried about you. I've never seen you this down before. Or this negative, normally you are more like Dad, always finding the good in a crappy situation."

"I'm fine. I just need to graduate and move away from Moncks Corner as soon as possible," I reply. Even I can hear the bitterness in my voice.

"It must have been scary being in the accident with Dad."

I don't say anything, so Violet continues. "Have you heard anything else about that whole blackmail thing?"

184

Yes, but I don't want to burden you with the secrets I know. I wish I would have left it alone like Dad told me to, I think. But I don't want to tell that to Violet, so instead I say, "I'm pretty sure that the accident was because of it."

"What? You're kidding, right?"

"Nope, they hit us three times, Violet. I don't think it was an accident."

"I still can't even believe that Dad has anything big enough to hide for blackmail."

You have no idea. "I think there is a lot we don't know about Dad, Vi. He may not be the person we have always thought he was."

"You can't really believe that, Genevieve," Violet whispers.

"I don't want to believe it."

Violet looks at me with a worried glance before saying, "Well, we need to get ready. We're supposed to go see Dad this morning. Mom stayed the night there last night."

I get up and make my way back upstairs to get dressed. My usual Christmas attire is a cheesy festive sweater and jeans, but this year I find my favorite comfy grey sweater and pull it over my messy hair. I pull on my jeans before brushing my hair into a ponytail and heading back downstairs. Violet gives me another worried look before we load into her car and drive to the hospital.

Dad looks better and smiles brightly at us as we walk into the room. His smile falters as he takes in my gloomy appearance, but he brightens back up and wishes us a Merry Christmas. Mom tells us that Dad is healing quickly now and the doctors think he will be able to come home soon. Dad asks Mom if she will take Violet and Konnie to go get us all some hot chocolate, and when they leave the room, he turns and takes a good look at me. I have trouble meeting his eyes.

"You doing okay?" he asks.

"Yep all healed up, just a tiny scar." I point to the spot on my forehead that had stitches.

"That's not what I am talking about, even though I am glad that you are all healed up. What's going on kiddo?"

I didn't realize just how much I had been missing my dad until now. Dad has always been the person I could talk to about anything. Tears fill my eyes and he pats the bed next to him. I walk over and sit next to him and he gives me an awkward side hug.

"Genna Bear, please talk to me," he says.

"I know what you are being blackmailed with, Dad." He turns to a statue next to me and his grip on my arm tightens, but he doesn't say anything, so I continue. "I found the newspaper articles and the letter from Charlie."

I finally get the courage to look at him. He looks terrified. His eyes are wide and he has lost all the color in his face. Our eyes lock.

"You can't know that information, Genevieve," he whispers. "I should have burned those things long ago."

"Are you really responsible for sinking that ship, Dad?"

"We didn't know what we were doing and I was actually in the infirmary when it happened, but I saw the aftermath."

I guess the part about Dad not actually sending the torpedoes in Charlie's letter makes more sense now. I know my dad and I know his character. I know he would never intentionally do anything like that, but I still can't believe that he would help cover something like that up.

"How could you lie about something like that?"

"We didn't have a choice, Genevieve. We were just following orders and it has haunted me my entire life."

"What would happen if you said anything?"

"Nothing good. I know it is hard, but I need you to try and forget all of this. Move on with your life and don't let my past ruin your future."

"How am I supposed to forget this, Dad? How is that even possible? You aren't even who I thought you were."

He flinches like I slapped him and whispers, "I'm still the same man who loves you and your sisters with everything that I am."

Deep down I know that he is telling me the truth. The men on that ship followed an order; they didn't choose to sink that ship, but if Dad can hide information like this, what other information could he be hiding?

"Everything just sucks, Dad. You aren't being honest with anyone, Livi won't talk to me, and Steve disappeared."

He looks startled. "What do you mean Steve disappeared?"

"He just left one day and didn't come back. Nobody can get a hold of him."

"That is really weird, I hope he's okay," Dad says with a frown on his face.

"I was worried for a while too, now I am just mad."

Unless the blackmailer saw Steve following Dad.

A knot forms in my stomach. I push my worry about Steve away, if he was truly missing the school or his grandma would have alerted the authorities by now. We would have seen something in the media. I think it is more likely that he just doesn't want to talk to me.

"Until you hear his side of the story, you should try to keep on open mind."

I know Dad is right, and I get the feeling he is talking about himself as well, but I am still so angry at all of them. Dad, Livi, and Steve. Violet brings Dad and me to-go cups of hot chocolate, and Konnie and Mom follow her into the room, ending our conversation.

We visit with Dad for a while longer before Mom pulls out a small gift for each of us. On a normal year, Mom elaborately wraps our gifts and we spend hours taking turns unwrapping while everyone watches. This year it is just one small envelope each that Mom tells us to all open at the same time.

I peek into the envelope and see cash; I don't even know how much is in there. I know Dad has been in the hospital and Mom has been extra busy. I know that I should be understanding and considerate of everything Mom has to deal with, but we have been home alone for most of the time and the envelope of cash still stings a little bit. I feel like a horrible daughter for even having hurt feelings.

"I know this Christmas hasn't been a normal one. Since I wasn't able to get gifts this year I thought I could just give you girls the amount I would have spent on gifts and you can use it for whatever you would like," Mom says, looking at each of us.

I try to put on a convincing smile. Konnie looks excited about the cash and Violet smiles and says, "Thanks Mom, you're the best."

There really is something wrong with me. My parents just gave me an envelope full of cash and all I can think about is how upset I am that Mom didn't get me a gift and wrap it up beautifully.

I try to look more convincing and smile and nod agreement with what Violet is saying. I meet Dad's eyes and I can tell I am not doing a very good job hiding my emotions by the worried look on his face. By the time Violet, Konnie, and I get ready to head back home, I feel like sprinting down the hospital hall just to escape the tension in the room.

When we pull into the driveway, Mark is waiting for us. He is holding a poinsettia and a small, wrapped gift. *Are you kidding me?* I didn't get Mark anything. Maybe I can give him some of the cash Mom just gave us. I laugh to myself. It is kind of ironic that I was just upset for getting a gift that wasn't presented in the way that I wanted it to be and I didn't even think to get Mark a gift. Violet parks the car and we all get out.

"Hey Mark, sorry we are a little bit late," I say as he gives me a hug.

"No worries. I haven't been here very long."

Konnie walks past us with a wave to Mark and heads into the house, but Violet stops next to us.

"Vi, this is Mark," I say, and Mark juggles the poinsettia and gift in one hand and holds out his other hand to Violet.

"I've heard so much about you Violet; it's good to finally meet you in person instead of over a screen," Mark says with one of his smiles I have learned he uses when he wants to try and be charming.

Violet looks at me and raises her eyebrows before shaking Mark's hand. "Nice to meet you in person too," Violet says. "Thanks for taking care of my little sister for me while I'm gone."

Mark turns that smile on me. "Anytime."

I can feel my face heat up. *Stupid blush. Why must it announce to the world every time I am even slightly uncomfortable?* To hide my scarlet cheeks, I turn and walk into the house with Mark and Violet following behind. We sit in the living room and Mark hands me my gifts. I don't tell him that I am horrible at keeping plants alive and open the wrapped gift. It is a new novel that I have wanted to read. I must have told him about it at some point, I feel even worse that he got me such a thoughtful gift and I didn't get him anything at all.

"Thank you so much, Mark. I've been wanting to read this book," I say trying not to cry. My emotions are all over the place today.

"Of course, I saw it and remembered you talking about it."

"I'm sorry I didn't get you anything," I say, feeling embarrassed.

"Seriously, don't worry about it, Gen, you've had a lot going on," Mark says with a smile. He looks and sounds genuine so it makes me feel better about not getting him a gift, but worse about my reaction to my mom's gift. I start to feel like the walls are closing in on me, everything has just been too much lately.

The doorbell rings and Violet gets up to answer it. She has a worried look on her face when she comes back into the living room with Livi trailing behind her. When Livi takes in Mark sitting next to me and the gift I am still holding in my hands, her face turns cold again.

I jump up. "What are you doing here, Livi?"

"I came to hear your side of the story, like everyone keeps telling me to, but from what I can see my side of the story is pretty accurate."

"That's not fair Livi, Mark and I are just friends."

"It sure doesn't look that way to me Genevieve. Where is Steve?"

"I don't know." I look down at my feet and bite my lip, trying to keep any tears from falling.

"So changing boyfriends like changing underwear is the way you roll these days, huh? Catching up for lost time since you didn't decide to start dating until senior year?"

Livi's comment stings, but it dries up my tears as a fresh wave of anger boils to the surface.

"Come on Livi, you know Genevieve better than that. Hear her out," Violet says which makes Livi turn her murderous glare onto her for a minute.

"What's wrong, Livi? Mad that all the attention isn't on you now? Can't share the spotlight with nerdy Genevieve?" I snarl.

Both Livi and Violet look shocked. I am shocked. I never talk to anyone this way, let alone my best friend.

"Screw you Genevieve and your holier-than-thou attitude. I do everything for you. I drive you to and from school, the only time you go out and do anything is when I take you to do something, and have you ever thanked me? No, it's just constant whining about not wanting to do anything that would actually be any fun."

"I'm sorry I try to keep you out of trouble, Livi. You know what? It has been nice these last few weeks not having to constantly worry about you getting yourself kicked out of school or arrested."

"Well, lucky for you, you still don't have to. I don't know why I let Violet and Mom talk me into coming over here in the first place. You're just a back-stabbing user and I want nothing to do with you."

Livi throws a small gift that I didn't notice she had been holding in my direction and stomps back toward the front door, slamming it hard on her way out.

Both Violet and Mark watch me in stunned silence as I pick up the small gift and drop it into the trash without looking to see what is inside. It hurts to know how Livi really feels about me. We have been best friends since we were three. I guess I just always assumed we would be best friends our entire lives. Even in my anger her absence makes me feel like a part of me is missing.

"Will you take me somewhere?" I blurt out.

"Sure, where are we going?" Mark asks.

"I want to show you one of my favorite places."

I tell Violet that I will be back in a while and try to keep myself from running to Mark's car. He unlocks the doors and I climb into the passenger seat. I give him directions to Mepkin Abbey, hoping one of my favorite spots can cheer me up. I look around inside Mark's car; I didn't really pay much attention to it when we were driving to the hospital. I don't know what it is, but I am pretty sure it is worth more than both of my parents' cars put together.

Mark pulls into the parking lot and parks by the gardens. We climb out of the car and walk through the peaceful beauty. As we walk down by the Cooper River, I am flooded with memories of my day with Steve at the Magnolia Plantation Gardens. Different river, different gardens, and he still manages to take over my thoughts. I sigh and sit down on a bench that looks out over the river. Mark sits next to me and we sit in silence for several minutes.

"Do you think Steve is coming back?" I ask.

"I don't know."

"Can we talk about something that doesn't have anything to do with boyfriends who disappear, best friends who hate me, and dads who are stuck in the hospital?" *Or hiding deep dark secrets.*

Mark chuckles. "Sure, what do you want to talk about?"

"Tell me more about you. You said you went to live with your uncle when you were little. Are you and your uncle close?"

I see a flash of something that might have been anger in Mark's dark brown eyes before he catches himself. "I'm not super close to Uncle Sebastian, but I am probably the closest relationship he has. He's an important man in New York; there isn't really anything that he can't make happen."

"Sounds intimidating."

Mark laughs bitterly. "You have no idea. Growing up with my uncle was far from living in a loving home."

"How come your mom sent you to live with him?"

"Like I said, when Sebastian tells you to do something, you do it."

He sounds like someone I think I am okay if I never meet. I can tell Mark doesn't want to talk about his family or childhood anymore, so I turn back toward the river and we sit in silence as the sun slowly starts to fade. Mepkin Abbey closes its gates at 6:00 p.m. and as the sun disappears, I know we need to leave but I really don't want to. We stand up and walk slowly back to the car as I try to soak in a little bit more of the peace that fills the gardens here. Mark trails along behind me. I am sure I look like a basket case, but he just follows my winding trail back to the car.

We get to the car and climb in but Mark doesn't start the engine. "Are you okay, Gen?" he asks.

"I'm really trying to be," I say.

"Is there anything I can do to help?"

"You could try and talk to Livi for me. Maybe she'll listen to you." I can't keep the bitterness out of my voice.

He reaches over and squeezes my shoulder. I flinch at the contact and hope he didn't notice. I don't want to push away the one person who is still talking to me.

"I'll try," he says and starts the car.

What a weird and depressing Christmas.

When Mark drops me off I say bye and go straight to my room without talking to either of my sisters. I smile when I see the new novel Mark gave me sitting on my nightstand. Violet must have brought it up here after I left, but the poinsettia is nowhere in sight. She must be hiding it to try and save it. I can't blame her; every plant I have tried to grow hasn't survived longer than a couple of weeks.

Maybe this Christmas wasn't as horrible as I thought it was, at least one good thing happened today. I prop myself up with pillows until I am comfortable and start to read.

Chapter 32

Steve

aking a final on New Year's Eve has got to be the most pathetic New Year's I have had yet. I guess I should just be glad that my teachers and the school have been so willing to work with me. I try to remind myself that I am taking this final on New Year's Eve, but it is weeks after everyone else took the final. The new semester has already started and I am still taking my finals for last semester.

I answer the last few questions and press submit. My last final done, now I have to play catch up with this semester's classes online. I really should just stop procrastinating and go through all of Gran's things so I can get back to school in person. Thinking about school reminds me that Mark still has not called me. I have left so many messages for him to call; there is no way he hasn't gotten any of them. I hope he told Genevieve where I am. It has been almost a whole month since I last talked to Genevieve and over a month since I saw her at Thanksgiving. I feel sick to my stomach wondering if everything is still okay between us. I wish Mark would call me back.

This Christmas was the most depressing Christmas I have ever had. At least after my parents and Jeremy died, I had Gran there for the first Christmas after. I spent this Christmas in a house full of haunted memories alone. I was hoping Mark would have given Genevieve Gran's landline number and she would call, at least that would have made Christmas bearable, but the phone never rang and I spent the day scrolling through Mark and Livi's social media trying to see what they have been up to since I left, but neither of them has posted anything new.

I have left so many messages with my dorm parents for Mark that the last time they seemed irritated with me. I still haven't heard anything. Mr. Langston tried to look up Mark's number to give to me but for some reason his number isn't in the school directory. He told me that it should be there and he will try to get the information. Thoughts of Mark trying to make his move on Genevieve tickle the back of my mind, but I push them away. He has been a fun friend and a good roommate; he wouldn't do something like that. *Would he?* I think about all the attention he has shown Genevieve these past few months and start to wonder.

I really need to get back to Charleston. There is nothing left for me in Brookhaven and I don't see myself staying here. Maggie and Claire have been great at helping me through all the hurdles that have come my way, taking care of everything after Gran's death. I am following the advice from them and Gran's lawyer, and decided to put Gran's house up for sale. I am sad to see the house go, but it will be for the best.

I should really be going through all the boxes I have piled in the dining room. The house is supposed to be ready to show next week. I look at the daunting boxes in the other room; they seem to stare at me with judgment.

My staring match is interrupted by a knock on the door. Jake and several of the others including Evie are there and ask if I want to go swimming at the local rec center with them. I look over my shoulder one more time at the pile of boxes before agreeing to go.

"Yeah, I'll go; I just need to borrow a swimming suit. I don't have one here," I say as I close the door behind me.

We all pile into Jake's van and stop at his house for a swimming suit before pulling up to the rec center. It is all indoors with slides and a wave pool included. I can't even count the number of hours I have spent here with my friends growing up.

I watch Evie flaunt out of the dressing rooms. She has always tried to push the boundaries of every rule. She is a lot like Livi in that department, but she puts even Livi to shame tonight with her swimsuit. I don't think it is possible to have a swim-suit with less fabric, definitely not leaving anything for your imagination.

Not that I need my imagination, been there done that.

It is irritating that Evie is still trying to flaunt herself in front of me. I have made it perfectly clear that I am going back to Charleston, back to Genevieve, as soon as everything is taken care of here.

Apparently, whatever plan she was trying to do isn't working and she comes and sits down right on my lap while Jake and I are talking in the hot tub. Jake raises his eyebrows and makes a quick retreat.

The traitor.

"You know," Evie says as she runs one of her long fingers down my chest. "I think it's weird that you never talk to your girlfriend. I'm not so sure you're as serious as you claim to be. If there even is a girlfriend."

"Like I have told you a million times Evie, there is a girlfriend. Her name is Genevieve."

"Well, what Genevieve doesn't know won't hurt her," Evie says with a smirk.

I look straight into her eyes and say, "Not interested," before standing up, making her slide off my lap into the hot tub with a splash.

I grab a towel and start to dry off heading to the locker room to change. Jake calls after me but I ignore him. I change quickly, but Jake catches me before I make it outside.

"Where are you going, Steve? I thought you were coming to the New Year's Eve party tonight?" Jake asks.

"I think I'm just going to walk home and catch up with you tomorrow."

"Are you sure you don't at least want a ride? It's a long walk."

"I'll be fine; a walk will do me good," I say as I push the heavy glass doors open.

Emotions and thoughts torment me on my walk home. I am irritated at Evie, mad at Mark, and play every horrible scenario in my head about Genevieve.

Maybe she is mad that I haven't called her, I am sure I would be if the roles were reversed.

Maybe she decided she likes Mark better and that is why he isn't returning my phone calls.

Maybe Genevieve and Mark are a couple now and I am just over here looking like an idiot standing up for our relationship when I haven't spoken to her in weeks.

I slam the front door harder than I mean to when I get home and walk straight over to the pile of boxes. I have got to get this done and get back to Charleston. The not knowing is worse than anything. I open the first box to find all the shirts from our vacations over the years that Gran was planning on making into a quilt.

"It will be our quilt of memories," she always used to say as she added another shirt to the pile.

This is too much for me right now. I close the box back up and plop down on the couch, turning on the TV. I am not even sure what movie I am watching, but I let it distract me until my exhausted mind finally gives in and I fall asleep on the couch.

January

Chapter 33

Genevieve

Dad is finally coming home. Konnie and I really should have made Violet help get the house clean before she left to go back to New York. I guess one nice thing about Livi not talking to me is that I have gotten ahead with my schoolwork so I should be able to help Dad.

I look around the kitchen to see if I missed anything that needs to be picked up. The sounds of a car pulling into the driveway float into the room. Hopefully the house is clean enough, we are out of time.

Konnie and I run out to meet Dad and Mom in the driveway and help carry everything in. Dad's bruises have healed, but he is still on crutches and has several new scars that are visible on his face. He has never been a big guy, but he has never looked this frail and weak either. An uneasy feeling coats my entire body as I watch Dad navigate into the house on his crutches.

It's weird to be around the table for family dinner again. It hasn't been that long since our last one, but it still feels strange having us all back together. Konnie helps Mom with the dishes while I help Dad get settled. He has a bed downstairs in the living room for now so that he doesn't have to go up and down the stairs until his leg is healed.

"Did the accident have anything to do with the blackmailing?" I ask, as I help Dad get comfortable by propping pillows under his arms.

He looks upset that I brought the blackmailing up again. "No Genna Bear, don't worry about that." He glances at my small scar on my forehead from that day and looks pained.

"Dad, I already know what's going on. Why won't you just talk to me?"

Sadness clouds his eyes. "Even if I did tell you everything, I don't have any information to give you. The screen on my phone broke during the accident. I don't know if they have sent any more messages. I really don't want you wrapped up in this, Genevieve. Please leave it alone."

I'm not sure I believe him, but I nod and finish getting him situated before going upstairs to call Mark. It has been over a month and neither of us has heard anything from Steve. I think it is time that I just try and forget about him. I am so mad that he just up and left, but it is hard to forget someone that you dream about every time you close your eyes.

"Have you been able to talk to Livi yet?" I ask Mark.

"No, she won't return my calls or texts. I'll keep trying though."

"Join the club," I grumble.

"You want to go see a movie later?"

A movie sounds fun; I haven't been to the theater since the last time the four of us went. "Yeah, that sounds fun. Can Konnie come with? Dad got home today and it has been kinda tense. I feel bad leaving her at home."

"Of course. Comedy or action?"

I am glad he didn't even bring up the new chick flick that came out. I don't think I could watch anything about a love story without thinking about Steve.

"Definitely action."

Mark laughs. "All right, I'll pick you guys up. See you soon."

I tell Konnie to get ready, tidy up my room a little bit, and read some more of the novel Mark gave me before he picks us up. We drive to the theater in comfortable silence and get in line to buy tickets. Mark hands me the big tub of popcorn he got for us to share and jokes about the popcorn fight we got into with Konnie the last time we watched a movie at the house. All three of us are laughing when I turn around and see Livi with some friends from school standing behind us.

My stomach plummets.

What does the universe have against me? What are the chances that Livi would decide to come to a movie on the same day as us? I wonder as I panic and just stand there staring at Livi, not knowing what to do. Mark tries to say hi to Livi, but she ignores him and he grabs my shoulder, steering me away from the group. We find our seats in the theater and I start to relax until Livi and her group come into the theater and sit just a couple of rows behind us.

Most uncomfortable movie EVER.

To make matters worse, Mark reaches over and tries to hold my hand, but I slide my hand away. I have a million different emotions hurtling through me. I am worried about what Livi's thinking, worried I am hurting Mark's feelings, and annoyed that Mark would try to hold my hand. Especially in front of Livi, not to mention that I still have no idea what is going on with Steve. I keep telling myself that it has been a month, I need to move on, but on the other hand I can't deny the strong feelings I have for Steve.

My boyfriend.

How long do you wait for someone to let you know they don't want to be with you anymore before it is okay to just assume you have broken up? Leave it to me to have the most dysfunctional first relationship ever.

I tense when I hear Livi say, "Looks like she found someone else to use."

"Just ignore her," Mark whispers, but Konnie ignores him and turns around.

"Genevieve doesn't use anyone Livi and you know that. As a matter of fact, it's been great not having you around, I actually get to hang out with my sister for once instead of you demanding all of her time."

I turn to peek at Livi who looks like she is fuming, but the people in the rows between us are telling both Livi and Konnie to be quiet. Thankfully Livi doesn't say anything else; we finish the movie in tense silence and Livi storms out of the theater as soon as the movie ends.

I was hoping the movie would help me relax. Let me have some fun and forget my problems tonight. But when Mark drops us off at home after the movie, I am even more confused than I was when we left.

Chapter 34

Steve

We are driving through the cotton candy fog again. I look over at Jeremy as he says he thinks if we stick our hands out the window we could grab some and eat it. I am startled to see Genevieve sitting in between us. I am filled with even more terror than normal as we drive through the thick fog. I know what is coming. Mom seems really nervous; she is telling Dad to slow down. Except when I look at the driver's seat, it isn't Dad driving the car. Mark is driving, hurtling us toward disaster. The fog parts and we slam into the back of my grandparent's car.

I sit up, frantically trying to free myself from the sheets and blankets that seem to be suffocating me. *What was that?* Seems like a pretty cruel trick for my own brain to play on me. Let's throw your current problems in with the worst day of your life.

Not cool.

There is no way I am going back to sleep anytime soon. I go sit at the computer and scroll through my feed. I roll my eyes at a bikini picture Evie has posted and then freeze.

It feels like someone has punched me in the gut and I forget how to breathe for a minute.

Staring back at me is a laughing Genevieve holding a huge bucket of popcorn and sitting next to Mark. Genevieve was at a movie with Mark and Mark felt the need to post about it. I click open messenger and sure enough, it says Mark still has not seen my message, and he couldn't even be bothered with checking his messages and responding. Not even a 'Hey dude, just trying to claim your girl while you're gone.' I could punch that smug smile right off his stupid face.

Livi isn't in the picture and when I go to Livi's page, she still hasn't posted anything new. Well, if Genevieve has moved on with Mark I guess there is no reason to be worried about what Genevieve would think about anything I do. Even though it is late, I call Jake and tell him to come over with some of the gang. Sure enough, when they show up Evie is with them. I let them all in and some of the guys start playing Xbox while everyone starts raiding the kitchen for snacks. I didn't quite think this through, I don't really have any snacks, but they find a bag of chips and start passing them around.

"Can you guys try and keep the house clean? I have a showing tomorrow," I ask as Jake spills some pop on the couch.

They all look at me like I grew another head and start to laugh.

"You need to chill, Steve," Jake says as he wipes at the wet spot.

When everyone else laughs again I realize that I have grown up quite a bit since I left for Charleston. Did I really used to act like these guys? I must have, because they haven't changed at all—now they irritate me.

Evie comes and tries to sit on my lap again and it takes all my will power not to shove her off onto the floor. Isn't this what I wanted? So now that they are here, why is it that the only thing I want is for them all to leave?

"You need to relax, Steve," Evie says as she runs her hands through my hair making my skin crawl.

"What I need is you to stop touching me and everyone to leave," I say through gritted teeth.

Everyone stops what they are doing to look at me.

"What happened to you? You used to be fun," Evie whines as she stands up and heads for the door.

Everyone gets up to follow her out, each of them throwing me glances, some in anger and some in concern. Jake is the last one to walk out the door.

"Call me when you chill out," he says, before he bounds down the stairs after the rest of them.

I close the door and lean my head against the doorframe. *I have got to get out of Brookhaven,* I think, before going to the stack of boxes and opening another one. This one is full of pictures and I sit down to go through them. I don't know why I am even bothering, it's not like I am going to get rid of any of the pictures, I should just put the box in the keep pile and move on to the next one. Instead, I look through all the pictures until early in the morning. I miss my family, I miss Gran, and I miss Genevieve even though I have no idea what is going on with her and Mark.

I slide the box of pictures over to the keep pile and stare at the rest of the boxes. There is an ache inside of me that I can't even try to ease. An ache that only Genevieve can try to fix, I hope I am not too late. Who knows what Mark has told her?

With a new determination I open the next box.

Chapter 35

Genevieve

"I just don't understand how you got that answer," I say, pointing to the answer in question on my chemistry paper.

"You mean how I got the right answer?" Mark teases.

I give him a shove with my shoulder and laugh. "I don't get how you or the book got that answer. This has never happened to me before."

"You've never gotten an answer wrong before?" he asks.

"Of course I have gotten answers wrong before, I'm just usually the one helping everyone else with their homework. This is the first time someone has been helping me."

He smiles that smirky smile that I am starting to crave and gets up. "Well, there's a first time for everything. I'll be right back," he says and heads toward the bathroom.

I shake my head and turn to focus on my homework again. After a while I realize that Mark has been gone for a long time and get up to go get some snacks. Walking down the hall I notice that no one is in the bathroom. *Where did Mark go?* I am about to go downstairs when I hear something in my parents' room. Dad shouldn't be up here and Mom isn't home. I push the door open and see Mark snooping around the room.

"What are you doing?" I ask.

Mark jumps and then laughs. "You scared the crap out of me, Genevieve. Your dad asked me to get him a pair of socks."

I walk over to Dad's sock drawer and open it pulling out a pair and handing them to Mark. Seems a little bit weird Dad would ask Mark for socks, but I follow him downstairs where he hands the socks to Dad.

"Thanks Mark, my toes were cold, but I keep getting too hot with the blanket on," Dad says as he pulls a sock on the one foot that he can wear a sock on.

When did I become so suspicious of everything? I wonder as we grab snacks and head back upstairs to my room. I try to get focused back on the homework, but my mind is thinking about everything other than what I want it to.

"Have you been able to get a hold of Livi yet?" I ask.

Mark shakes his head with a mouth full of chips. He hurries and swallows. "She hasn't returned any of my calls or texts, but I'll stop by the apartment on the way home tonight and see if I can get her to talk to me if I show up on her doorstep."

Seems like a better plan than we have had so far. Even if Livi wants to slam the door in Mark's face, I doubt Darla would let her. *Why didn't I think of that?*

Konnie is sitting at the dining room table with two cups of hot chocolate after I say goodbye to Mark. I sit down and take a sip of the delicious chocolate.

"Would you hate me if I told you I kinda hope you and Livi never stop fighting?" Konnie asks.

"Why would you want us to keep fighting?"

"Because I actually get to hang out with you now."

"We hung out before," I point out.

"Not the same. I actually get to go do fun things with you. Mark never minds if I tag a long, but Livi was always mean when I wanted to come with you guys."

"I promise if Livi and I do stop fighting, you will get to go with us more often."

Konnie smiles. "Thanks. It has been really nice getting to spend more time with you. I'm sorry it's because so much is going on."

"Thanks Konnie. I have had fun hanging out with you too."

She gives me a hug before she heads upstairs. I rinse both of our mugs out and put them in the dishwasher. On my way out of the kitchen I hear Dad's cell phone get a text. Mom got the screen fixed today; I can't help but wonder if there are any new messages from the blackmailer. I know I shouldn't, but he is sound asleep so I pick up his phone and open the text from a blocked number.

The accident was just a warning.

You're out of time.

My heart starts to race. Whoever is blackmailing Dad was responsible for the accident. My body is buzzing with nervous energy.

What does the text mean?

And what happens when his time runs out?

Chapter 36

Steve

The nightmares are relentless. Every night I have some version of my family's car accident replay in my dreams, only now Genevieve, Mark, and sometimes Gran are in the car too. I have to watch everyone I love die each night before I wake up drenched in sweat.

It doesn't help that Mark has been posting pictures of him and Genevieve regularly. Livi is never in the pictures and she still hasn't posted anything new since before I left Charleston. None of the messages I have sent to Livi or Mark have been read. It has been almost two months since I have talked to any of them.

At least Gran's house sold quickly. I got an offer for full asking price last week that I accepted without even thinking about it. I am ready to get out of Brookhaven; I haven't wanted to hang out with Jake and the rest of the group since the night they came over to the house. I just want to get back to Charleston, even though I don't know what will be waiting for me when I get there.

I am in the lobby waiting to see Gran's lawyer. This appointment with the lawyer and the appointment to sign the closing papers and hand over the keys to the house tomorrow morning are the last things I need to do before I can leave.

I have finally made it through all the boxes. I decided that I don't want to leave anything here in Brookhaven; I don't want to have to pay for a storage unit or come back to get stuff. I have sold and donated everything that I am not keeping and everything I am keeping is packed into the Jeep. I don't even have anything left in the kitchen so I have resorted to eating off the value menus at fast food restaurants for every meal the last few days. Not going to lie, I am starting to not feel the greatest. Maybe I should get a salad for dinner tonight.

Gran's lawyer calls me into his office and I sit down. This definitely looks like a lawyer Gran would get along with. His office is covered in a collection of random trinkets from various places. He apparently likes to travel.

The lawyer shuts the door and sits down behind his desk. "Thank you for coming Mr. Adler. Now that the house is sold, we just need to go over some things before you head back to Charleston."

He pulls a file from a file cabinet behind him before continuing. "Your grandmother placed all your parent's life insurance money into some high interest accounts for you after their deaths. The accounts have made quite a bit of money over the years."

He pushes a paper toward me and points to the balance at the top of the page. I'm in shock. I can't form any words before he continues talking. "There are some stipulations: most of the funds cannot be accessed until your twenty-first birthday, although some of the accounts can be used for educational expenses. That does include housing."

He looks at me like he is waiting for me to say something, but words still evade me and I just stare at him so he continues. "Between these accounts, your grandmother's life insurance policy and the sale of the house, you shouldn't have to worry about any tuition or housing costs for the rest of your senior year and your college education."

He has me sign several forms, gives me a pile of papers to take with me and then walks me back out to the lobby where I'm finally able to muster a thank you before walking out to the Jeep.

We have never had a lot of money. We did fine, but we always had to be careful with finances. The amount of money in those accounts is almost too much for me to even comprehend. Granted, most of the kids at Charleston Academy probably have this much in their own accounts, not including their parents' net worth. It is still more money than I ever thought I would have.

I don't have to work while I am in college, I realize. Which is probably a good thing with my tendency to procrastinate my schoolwork, but I really enjoy the ghost tours so I will probably continue with that job at least until I leave Charleston Academy. It's probably a good idea to save as much of this money as I can, I don't know what the future holds and I may need it.

I pull into the cemetery before driving home. I don't know when or if I will be back in Brookhaven and I want to say goodbye to my family before I leave. The newly placed bright green sod over Gran and Grandpa's grave is drastically different from the well-established dark green grass over my parent's and Jeremy's graves. It rarely snows in Brookhaven and the grass is still green in January even though it doesn't have the vibrant green colors like it does during the spring and summer months.

I place Gran's and Mom's favorite flowers on the graves, lilies on Gran and Grandpa's grave, and daisies on my family's graves. I know Gran hates goodbyes so instead I say, "See you later," before I turn and walk to the Jeep without looking back.

When I get back to the house, I walk through its halls making sure I didn't miss anything. Everything is clean and there is nothing in the house except for a small bag with some clothes and toiletries I am still using and a blanket that I will sleep on the floor with tonight before leaving the house for the last time tomorrow morning.

The glint of the stained-glass window in the back door catches my eye.

When I was eleven, I broke the window out playing baseball with my friends. I thought Gran was going to be livid, but she just cleaned up the glass and said, "I've always wanted a stained-glass window there anyway."

I smile as I relive all the memories I have in this house with Gran. Some say that the experiences of my childhood were tragic, and they were, but I grew up in a loving home full of laughter and happy memories. There have only been two people in my life that I have truly felt like I could be myself with: Gran and Genevieve. I really hope I am wrong about Genevieve and Mark, but my stomach tightens and I feel sick thinking about what I might find when I get back to Charleston.

Chapter 37

Genevieve

"We need to talk."

I have gotten so used to keeping to myself at school, Livi's voice startles me. She doesn't wait for me to answer before she starts again. "Meet me at my car after school."

It has been horrible not having my best friend the last month and a half and I hate riding the bus too. I hate to admit it after she accused me of using her, but being able to ride to school with Livi is a definite bonus to being her best friend.

After school I walk out to the parking lot. Livi is already sitting in her car. Taking a deep breath, I open the passenger side door and sit down.

"Livi, you don't even have to say anything, just listen to my side of the story and then I'll leave."

"I'm the one who told you to come here, remember?"

Oh yeah. I giggle and a small timid smile shows up on Livi's face. "Genevieve, I'm really sorry that I have been so horrible this last little while. Mark stopped by my house and told me I really do have it all wrong. I figured I should give you the chance to tell me your side of the story."

I clear my throat and wipe my sweaty palms on my jeans. "Mark was only at the hospital that day because I had called him to ask if he had heard anything from Steve. He was on the phone with me when Dad and I got into the accident. He actually helped me get out of the truck. When you walked into the waiting room that day Mark was just giving me a hug because I had just gone through a lot."

Livi isn't saying anything, but her face relaxes a little bit so I keep going. "I'm honestly not interested in Mark that way at all, but he has been the only person here for me during all of this. I haven't heard anything from Steve. I have no idea where he is."

To my surprise, when I look back at Livi she has tears in her eyes and almost bonks my head on the window trying to give me a hug. "I'm so sorry, Genevieve. I should've been there for you, I was already frustrated with Mark and when I walked in and saw you guys hugging I just got so mad."

I squeeze my best friend back. "I would never do anything to compromise our friendship, Livi."

"Deep down I knew that all along. I don't know why I was so mad, but every time I would see you, especially if you were with Mark, it just made me even madder. I've missed my best friend sooo much."

"I've missed you too," I say, tearing up myself.

"And what do you mean you don't know where Steve is?"

"He ghosted me. He even left school without saying anything to Mark."

"You really haven't heard anything from him?"

"Nothing," I say trying to hold back tears.

"What a jerk. Has Mark seen anything on Steve's social media accounts?"

Wait, what? Mark has social media accounts? "I didn't even realize Mark had accounts. I have never seen him on any."

"Yeah, he does. I would look for you, but Mom took my phone and grounded me from all social media after I threw the tantrum at the hospital. She still hasn't given either of them back."

Well, that makes more sense why Livi wasn't responding to any of our calls or texts. I will have to ask Mark if he has tried getting a hold of Steve through social media.

Smiling at Livi I ask, "Do you think you would be okay hanging out with Mark again? We don't have to, but he really has been the only person I have been hanging out with lately and I don't want to ditch him. It would be nice if I could hang out with both of you together."

"Yeah, I've actually thought about it a lot since Mark stopped by. I don't think he is into me like I wanted him to be, but it would be nice to have my friends back."

"I honestly don't know how Mark feels about you, but I think it might be a good idea if we're all just friends for a little bit before we broach that subject.

How about you come to karaoke with us tomorrow night? We've been planning on going for a while and it will be fun for all of us to go."

Livi smiles. "That sounds like fun, I'll be there. How is your dad doing?"

Would it be safe to tell Livi about the blackmailing? I can't talk to Steve about it and Violet always seems to just brush it off when I bring it up. I haven't said anything to Mark about it either and now that I know about my dad's past, it is even more important to keep it to myself. That is all I need—getting myself into trouble with the U.S. Military on top of everything else.

"I'm worried about him, but he seems to be healing."

"I'm sure he'll be as good as new soon." Livi grins excitedly. "I really want to go on another ghost tour! I've been missing the tours so much, but I didn't want to run into Mark or Steve and it felt weird going without you. Can we go to one on Friday?"

Karaoke and a ghost tour back-to-back. We have only been talking again for a matter of minutes and Livi is already pushing me back out of my comfort zone, but I don't know how fragile our new-found peace is. "Sure, why not. We do need to try and include Konnie more though."

Livi groans. "How about we start letting Konnie come with us next week, I haven't been able to talk to you in ages."

That was your own fault, I think but say, "Okay, starting next week."

Livi squeals and gives me a bone-crushing hug. "Gen, I really think you should try to put Steve behind you. We can find a new hot guy to replace him."

I sigh and tell Livi I need to get home and check on Dad since Mom is working this afternoon.

I smile and wave goodbye as Livi drops me off. Violet and Mark have both told me the same thing about Steve. I want to put him behind me and move on, but I don't know how. He is the first boy I have ever felt this way about and maybe it is the not knowing, but it feels so abrupt and unfinished. I still have no idea where he went and I think I just need some closure before I can truly move on.

I haven't even been able to go back to Cypress Gardens without remembering walking around the black water swamp with Steve in the dark. He has turned one of my favorite places into a place where I can only remember the one night I was there with him. I bite my lip thinking about going on a ghost tour with Livi and Mark. A ghost tour is going to bring back so many memories.

Walking toward the front door I notice movement in the tree house. *Who could possibly be up there?* I thought Konnie was staying after school for a project. I don't think she would be home already. As I get closer to the house, I am surprised to see Dad hobbling down the ladder with his broken leg.

"Dad! What are you doing?"

Dad flinches at the sound of my voice. "I just hadn't been up in the tree house for so long, I wanted to check everything out. I have been getting a little stir crazy."

Well, I guess that makes sense, he has been trapped inside for a while, but I still don't think he is telling the full truth. "Do you want to break your neck too?" I ask.

He lets out a strained laugh. "You're right, probably not the best idea, let's go inside."

I hand Dad one of his crutches that fell to the ground and follow him into the house. He seems jumpy and his eyes never focus on one thing for long, like he is continuously searching his surroundings.

"Are you okay, Dad?"

"I'm fine, kiddo. Just need to sit down for a little bit."

I can tell he isn't being completely honest, but I don't know if he is jumpy from everything that is going on or if he is hiding something else.

"Do you want to work on the blueprints? We're almost finished."

With the mention of blueprints, I can see a terror in his eyes that has my heart accelerating, but almost as quickly as the terror came, it leaves his eyes and he smiles. "I would love that, Genna Bear."

When Mom tells us it is way past our bedtime, we stay up just a little bit longer and put the finishing touches on my dream house we have been designing for so long.

"It's perfect," I say.

He wraps his arm around me and squeezes my shoulder. "I can't wait to see you bring it to life. I love you, Genna Bear."

I smile up at him. "Love you too, Dad."

Despite what I have learned about Dad's past, I realize that he had no control over what was happening to him either. He has been put into difficult situations his entire life, and even with the skeletons in his closet, he is a good person. He is still the same man he has always been. There has to be a way to make everything right. We just have to figure it out.

I walk upstairs to go to bed. Life is never easy and it never goes exactly how you expect it to, but if you look closely enough you can find beauty in the little moments. And the little moments are truly what make life worth living.

February

Chapter 38

Steve

How can a ten-and-a-half hour drive feel like seconds? The entire drive back to Charleston I have been trying to figure out what I am going to say to Mark when I see him and whether or not I should just drive straight to Genevieve's house or go to Charleston Academy first. I decide I want to change my clothes before I see Genevieve.

Being back on campus is weird. It feels like I have been gone for a lot longer than two months. I walk into the dorm room I share with Mark and I'm surprised to see Mark there getting ready to leave. I don't know what I was expecting. I know he lives here, but Mr. Langston said that he could never catch Mark at the dorm so I guess I just assumed I wouldn't have to see him right away. Mark looks just as startled to see me walking through the door. His wide eyes and raised eyebrows are almost comical, but I don't feel like laughing.

I walk in and drop the boxes I am carrying onto my bed before whirling around to face Mark. "Why didn't you return any of my messages?"

"Well, hello to you too, roomie," Mark says with that stupid smirk of his. Apparently he has recovered from his shock.

"I've been trying to get a hold of you this whole time."

"We've been trying to get a hold of you, too. Ever heard of returning a text or a phone call?"

Is he really going to lay the blame on me? "I haven't had a cell phone this whole time, Mark. I left multiple messages for you at the dorm with Gran's landline number. I even sent you messages online."

"I never got any of your messages here and I don't have the messenger app on my phone, so I don't get any messages sent to me through social media."

Okay, not having messenger on his phone can explain him not seeing those messages, but it seems farfetched that he didn't get any of the messages left for him at the dorm.

"Where are you headed off to?" I ask, trying to keep the anger out of my voice.

"I'm meeting Genevieve and Livi for karaoke."

Genevieve is going to karaoke now? How can so much change in less than two months?

"Mind if I tag along?" I ask, so much for changing my clothes.

Mark looks irritated but says yes and I follow him out to his car and climb into the passenger seat. When he starts to drive, I realize that he is driving to Moncks Corner for karaoke and it crosses my mind that I should have driven the Jeep in case I wanted to go over to Genevieve's house after. What am I going to say to Genevieve when I see her? I don't even know what to expect. Is she mad? Will she be happy to see me?

I glance over at Mark. "So what is going on with you and Genevieve? I've seen all the pictures you've been posting. How is she doing?"

"She has been pretty pissed that you haven't called and left without telling her."

I notice he didn't answer my question about what is going on between the two of them, but I am mostly irritated that none of them seem to be trying to be understanding at all about my situation. I don't have a chance to ask anything else before we pull up to the bowling alley, where they have regular karaoke nights, and Mark gets out of the car.

I follow him in and I am both relieved and disappointed when Livi is the only one waiting for us. She looks shocked to see me too, but it doesn't last long before she walks straight up to me and slaps me across the face.

"Where in the heck have you been? You're such a jerk!" Livi yells at me.

I look around at all the faces turned toward us. I definitely wasn't expecting this reaction.

I glare at Mark and turn back to Livi. "My grandma died and I had to leave suddenly, I told Mark to tell you guys. I haven't had a cell phone this whole time."

Some of the anger seems to leave Livi as she looks at Mark in confusion. "Why didn't you ever tell Genevieve where Steve was?"

"I never got a chance to. Where is Gen by the way?" Mark asks.

"You've been with Genevieve regularly, how have you not had a chance to tell her?" Livi asks incredulously. "Genevieve isn't coming tonight, she isn't feeling well."

Mark never told Genevieve why I was gone? This situation is a lot worse than I thought it would be. My suspicions about Mark seem to be true. There is no other reason he wouldn't have told her why I left, unless he was trying to win her over. I really should have driven. I do not want to ride clear back to Charleston in the same car as Mark. I wonder if I can switch to a different dorm room while I am at it.

Ignoring Mark, I turn to Livi, feeling desperate. "Can I get Genevieve's number from you? Actually, can I borrow your phone to call her?"

"I don't actually have a phone right now either. My mom took it."

Well, I guess that explains why Livi hasn't been on social media and didn't return my phone calls. I turn to Mark. "Give me your phone."

"No."

"Are you kidding me?" I don't care that Mark is the Hulk, I am going to deck him right in the face.

Luckily for probably both of us, Livi steps in between us. "Steve, Genevieve's had a really rough couple of months too. There is too much to explain right now, but she isn't feeling well tonight and we probably shouldn't dump this on her. You know how she hates surprises. Why don't you come on the ghost tour with us tomorrow and I'll give her some warning before she sees you."

A tour? I guess I just assumed that they wouldn't be going on tours without me. Not sure why, Mark works there too. It still stings.

"I'll warn Genevieve," Mark says. "You two aren't on the best terms either, Livi."

Genevieve and Livi aren't on good terms? A lot has happened while I was gone. I wasn't sure what I was going to be coming back to when I got back to Charleston, but everything seems just as broken here as it was in Brookhaven.

Chapter 39

Genevieve

Livi screeches to a halt in front of my house at seven o'clock on the dot. I can count on one hand the number of times Livi has been on time and this is one of them. Running down the stairs, I open the front door.

"You're not wearing that," are the first words out of Livi's mouth. "Get back upstairs, and change your clothes!"

Livi is wearing tight jeans and a black spaghetti strap shirt that is showing most of her midriff. I look down at my faded jeans and baggy hoodie. It's just Livi and Mark, why can't I be comfortable?

"What's wrong with this? It's supposed to be cold tonight, you're going to freeze."

Livi doesn't seem to hear any of my complaints as she pushes me up the stairs. About twenty minutes later we grudgingly make a compromise; I am still wearing my faded jeans, but have switched my hoodie out for a halter top and a jacket.

"So what tour are we going on for the millionth time?" I ask sarcastically as I climb into the front seat of Livi's Mustang.

Livi's wicked smile returns. "The Haunted Jail tour. This one won't be boring though, don't worry."

I sigh. "Livi we've been on all of the ghost tours multiple times, no matter what one we go on it's going to be boring."

Livi grins. "I think you'll change your mind when we get there." Turning up the radio, she ends the conversation.

The drive to Charleston goes by without conversation and Livi blasting country music with the windows down. How she isn't an icicle by now is beyond me. By the time we park, my head is throbbing from the hour of blaring country music, or maybe it is residual from my migraine yesterday. I was upset when I missed out on the first get together with the three of us again, but I really wasn't too sad about missing karaoke.

I follow Livi down the crowded street pulling my jacket tighter around my shoulders. It is already starting to cool down. About a block away from the building the sky lets loose and rain starts pouring down on us. Livi shrieks and starts running. *Could tonight get any worse?* I wonder as I follow Livi into the tour office. There was a huge line but it is starting to dwindle as people decide they don't want to do a tour in the rain.

I stand in line with Livi, wondering why anyone would be idiotic enough to spend $18 to walk around Charleston during a rainstorm, which reminds me of walking through Magnolia Gardens in the rain with Steve.

Apparently under the right circumstances, I would.

Livi steps up to the counter and asks for the tickets reserved under her name. The lady at the counter hands Livi the tickets and says, "All right, you're all set for the 10:00 tour with Mark. He left a note saying the tickets have been paid for. Meet on the corner in front of our office building at 9:45. Have a spooky adventure." I roll my eyes and follow Livi outside.

Livi turns around and smirks. "This is going to be awesome! I've missed the ghost tours!"

What in the world does she keep smirking about? I text both Mom and Dad letting them know the tour doesn't start until ten and I might be late. It's a weekend so my curfew is midnight, so it is possible we will be home on time, but I doubt it, unless we leave immediately after the tour ends.

Neither of them responds, which is strange.

My head is pounding and I am done with Livi's cryptic optimism. Livi is a bubbly person, but she is over the top giddy tonight.

"Great. We're going on a tour we have memorized, in the dark, and it's raining." I look at the time on my cell and groan. "What are we going to do until 9:45? I think I need to eat something before the tour starts."

Livi shrugs. "Let's get dinner while we wait. And just for the record, I didn't pick the Haunted Jail Tour again, Mark gave us the tickets."

I am so hungry.

Maybe some food will stop the pounding in my head. I follow Livi as we sprint through the rain to the restaurant. She picks The Noisy Oyster which has always been a favorite restaurant of mine. Livi knows me too well. I order my favorite sesame crusted tuna and start to relax. After talking and laughing with Livi, my mood starts to improve. If I am being totally honest, I was probably a little bit hangry.

It doesn't seem long before it is time to meet for the tour. Thankfully, the rain has stopped for the time being. Hopefully it will stay that way, at least until we can get into the jail.

When we get to the corner, there are already a few people waiting. There is the usual group of college kids and a couple who can't keep their hands off each other. No sign of Mark yet. The air is still heavy and humid; the rain could start again at any moment. Livi nudges me and points down the street; she has a huge grin on her face. I look where Livi is pointing and my heart stops.

I think I forget how to breathe.

Steve is walking down the street next to Mark.

He looks even better than the last time I saw him if that is even possible.

"I told you," Livi giggles.

I had thought I would be ecstatic when he was back, but I'm not. The anger builds even more as I watch him walk toward us.

I am straight up pissed off at Steve.

It hurt so much when he left without saying goodbye, and I was devastated when he stopped texting and calling. How dare he just show back up looking all perfect without any warning?

It is starting to make a bit more sense why Livi was so adamant about me changing. I mean, she usually wants me to change my clothes, but she usually gives up a lot easier than she did tonight. Thinking about Livi, I realize that she knew Steve was back.

She knew he was back and didn't tell me.

He walked here with Mark, so apparently Mark knew too. How long has he been back? Realizing that I am starting to spiral into my anxiety ridden emotions, I glare at Livi and try to look unaffected.

Steve walks up with those blue eyes focused on me. "Hey Gen. How are you?"

"I'm fine," I say, before turning around and facing the group. I desperately want to ask him where he has been all this time and why he didn't call or text, but I don't want to have this conversation here in front of all of these people.

Mark looks smug as he walks up to the front of the group and introduces himself. Livi shoots me an apologetic look and follows Mark. She keeps glancing back at us every so often with a worried look on her face. I must not have reacted how she was expecting me to. I am not reacting like I thought I would if I ever got a chance to see Steve again either.

This is what I wanted, wasn't it?

"Hey Gen, you okay?" Steve asks. He looks like he is trying to approach a wild animal.

All that comes out of my mouth is an almost silent, "Yep," before I start to follow the group down the sidewalk.

Livi waits for us to catch up to her. "You okay?" she whispers.

"What do you think?" I snap.

Livi flinches like I slapped her. "I thought you would be excited to see him," she whispers frantically.

"How long?"

"How long what?" She looks confused.

"How long have you known he was back?"

"I swear I didn't know until last night at karaoke. Mark said he was going to warn you Steve was back. We know how much you hate surprises."

I turn to look at her. "Well, consider me surprised."

"I am so sorry. I …"

"You sure you're okay, Gen?" Steve interrupts.

I don't even respond. Livi glances at me one last time and hurries back to the front of the group to walk with Mark.

Steve sighs next to me. "Can we talk?"

"Now you want to talk?" I snap.

"Please let me explain what happened."

"Yes, please enlighten me. I am dying to know why you ghosted me for months!" I whisper yell at Steve, loud enough that some of the others on the tour turn to look at us. "Are we even still a couple?"

His eyes seem to fill with sorrow. "Gran died." He says quietly before locking those sad blue eyes with mine. "And I hope we're still a couple."

Okay now I feel like a jerk, but it still doesn't explain not talking to any of us for months.

Not talking to me for months.

I have no idea what to say. I have so many questions. The group is walking faster than we are and we are falling behind.

In my silence Steve changes the subject. "So are the tours still scary or are they mostly boring now?"

"The tours were boring before you disappeared."

What is wrong with me?

He just told me his grandma died and he does still want to be with me, but I am still so angry. He doesn't need to know that the tours were never boring when he was still here. I could listen to him tell the stories over and over and I would have never been bored.

Steve sighs again. "Well, I guess we'll just have to make this tour a little more exciting then, what do you say? Should we scare the crap out of some people?"

Steve turns down one of the alleyways away from the group. I still need to know so much information about these past few months, but I can't help it, even though I am still mad, I am drawn to him. I sigh and follow him down the alley between the old buildings; he picks up his speed and leads me through a maze of streets. When we finally stop, we are in front of the old jail and Steve pulls out a key.

Panting from the brisk pace I ask, "How do you have a key?"

Steve puts his finger to his lips and whispers, "I still work for the tour company. Hurry, they'll be here soon!"

As Steve reaches to put the key in, his fingers bump the gate and it swings open effortlessly. He looks confused. "I was the last one that gave a jail tour and I swear I locked it up behind me. I must have not latched it right or something."

He looks worried but grabs my hand and pulls me through the gate, locking it behind him. We walk around the side of the building to the door the tours exit and enter the decaying jail. I follow him into the dark building and he turns and locks the door.

My heart rate skyrockets. "Wait, what are you doing?" I hiss.

The jail is way creepier without a group.

My pulse starts to pick up speed again. I am standing so close to Steve. He smells so good, his woody citrus scent washing over me. *Did I brush my teeth before I left the house?* What am I even thinking? It doesn't matter if I brushed my teeth or not. Steve didn't even text me for two months we're not going to have a make out session no matter how good his excuse is.

He laughs. "I'm not locking us in or anything, they have to think everything is normal when they get here, or we aren't going to be able to scare anyone."

Good, he thinks I am freaked out about the jail, not being in close proximity to him.

I look at him skeptically through the dim orange lights that are coming from the fixtures on the walls.

"I guess that makes sense," I say and then against my better judgment I follow him down the dimly lit hall.

We walk up a few flights of stairs and turn toward the front of the building. Steve stops and motions for me to come closer. *Why does he smell so good?* It sounds like he has been working all day. I can walk down the street in the South Carolina humidity and stink within five minutes.

"Okay, so I have three different ways that we could make this tour extra scary and I think that we can do all three if we work together. First, we should be here on the third floor. When they enter the building and start up the stairs, we'll slowly walk down the hall toward Lavinia's cell. This floor is so old they should be able to hear our footsteps clearly."

"Sounds easy enough."

"Then part two would be all you if you're up for it?" he asks in a whisper.

"It depends on what I would have to do."

"It's easy, I'll unlock the door next to Lavinia's cell and when Mark is telling her story he will end the story with her last words. You remember her story, right?"

I nod. How could I forget? She is only one of the creepiest people I have ever learned about.

"All you need to do is recite her last words along with him loud enough for the tour to hear. I would do it, but I think I might have a hard time sounding like a woman." He chuckles.

"What were her last words again?" I ask nervously.

"I thought you had these tours memorized," he jokes. "Don't worry, it's an easy line. 'If you have a message you want to send to hell, give it to me—I'll carry it.' Even if you're not perfectly on cue I'm sure it will scare the crap out of at least one person on the tour."

Once again I want to ask him about what has happened while he was gone, but Steve puts his finger to his lips as we hear the tour group approaching the front doors of the jail and Mark going into his spiel on the building. "The Old City Jail was in operation from 1802 to 1939. It housed 19th century pirates, civil war prisoners, and Charleston's most infamous criminals. Most of the jail's structure is still intact, including the cells and the warden's quarters. It was originally four stories high with a two-story tower. Several expansions were added to the main building in 1855. In 1886 an earthquake badly damaged the tower and top story and they were removed, thus the reason why you do not see a tower today. Now if you follow me, we will enter the most haunted building in Charleston and proceed up the stairs to the second level."

I hear the door open and feet shuffling into the building. They must make it to the second floor because the noise dies down and Steve is tugging on my hand to follow him. We slowly, but purposefully walk the length of the hall to Lavinia's cell. I stifle a giggle when I hear several of the group saying, "Did you hear that?" and "I just heard footsteps up there!"

We reach Lavinia's cell and frantically I lean over and whisper, "You never told me the third step, and I already forgot my line!"

Steve unlocks the door next to Lavinia's cell and we scramble in. "Just follow me after you say your line," he whispers and then repeats my line to me.

Soon, we can hear the group walking down the hall to the cell. Through the cracks I can see Livi looking around trying to find us. I hope that since we are in the dark and Lavinia's cell is lit with the dim orange lights, no one will be able to see us. After they are all in the cell, Mark starts the story.

"We are currently in the cell of the late Lavinia Fisher. She is famous for being the first female serial killer in the United States of America and is our most seen ghost on the tour," Mark continues with the creepy story of Lavinia and John.

"They were found guilty and sentenced to be hanged on February 18, 1820. Lavinia wore her wedding gown to the execution and her last words before they were both hung were, 'If you have a message …' Mark stops talking when he hears my voice speaking along with him finishing Lavinia's sentence, 'you want to send to hell, give it to me—I'll carry it.' Several of the college girls scream. Mark and Livi look startled at first, but they both know my voice so well they are trying not to smile as the rest of the group panics. Steve gives me a thumb up as we wait for the group to calm down and follow Mark to the next stop on the tour.

"That was awesome!" Steve whispered when the group is out of earshot. Laughing he asks, "Did you see their faces?"

I start to laugh too. "I'm just glad I remembered the words."

Steve grabs my hand again. "Follow me; we're going to have to be super quiet." He slips out the door and starts to walk back toward the stairs. "Just stay close, you'll figure out what we are doing. We have to hurry though."

I follow him back through the hall and down the stairs; we are on the main level now and walking as quietly as we can through the big hallway. When we reach the thick metal doors that block entry to the basement, Steve pulls out his keys and unlocks them. I have never been in the basement before. The tours aren't allowed down there. Unlike the hallways in the main building, down here, there are no lights.

Goosebumps pop up on my arms and I can feel the hair on the back of my neck stand up. I pause. It is so creepy down here. Steve grabs my hand and starts to lead me farther into the darkness. The farther we walk the more disoriented I am. It seems like we have been walking for miles, when I know in reality we can't have gone far.

Steve stops short when we hear a commotion above us. The old wooden floors don't do much to stop any sounds from coming through. I can't see Steve, but I can feel him tense up next to me. It sounds like there might be a fight going on upstairs, several of the group members scream.

Steve whispers, "Stay here for a minute; I'm going to grab one of the flashlights." And then he is gone.

After a few seconds, I can't hear Steve moving anymore.

"Steve," I whisper. "Where are you?" No answer. I wait a few seconds and then whisper again, "Steve! Are you there?"

I start to panic. Where is he? I am too turned around to try and find my way back to the stairs. Did he lock the door behind us? Fighting tears, I sit down on the grimy floor and try to figure out what to do. I hear someone scream again.

Is Steve scaring the group? I wonder. More screams filter through the floor. Not just startled screams, but bloodcurdling screams. They aren't just scared, they are terrified. I can hear the group start running in all directions above me. I start to breathe faster.

Something is wrong.

Chapter 40

Steve

Something horrible is happening upstairs. It's normal to have the occasional group that screams more than others on the tours, but not to this extent. I haven't made it to the stairs where I can get a flashlight yet, but the need to get back to Genevieve outweighs the need for light right now, she has to be terrified. *Why did I leave her alone?* I slowly make my way toward the area I left Genevieve.

When I find Genevieve, I try to let her know I am there without saying anything by reaching for her hand and she goes ballistic. She is thrashing around like a wild animal, kicking, clawing, and to my horror, she inhales deeply like she is about to scream. I manage to get through her flailing limbs and clamp my hand over her mouth.

"Stop, STOP! It's me, Steve," I whisper frantically.

She goes limp with relief in my arms, and I move my hand off her mouth. It feels so good holding her in my arms again.

"What in the world did you do? You scared the crap out of them! I was terrified and I'm not even up there!" she asks.

I can hear slow heavy footsteps above us. "You need to be quiet." I try to keep the fear out of my voice, but the way Genevieve tenses, I know I didn't do a good job.

I grab her hand and tug her farther away from the stairs. "That wasn't me. I was still trying to find a flashlight when all the screaming started."

"Well, did you find one?" she asks in a panicked voice.

"No, I rushed back here to you."

We stop walking and listen for any sounds coming from above. I can still hear footsteps running. An occasional scream. Quick footsteps above us rain dust and debris onto our heads.

I don't know what to do. Should we hide in the basement? I don't know my way around down here; we don't bring tours into the basement. Maybe we should try to sneak back upstairs and out the front door. Slowly we start to make our way back to the stairs.

She tugs on my hand. "Steve, we have to find Livi," she whispers. I can tell she is trying to hold back tears.

"Livi is with Mark, he'll be able to get her out." I hope I am telling the truth. Mark is a big guy; he definitely has a better chance than most.

I can make out the dim light from the stairs in front of us. Slowly we creep up the stairs. We stop when we hear voices.

"They've all seen our faces. We can't let any of them live."

There is no way I heard that right. I peek my head around the corner and see two men, one of them his holding a sobbing girl by the arm.

"Please, I won't say anything to anyone, please just let me go," the girl pleads.

To my horror, one of the men pulls out a knife and stabs the girl. She whimpers and hits the floor with a heavy thud. My heart stops and then picks its frantic pace back up again. Genevieve's whole body goes rigid and I clamp my hand over her mouth again. She can't scream right now. They are right around the corner.

When I am sure Genevieve isn't going to scream, I move my hand back off her mouth and grab her hand, adrenaline courses through my body. I have to get Genevieve out of here. I'm a tough guy, but I don't think I would be able to get Genevieve past these guys safely. I slowly start to back up, pushing Genevieve behind me and into the darkness. I really hope she doesn't fight me on this.

At the bottom of the stairs, I turn around and bend my head down to Genevieve's ear. "Run!" I whisper and give her a gentle nudge.

I sigh in relief as she doesn't question me and takes off running into the pitch-black basement. I try to follow the sounds of Genevieve running, but running blindly in the dark is super disorienting and soon I'm not sure where she is. The noise sounds like it is coming from every direction and the sound of my own heartbeat in my ears almost drowns out any other sounds around me.

THUNK. I hear Genevieve whimper somewhere up ahead. *What was that? Is she okay?* I pick up the pace toward where I think the sound came from and smack right into Genevieve and a wall.

Pain shoots through my head and Genevieve starts fighting to get away from me until she realizes it is me. I gingerly touch my forehead and I can feel the warm sticky blood coat my fingers.

Great.

"Steve, what's going on?" she whimpers.

"I have no idea, but we need to get out of here."

I frantically try to think of a way out other than going upstairs. I don't know the layout of the basement well enough, but I am pretty sure our only option of getting out is upstairs.

Unfortunately, we are in a building that was built to keep people in.

The sound of Genevieve's cell receiving a text makes both of us jump before she scrambles to pull her phone out of her pocket.

"It's Livi," she says in relief and starts to text back.

I grab her hand covering her phone in the process. "Don't text back. It might not be her. I thought Livi didn't have a phone right now?"

"Darla gave her phone back to her this morning."

"Let me see your phone."

She hands me her phone and I turn on the phone's flashlight. Why didn't I think to ask her if she had her phone with her earlier? We navigate further into the basement with nothing more than the light from the phone. Looking down at the screen, I see it is jumping between one bar and no service and the battery is almost dead.

Maybe if we find a window we can get enough service to call 911.

The light reflects off of something ahead of us, I pick up the pace when I realize it is a window. I hand the phone to Genevieve and she points the light at the window as I tug on the bars. For being hundreds of years old they are still remarkably strong and don't budge. I grab the phone from Genevieve and hold it up to the window.

Two bars! I dial 911.

"911, what is your emergency?"

I sigh in relief. "We're on a ghost tour in the Old Charleston City Jail and something happened. I think people are hurt."

"Can I get your name, sir? What happened?"

"Steve Adler. I don't know everything that is happening, but there was a lot of screaming and someone got stabbed."

"Did you see someone get stabbed, sir?"

"Yes."

"Is the victim breathing?"

"I don't know. We ran from the group. Please send help."

The phone goes silent and I pull it away from my ear.

The battery died.

I don't even know if they will send help. They have to, right? I sure hope so.

Sliding down the wall, I sit on the damp floor. Genevieve sits down next to me.

We sit in silence for several minutes before Genevieve quietly asks, "Where have you been? How come you didn't call?"

She sounds broken and I hate that I had anything to do with hurting her. This whole time I thought that at the very least Mark had told her where I went.

"I had to go home. On the drive to the hospital my phone battery died and I forgot to bring a charger." I sigh before continuing. "When I found out Gran died before I got there, I threw my phone at the wall. I didn't have anyone's numbers memorized and I couldn't get any information off my phone."

She doesn't say anything, but reaches out and laces her fingers through mine. "I asked Mark to tell you where I was going and I left him multiple messages at the dorm asking him to call me on Gran's phone."

"Mark knew where you were this whole time?" she asks quietly.

"Yeah, when you didn't answer that night, I called Mark and asked him to tell you what was going on."

"I thought you had ghosted me. Mark said he had no idea where you went. If we live through this I am going to strangle Mark. Not really, but you know what I mean."

I didn't know it was possible, but I get even angrier at Mark. He was supposed to be my friend. How could he purposely put Genevieve and me through so much pain? I felt completely alone dealing with Gran's death and he just watched as Genevieve thought I left and was ignoring her. Genevieve may not actually want to strangle Mark, but I do.

"Genevieve, I can't even tell you how much I wanted to hear your voice these past two months. I've never wanted anything so bad in my entire life."

"I'm so sorry about your grandma," she says quietly and leans her head on my shoulder.

She must be exhausted, because after a few minutes of silence her breathing switches to the quiet deep breaths of sleep. I rest my head on her head and listen for any signs of danger.

Chapter 41

Genevieve

A quiet sound startles me awake. My head is lying in Steve's lap and I can hear his slow, steady breaths. He must have fallen asleep too. *How could I fall asleep at a time like this?* My brain quickly flips through what I have learned about adrenaline spikes and the exhaustion afterward. I have read about it, but this is the first time I have experienced it. I listen intently, trying to figure out what jolted me awake.

Guilt crushes me. I have spent these last two months so angry with Steve and he has been dealing with his grandma's death alone. How could Mark not tell me? He spent these last two months pretending to be my friend.

I trusted him.

I hear movement coming from somewhere in the dark basement. I sit up and shake Steve awake. The sound of voices echo down the hallway and Steve is instantly alert. He scrambles up and pulls me to my feet, looking around frantically for someplace to hide.

Not very many places to hide in a hallway full of closed cell doors.

Out of time, he pushes me in the corner, hiding me with his body just as the hallway illuminates with light. Peeking around Steve, I can see two men in the hallway. Are they the men responsible for whatever is happening upstairs?

"Find them." I recognize Mark's voice. Find them? I guess I just assumed it would be the police that came looking for us, not Mark.

Something doesn't feel right.

The beam of his flashlight lands on Steve. "There you are. Where's Genevieve?"

236

Mark's flashlight seems so bright in the dark basement, but he still hasn't spotted me tucked behind Steve.

Stepping out from behind Steve I ask, "Where is Livi? What happened upstairs?"

"There you are. I thought Steve had already lost you again. I keep telling you to forget him and move on," Mark says with that signature smirk on his face.

"How come you didn't tell me where Steve was?" I can't mask the hurt in my voice.

Before Mark can answer Steve punches him in the face with a satisfying thud.

He looks as if he has wanted to do that for a while now. Mark stumbles backward a few feet before righting himself. The rage in his eyes is terrifying as our gazes meet. Steve winds up for another punch, but stops short when Mark pulls a handgun from under his jacket and aims at Steve's chest.

Time seems to freeze for a moment as I stare at the gun pointed at Steve and then drag my gaze back up to Mark's eyes.

The warmth of the boy who was finally able to get me to laugh at my lowest is gone.

He looks like a stranger to me, not someone that I have spent most of my free time with for months.

"What are you doing Mark?" I ask.

Mark uses his free hand to wipe blood from his lip. He looks at the blood on his fingers. "You know, I really didn't think you had it in you, Steve. I've been flirting with your girl since you introduced us and you haven't done anything about it."

The only voice that has given me comfort for the last two months now fills me with terror.

I grab hold of Steve's hand to stop him from trying to punch Mark again. Steve's jaw is tense and I can tell he wants to. Mark doesn't even seem to notice.

Mark grabs my arm and shoves me in front of him. The force rips my hand from Steve's. With one hand still grasping my arm, Mark turns to grab Steve's and pulls him up next to me so that we are both walking in front of him. Steve reaches over and grabs my hand again giving it a squeeze. I have no idea how or if we are going to get out of whatever situation we are in, but the squeeze of Steve's hand gives me at least a little bit of comfort.

Mark walks behind us with his gun aimed at Steve, the other man trailing along behind us with Mark. I can see the dim light from the upper level shining down the stairs as we get closer. I knew something bad was happening above us, but nothing could have prepared me for the scene in front of me as we climbed the stairs. Several bodies litter the hallway and the floor is sticky with blood. I walk through the bodies not wanting to look at the gruesome scene, but also searching each of the faces for Livi.

Mark takes us to what was once the warden's office if I remember correctly and I let out a relieved sob when I see Livi and several other members of the tour group still alive and sitting on the floor along the wall, gagged, and with their hands tied behind their backs. There is another man I haven't seen before with a gun pointed at the group. The man with Mark ties and gags Steve, before shoving him down on the ground next to Livi.

Livi's terrified eyes meet mine for a moment before Mark roughly ties my hands behind my back. I am expecting a gag and to be shoved to the ground with the others, but instead Mark roughly pushes me into a chair.

"Where would your dad keep blueprints?" Mark asks.

What? Why is Mark asking me about blueprints?

The blueprints for the dream house that we designed flash through my mind. Dad keeps those and all the other fun blueprints he has made in his gun safe, not because they are worth anything, but because he wants them to be protected if there is ever a fire or flood. The gun safe protects them from both.

I rack my brain for reasons Mark would want blueprints from Dad when it dawns on me. My eyes lock with Steve's and I can tell he has come to the same conclusion.

Mark has something to do with Dad's blackmail.

I thought I had already felt the pain of Mark's betrayal, but grief washes over me. I trusted Mark. He has been my rock through these last few months. I thought he genuinely liked me and my family, but all he was doing was trying to get closer to whatever blueprints Dad has that they want.

"Mark, why are you doing this?" I ask.

Ignoring my question, he lifts my chin up with his gun, the metal is cold on my skin. "Where would your dad keep blueprints?"

Anger replaces my grief as I look into Mark's cold eyes. "What blueprints? He keeps the blueprints we work on together in his gun safe." My voice sounds surprisingly calm, I feel anything but calm right now.

"The blueprints we're looking for weren't in the gun safe."

They have been to my house? Dread fills my body.

"Why don't you just ask my dad?"

Mark smirks at me. "I would if I could, but dipstick over there got a little bit trigger happy." Mark waves his gun in the direction of the other two men.

I can't breathe.

Did Mark just say one of those guys shot Dad? Is Dad dead? Just because he got shot doesn't mean they killed him, right? He could just be unconscious or something.

Whoever these people are, it is obvious they aren't afraid to kill—a walk through the Old City Jail hallway proves that.

I can't wonder if Dad is okay right now. Right now, I need to get them away from the rest of the tour group.

Away from Steve and Livi.

"Which safe did you check? The one in the office or the one in my parents' room?" I ask Mark. There is no safe in my parent's room, the only safe is in the office at home, but I am hoping Mark doesn't know that.

He turns to the men. "Did you guys check the second safe?"

"We never saw a second safe," one of the men replies in a gruff voice.

"You idiots were supposed to search the whole house," Mark says angrily.

"We did, we didn't see another safe," the same man replies testily.

Mark jerks me to my feet and starts walking me toward the exit. "Bring those two," Mark says pointing to Steve and Livi. "We may need to use them to get her to cooperate. Take care of the rest."

Mark pushes me down the hall, leaving Steve and Livi in the room with the two men. We walk through the exit and down the front stairs outside.

"Drop the weapon and put your hands where I can see them!"

Mark's head whips toward the voice. I can see a police officer in front of the jail. Several tense seconds go by before Mark wraps his arm around my throat and pushes the cold end of the gun's barrel against my head.

"Come any closer and I pull the trigger," Mark snarls and drags me away toward the back of the building, keeping me in between him and the officer.

We round the corner and stop. I don't know if I am relieved or terrified when there is another officer. The first officer moves toward the second, the crackle of the radio is muffled as he radios for backup.

I can see both officers now and Mark's arm around my neck loosens a little bit, letting me gasp in a deep breath of cool damp air.

I can already hear sirens. Help is on the way, but I'm not sure it will get here in time.

I can't make out every word that is being said on the officer's radios, but it sounds like there are already officers inside the jail. I hope they make it to the rest of the hostages before it is too late, realizing that they have no idea the situation they are walking into. Steve only told them someone got stabbed.

Mark chuckles in disbelief as more officers arrive.

My blood runs cold when he says, "If you have a message you want to send to hell, give it to me—I'll carry it."

Mark removes his arm from my neck.

He moves the gun from my head, aims toward the police officers, and pulls the trigger.

The deafening crack of Mark's gunshots ring in my ears as I collapse to the ground.

Chapter 42

Steve

One of the thugs looks at the other one angrily. "I am sick and tired of having to take orders from the kid."

"He's the boss's nephew and second in command, it doesn't matter if you are sick of it or not, if you don't want to risk the wrath of the boss, I suggest you do what he tells you to."

I thought it was weird that they were taking orders from Mark, but it is starting to make sense. I jump as the sound of the first gunshot ricochets off the walls in the small room.

This can't be happening, I think to myself as I watch the two thugs aim at two people in the group. What spineless pricks, shooting innocent, defenseless people.

Lining them up for slaughter.

Livi is sobbing hysterically next to me. I watch the first body slump over; it is one of the college kids I noticed when the tour started. The girl sitting next to him meets my eyes with hers, tears streaming down her face.

"Put your guns on the floor and step away from the hostages," a voice says from the door.

The two gunmen whirl around to face the police officer standing there. The bigger one points at the officer and pulls the trigger. I hold my breath, but it isn't the officer that drops. The gunman collapses onto the floor with a surprised look on his face.

The gunshot is deafening and my ears slowly start to register sound again as the officer yells at the other gunman to drop his weapon. He drops his gun on the ground and lifts his hands above his head.

As the police officer yanks his hands behind his back and secures him with handcuffs, another officer comes into the room and checks the gunman who was shot. He lets the other officer know that the gunman he shot is deceased and starts to untie the rest of the group.

Livi sobs loudly as they remove the gag from her mouth and untie her hands. The college girl who almost got shot stares at her friend slumped over on the ground.

I have to find Genevieve.

The officer unties me as the sound of gunshots from outside fill the air.

"Genevieve!" I scream and run toward the exit.

I vaguely comprehend the officers inside yelling at me to stop.

I make it to the door and look out into the courtyard just in time to see Mark drop to the ground. Genevieve is already on the ground.

I panic. *Did she get shot? Did Mark shoot her before the police shot him?*

I rush out of the building toward Genevieve. I can hear the officer behind me yelling to the officers outside that I am not a threat. Realizing too late that I could have looked like one of the gunmen running out of the building.

I drop to the ground next to Genevieve and gently lift her long auburn hair that is covering her face. I sigh with relief when those dark green eyes meet mine.

Genevieve is alive.

"Genevieve, are you okay?" I ask gently.

"I think so," she replies in a shaky voice.

I help her up, untie her hands from behind her back and look her over for any injuries before crushing her to my chest.

I am never letting go of her again.

One of the police officers ushers us away from Mark's lifeless body.

Genevieve reaches for one of the officers. "My family is in trouble too."

The look on the officer's face isn't reassuring as he leads us to one of the patrol cars. I think he might know something he doesn't want to tell us.

The officer glances at one of the other officers before responding. "We'll check into it."

I watch as the other officers walk the rest of the tour group out of the building. When Livi sees us, she breaks into a run and crashes into Genevieve, clinging to her like she will float away if she lets go.

I know exactly how she feels.

Genevieve hugs Livi, but has a vacant look in her eyes.

I feel numb too. We all can't help but watch as officers take pictures of the whole scene before medical personnel move Mark's body into a body bag and take him somewhere out of our view. I glance at Livi and Genevieve who watch as his body is taken away.

Livi has tears streaming down her face, but Genevieve's face is tear free. Even though she isn't crying she looks like she might shatter into a million pieces at any moment. Disbelief and pain etched into her beautiful features.

The officers load the three of us into one of the patrol cars and take us to the police station. Genevieve has a death grip on my hand, but stares out the window the whole drive without speaking.

Darla is waiting at the station and wraps Genevieve and Livi in her arms, sobbing. I can tell that there is more going on than we know. Darla looks at Genevieve like she might break.

The officers lead us into a room where we sit down and wait a few minutes before a detective comes in.

He introduces himself as Detective McAllister and asks us to tell him what happened, asking questions for clarification when needed. He almost looks too young to be a detective. I have always pictured detectives as middle-aged men with a permanent five o'clock shadow, but Detective McAllister doesn't look much older than us. His dark copper toned skin is clean shaven and his dark hair short in a high and tight hairstyle. A flawlessly pressed suit and stiff posture make him seem unapproachable, but his dark eyes are kind.

His kind, yet sad eyes are what make me feel like he genuinely cares about what happened to us tonight despite the no nonsense vibe he gives off. I am answering as many questions as I can and Livi is tearfully answering questions as well, but Genevieve doesn't seem to be hearing or processing anything that is being said.

Detective McAllister has to say her name more than once before she focuses a vacant gaze on him.

"I'm so sorry, Miss Clark; there was an incident at your home this evening. We think it might be connected to the ordeal you have all just experienced." He places his hand on Genevieve's knee before continuing. I look at Darla with her tear-streaked face and know whatever is coming next is not good news. "Two bodies were recovered from your home. It's presumed that the bodies are your father and mother that were killed during the altercation. Can you think of anyone who might want to hurt your parents?"

"No." Genevieve hesitates for a minute. "My dad was being blackmailed. I don't know who's all behind it, but I know that Mark, one of the guys at the Jail, had something to do with it."

"Do you know what they wanted from your dad?"

"Some kind of weapon from work."

"We've been trying to put the pieces together; we'll keep working on it." Detective McAllister turns to someone behind him. "We need to get in touch with Mr. Clark's commanding officer."

"Where is my little sister Konnie?" Genevieve asks.

"We haven't been able to locate her yet; we have units searching the area around your house."

Thank heavens Konnie may be okay.

Genevieve looks at Livi and me before turning back to Detective McAllister, the desperate look in her eyes worries me. "What about my sister in New York, are officers checking on her too?"

"We have contacted the NYPD; they are checking on her and will let her know what has happened." Detective McAllister inhales deeply, like he doesn't want to ask his next question. "I hate to ask this of you right now, but when you are feeling up to it, we need you to identify the bodies."

A sob escapes Darla's lips and Livi has stopped crying, she looks like she is in shock. I look at Genevieve and it is like all the pain from my own losses hits me all over again.

She looks broken and haunted, like she is trying to wake up from a horrible nightmare that just won't end.

I clear my throat. "Is it okay if I come with her? I don't want her to be alone."

Detective McAllister nods and I squeeze Genevieve's hand trying to lend her some comfort.

I know what it feels like to be alone during the worst days of your life. I will not leave her side.

Chapter 43

Genevieve

There are two tables with sheets draped over them. I can tell that there are bodies under the sheets. The morgue doesn't look like I thought it would. It is brightly lit and cold. I pull my jacket around me tighter—I guess I was expecting it to be dark and dungeon-like.

I really don't want to do this.

I must look like I am about to panic, because Steve lets go of my hand and wraps an arm around my shoulders and gives me a hug.

"I know this is going to be hard. I'm so sorry that you have to do this, Genevieve," Steve whispers in my ear, before ending the hug and grabbing my hand again.

I can't speak. I just nod and Detective McAllister walks me over to the first table. I realize that we aren't alone in the room. There are others there as well. Probably the coroner and an assistant. Whoever they are, one of them walks over to the table I am standing in front of and lifts down the sheet exposing my father's face.

They have cleaned him up; there is no blood that I can see. He looks as if he could be sleeping. I half expect him to wake up and tell me one of his corny jokes.

I nod with tears streaming down my face.

"Ye ..." I have to stop and clear my throat. "Yes, that is my father."

Detective McAllister walks over to the next table. The look on his face indicates that he likes this about as much as I do. The man, who I am now assuming is the coroner, pulls down the next sheet.

I involuntarily gasp.

My mother. My beautiful, vibrant mother.

She also looks like she is sleeping with her bright auburn waves cascading around her face. Looking closer, they don't really look like they are sleeping.

I can tell they are gone, leaving behind a shell that can no longer hug me when I have a bad day, take me on wild silly adventures or argue about what color to paint a tree house.

Steve gives my hand another squeeze and I hold on to his hand like it is a lifeline thrown to me.

I definitely feel like I might be drowning.

I collapse onto the floor and sob. Steve gets down on the floor with me, untwines his fingers from mine and wraps his arms tightly around my trembling body.

"Can you identify the body, Miss Clark?" Detective McAllister asks.

I nod. It takes me a minute to compose myself enough to say, "That's my mom."

Detective McAllister nods at the coroner and he pulls the sheet back up over Mom's face. Steve helps me up off the floor and half leads, half carries me back up to the room where Livi and Darla are waiting.

I don't think I could have walked on my own. I don't even see anyone or anything on the trip back up from the morgue. Next thing I know I am sitting back down in a chair and Darla is hugging me tightly, stroking my hair, just like Mom used to when I would have a bad day.

Thinking of Mom brings fresh tears to my eyes. *Is there a point when your body runs out of tears?* I wonder.

At some point, Admiral Smith comes into the room. He walks over and gives me a tight embrace before asking me any questions.

"Genevieve, I'm so sorry for everything that has happened to you tonight. Do you know where your dad would have put the blueprints if he had them?"

I shake my head. He doesn't ask if I know what Dad was being blackmailed with and I am glad.

"Let me know if something comes to mind. And please let me know if you or your sisters need anything. Anything at all."

I just nod and Admiral Smith leaves the room. I don't know how much time has passed when Detective McAllister comes back into the room. "They found Konnie hiding in the woods behind your house. She is a little bit beat up, but alive. They're taking her to the hospital to get checked out. And NYPD officers were able to locate Violet, she is safe and on her way here."

Some relief flows through me, but it doesn't even touch the pain I am feeling. I hear Detective McAllister telling Darla something about not being able to go back into the house until the crime scene had been processed and that they would have a unit outside Darla's apartment complex until they are sure there is no longer a threat, but now that I know my sisters are safe I feel like I can't handle any more.

The pain starts to turn to numbness.

"Sweetie, Detective McAllister says that you can come home with us for the night if you want to. You can get cleaned up and borrow some of Livi's clothes."

"Okay," I say. My voice sounds raspy, like it hasn't been used for years or like I am a chain smoker.

— • —

The next few days go by in a blur. I feel like I am dreaming, not quite in the real world.

I don't feel anything.

No emotions at all.

Steve sleeps on Livi's couch and is always there to squeeze my hand or give me a hug when he thinks I need one, but I don't think I have spoken since we left the police station. I just can't muster up the energy to respond to anyone.

At some point Violet shows up. She comes into the room and tries to get me to eat something after giving me a long hug, but I don't talk to her either.

I just lay on Livi's bed, curled up under the blankets, hoping that this is all a horrible nightmare and I am going to wake up any minute.

I didn't know it was possible to feel so broken and empty.

Chapter 44

Steve

We can't get Genevieve to eat anything.

She hasn't said a single word since we left the police station. I thought that Violet would be able to break her out of her sorrow when she arrived, but Genevieve has ignored Violet just like she has ignored the rest of us.

I wish I was meeting Violet under different circumstances.

I had talked to her over the phone on Thanksgiving, but to meet her in person under this much stress doesn't help the situation. She has been splitting her time between being at Darla's with Genevieve and being at the hospital with Konnie, who needed surgery on a badly broken arm and some internal bleeding.

Who knows what Violet heard about me while I was gone, but judging by the daggers she shoots at me with every look, I am assuming it was not good. I am going to have to win her over if she is going to let me stick around.

Darla has been letting me sleep on the couch. Because Mark and I were roommates, our dorm room is also a crime scene. The dorm parents wanted to just move me to another room, but because I would have adult supervision from Darla and I am still doing online classes, Mr. Langston was able to convince the school to let me stay here for now.

I owe Mr. Langston so much; I don't know how I would have survived Gran's death without him. I think he knows that leaving Genevieve during this time would break me even more than I already am.

Detective McAllister updates Violet about the investigation regularly. They were able to get a lot of information out of the one gunman who survived, but they still haven't been able to track down Mark's elusive uncle, Sebastian, who was behind the whole blackmailing.

When someone was sent to his offices and mansion in New York, it was as if he had vanished into thin air.

Now that Tony is gone and they have combed through all his interactions with the blackmailers, Detective McAllister is confident that Violet, Genevieve, and Konnie are no longer targets. The girls would have no way to gain access to confidential military information.

I will still sleep a lot better when they catch him and I know that they are safe.

Violet still won't talk to me very much, but she doesn't seem to mind talking to Darla about everything while I am there too. It is hard to avoid each other when there are five people all staying in one small apartment.

Violet sighs at the kitchen table. I really want to show her that I'm not the jerk that Mark made me out to be. I think Livi must have told her a little bit about where I disappeared to, because she doesn't seem to be quite as frosty as she was when she arrived a few days ago. I close my laptop and walk into the kitchen.

"Is there anything I can help with?" I ask Violet and sit down at the table with her.

"I don't know." She rubs her temples while staring at the piles of papers in front of her. "There is just so much that needs taken care of."

I think back to my time trying to sort out everything after Gran's death. I am so glad that I had Maggie and Claire to help me figure most of it out.

"What do you want me to take care of? I just did a lot of this for Gran, so I kinda know what to do."

Violet looks up at me. I think it is the first time she has really looked at me since she got here. "Thank you, Steve. I would really appreciate the help."

I slide my chair next to her and dive into all the details that nobody really thinks about until they have to. We stay up late into the night going through the financial side of things, going through Tony and Charlotte's will, and planning the funeral.

In the early morning hours, when we have done all we can do for now, Violet's eyes are heavy with sleep.

"Do you think we'll be okay?" she asks quietly.

"It is going to be hard and you are going to have to lean on those who care about you. Give yourself time to heal Violet, let yourself process the pain. Don't shove it down and put it away for another day. It doesn't just disappear; at some point you are going to have to let yourself feel the pain too."

"I have to take care of my sisters."

"Genevieve is dealing with all of this in her own way, she will snap out of it eventually." *I hope.* "And Konnie will heal. Focus on the good and happy things, but don't ignore the hard things."

She nods and disappears into the room that she is sharing with Genevieve. I lay on the couch and try to fall asleep. It is time that I take my own advice and focus on all the good in my life and not dwell on the negative.

I just hope that I can help Genevieve do the same.

Chapter 45

Genevieve

I don't even know what day of the week it is.

I got up and got dressed in the long black dress Violet set out for me and followed Violet and Konnie into the church for the funerals.

I don't even know how long Konnie has been out of the hospital and I am not even sure what is being said during the funeral.

When I look at the coffins and the smiling pictures of Mom and Dad next to them, all I can remember is the cold, brightly lit room of the morgue.

So I pick a spot on the back wall and stare at it for the rest of the service. I know at some point I am going to have to feel something again.

Unless I am permanently broken.

I sure feel broken; maybe my pieces can't be put back together again.

Steve grabs my hand and we follow Violet, Konnie, Livi, and Darla out of the church and drive to the cemetery.

It starts to drizzle as Steve parks his Jeep and we get out and walk to the gravesites. The rain is cold, but I still don't feel anything.

As we get to the gravesites and sit down, I stare at the large holes waiting for my parents.

One next to the other.

A dense mist coming up from the ground creates an unnatural looking fog. It looks like something you would see in a horror movie.

And like the flip of a light switch, I feel again.

The pain feels like it is crushing me.

I can't breathe.

I can't sit and watch as they place my whole world into the ground.

I startle several people, including the pastor, as I jump from my seat, knocking over my chair with a loud thud.

Everyone's sympathetic eyes are on me and it makes the pain even heavier.

With one last look at those empty holes, I take off running toward the wooded area that lines the backside of the cemetery.

The heels I am wearing just slow me down, so I take them off and leave them as I pick up speed.

The fog is so thick I can't see the ground and as I run, I trip over several headstones before I find the edge of the cemetery.

When I get to the line of trees I don't slow down, continuing into the woods before finally stopping.

My ragged breath burns as it fills my lungs and I collapse onto the ground, covered in thick vegetation. I know I should be worried about things like snakes, ticks, and chiggers, but I don't even care what happens to me as the tears finally come and I curl up on the ground, letting the sobs rack my body.

Steve must have followed me into the woods. He lies down next to me and wraps me in his warm embrace. He doesn't say anything. He just lets me cry as the thick fog covers us, hiding us from the cruel world we live in.

How can I go on without Mom and Dad?

In the back of your mind, you always know that at some point in your life you are going to lose a parent, but I didn't think it would be now.

I still have so many things that I need my parents there for; they aren't supposed to be gone until they are old and wrinkled.

Not until after they see me graduate and Dad walks me down the aisle on my wedding day.

They were supposed to be grandparents and spoil my children with cookies and bad jokes.

Mark took this from me.

And it hurts even more that I feel the loss of Mark too.

I shouldn't feel sad that he is gone.

He took everything from me.

But knowing I will never see that smirk again hurts. In my mind I know that Mark was never truly my friend; that he was playing a part, but he was there when I felt like I had no one else.

It makes me angry that I am mourning him at all, but there is a part of me that hopes that maybe not all of it was an act.

Steve holds me until my tears finally stop. When I look at him for the first time since that horrible night, the mirrored pain in his own eyes brings tears to mine again.

"Just take one day at a time Genevieve, and if one day feels like too much, just take one hour at a time. If one hour feels like too much, just take it one minute at a time. You'll get through this, and I'll be here for every second of it." He helps me stand up and wipes the tears from my eyes, kissing the top of my head.

One minute at a time. Make it through sixty seconds of immense heartache. Maybe I can handle that.

March

Chapter 46

Steve

The house is a wreck.

It is no longer a crime scene and the living room has been cleaned. Darla checked to make sure there wasn't anything disturbing left before the girls came over to go through their things. The rest of the house is a mess from the two thugs looking for the blueprints. Drawers are dumped of their contents; closets are empty with everything thrown onto the floor, even some of the beds are on their sides.

The blood may be gone, but the house is still disturbing.

I follow the girls through the house as they take in the destruction.

Violet stops in the kitchen and starts picking up utensils off the floor. Genevieve quietly climbs the stairs. I watch as she disappears into the upstairs hallway and turn to Violet.

"Can I run an idea past you?" I ask.

Violet stops her sorting of silverware and looks up at me. "Sure."

"I want to go to New York with you guys."

Violet looks defeated as she contemplates my request. She has already made arrangements with the high school for Genevieve and Konnie to finish this trimester and then switch to online classes so that they can be in New York with Violet. I have been doing okay with the online school this time, so I am hoping that Mr. Langston can help me convince the school to let me continue with my online classes as well.

I know what it feels like to have everything you love taken away from you.

I can't watch Genevieve leave and I don't ever want her to feel like she is completely alone either. I know her sisters will be in New York with her, maybe I am just using Genevieve's need for support around her as an excuse.

The thought of having to walk Charleston Academy's campus with the ghost of Mark following me around scares me. For someone who loved the stories and the thrill of the ghost tours, I am okay with never running into Mark as a ghost. I have a feeling he would not be a friendly one.

Violet pulls me out of my thoughts. "I think it would be good for Genevieve to have someone else besides me for support. Where would you live?"

"I haven't quite figured that out yet."

"Rent in New York is crazy expensive. I've been trying to figure out our living arrangements too." She sighs. "I think we're going to be leery of having roommates we don't already know after everything that happened with Mark."

"Yeah, pretty sure I'm going to have trouble with that too."

"We have quite a bit of money from the life insurance and we'll get more if the house sells. Not sure how easy a house that just had a double homicide in it will sell though."

She looks out the window into the dense woods behind their house for a few long seconds before continuing. "I'm worried that we will burn through the money too fast between school and rent if it is just us. We're going to have to have roommates."

"Well, I have some money. I would be happy to help if you don't object to me being one of your roommates."

"I've been thinking about it. Genevieve is eighteen, she technically can do what she wants, but at the same time I keep wondering how Mom and Dad would feel about it. We need the help with rent and not having to share our space with someone we don't know would be a benefit." She runs her hand through her dark hair. "I think it's a good idea, as long as you have your own room."

"Of course. I am totally fine with that." I sigh in relief. I can check Violet off my list of those I need to convince; now it is just Mr. Langston and Charleston Academy.

"Thank you for all your help, Steve. I really appreciate it; sorry I was not the nicest when I first got here."

I chuckle. "No worries, I totally understand. I probably would have acted worse in your situation."

She smiles and starts picking up and sorting the utensils again and I head up the stairs to find Genevieve.

She is sitting on her bed staring at the mess in her room. I know she needs time, but I am worried. We still can hardly get her to eat anything and she still hasn't spoken. I sit on the bed next to her, not sure what to do.

"I'm really sorry about everything, Gen. I wish I never brought Mark into your life. I shouldn't have taken you down into that basement. I wish I could redo a lot of things. Like not breaking my phone for starters."

I sigh, not expecting Genevieve to respond, so when I hear her quiet voice, it brings me hope that we will all be okay. "You didn't bring Mark into our lives. Dad was already being blackmailed before he was your roommate. He purposely inserted himself into our lives. I'm sorry that you got pulled into this mess and I am so sorry that I was so mad at you for not calling. The fact that you had to deal with everything alone makes me feel horrible." She wipes a tear off her cheek. "And taking me down to the basement may have saved my life."

We sit in silence for a few minutes before Genevieve speaks again. "I guess I need to start packing."

We spend the next few hours packing boxes to go to New York and making piles for donations and a pile for trash. We have made it through most of the upstairs when we hear Darla and Livi downstairs.

"We brought pizza!" Livi yells up the stairs.

Making our way downstairs, I am surprised how much Violet got done while we were working upstairs. Darla pulls out some paper plates and napkins and we start eating. There is a collective sigh of relief when Genevieve grabs a slice and starts to chew.

Darla asks about all the arrangements for the girls to move to New York and Violet explains what she had been planning, leaving me out of the explanation.

"Are you okay with all of these plans, Genevieve?" Violet asks.

Genevieve's eyes find mine, but before she can say anything, Violet smiles. "Don't worry, Steve is coming to New York too. How about you, Konnie?"

Konnie nods. Darla looks startled by the news that I am coming with them and Livi pouts. "Why does everyone get to go to New York besides me? Can I come too?"

We all laugh, including Genevieve, at the incredulous look on Darla's face. She regains her composure quickly and says, "How about we talk about it after you graduate high school."

In true Livi fashion, she rolls her eyes.

Konnie stares out the kitchen window at the wooded area behind the house. Tears start to stream down her face.

Genevieve notices and wraps an arm around Konnie. "I'm sorry I've been absent. I'm here now if you need to talk."

We have all been wondering what happened that night. None of us were with her when the police questioned her, but we haven't wanted to make her relive the moment either.

Konnie sniffs and wipes her eyes. "We thought you forgot something when you left for the ghost tour, but when Dad went to the front door to see what you needed it wasn't you coming through the door." Konnie doesn't take her eyes off of the trees behind their house. "Dad yelled to us, telling Mom and me to run and get out of the house, but he couldn't move fast enough with his broken leg and they caught up to him pretty quick."

We all sit in silence, not sure what to say.

"When we got to the back door, Mom took my face in her hands and made me look into her eyes. She told me she had to go back and help Dad and I needed to run into the woods and hide." Tears are streaming down Konnie's face now. "She told me not to come back no matter what I heard. I kept running even after I heard gunshots. It was so dark I couldn't see where I was going once I was in the trees. I tripped and fell hard onto some logs or something. I don't remember anything after that until I woke up in the hospital."

Both Genevieve and Violet wrap their arms around Konnie as she cries. "I should have gone back to help them."

Violet wipes her own eyes. "There wasn't anything you could do Konnie, this isn't your fault. We're just glad you got away."

The sisters stand with their arms wrapped around each other for a long time, looking out into the trees before we head back to Darla and Livi's house for the night.

Chapter 47

Genevieve

The quiet tranquility of the swamp washes over me.

I'm glad I asked Steve to bring me to Cypress Gardens one last time before we leave for New York. We walk the trails in silence, listening to the sounds of all the animal life.

I will always be grateful for Steve and his understanding support. Not once has he made me feel like I am being rude or crazy during my silence.

Everyone seemed relieved when I started talking again. I didn't realize how much I was stressing everyone out, I just kind of shut off for a little bit.

"Do you want to go on one of the boats?" I ask.

Steve smiles that dazzling smile. "Sure."

We walk to the boat dock and rent one of the boats for the self-guided tour. I slide on my life vest and we paddle out into the swamp. Looking down into the inky water, I remember the first time Dad brought me here.

He rented one of the self-guided tour boats and paddled out, cracking corny jokes and pointing out different animal or plant life as we passed. After a while we got turned around and Dad had no idea where we were. I smile thinking about Dad trying to act like he wasn't lost, pretending he just wanted to explore every little nook and cranny of the swamp.

My smile quickly fades. Will I ever be able to remember happy memories with my family without the crushing sadness following close behind?

I think about all the countless hours I watched Dad draft the blueprints for our tree house and then helping him with the blueprints for my dream house. As we cleaned and packed up the house, the blueprints were nowhere to be found.

Not only are the blueprints that got my parents killed missing, but the blueprints that now mean more to me than I ever thought they would are missing too.

And there it is again, happy memories followed by my painful reality.

"Are you okay with me coming to New York with you guys?" Steve asks.

I turn to look at him. He looks anxious, like he is worried I wouldn't want him with me.

I smile. "Of course I want you to come." I sigh and my smile fades away again. "Those two months while you were gone were horrible; I definitely don't want to miss you like that again."

That smile of his returns. "You missed me?"

I reach down and splash him with some of the water. "Of course I did. Did you miss me?"

"Every day."

I wish we weren't in the boat right now. I can't even look at him properly as he paddles behind me. I start paddling again too.

"Instead of flying to New York, do you and Konnie want to drive with me?" he asks.

"Sounds good to me." I sigh and stop paddling again. Laying my paddle across the boat I lean back into Steve's lap and look up at him. His bright blue eyes look down into mine.

"Do you think it will ever get easier?" I ask.

Steve sighs and tucks a strand of my long hair behind my ear. "It never gets less painful, but you learn how to live with your new normal and the pain becomes bearable. Then eventually one day you realize that when you think about those you love that have left this Earth, you don't feel sad anymore, you remember the good times. The good times can always overshadow the bad times if you let them."

"When did you get so wise?" I tease.

"It just comes naturally."

A giggle escapes me and I feel the joy for a minute before the guilt comes crashing back down onto me. "Do you think I am partially responsible for what happened to my parents?"

Concern and sympathy wash over Steve's features.

"Genevieve, look at me." I gaze up into those sparkling eyes. "None of this is your fault. There is nothing that you could've done."

He says it with such conviction that I almost believe him.

Chapter 48

Steve

It's really happening. I am moving to New York with Genevieve, Violet, and Konnie.

If Livi gets her way she will be joining us after graduation, she even told her Mom she would apply to a college in New York if it would convince her to let her go. Today is Genevieve and Konnie's last day of their trimester; we start our drive to New York tomorrow morning.

I pull up to the high school and lean over for a kiss before Genevieve and Konnie hop out and walk into the school. I watch them disappear into the building before I leave and drive to Charleston. I have been dreading this day, but I can't put it off any longer.

The dorm room is musty and smells of mildew. I open the window and look around the small space.

Mark seems to be everywhere in the room.

I still feel a little bit stupid that he fooled me so easily. I don't know if it was the school or the police who removed all the belongings on Mark's side of the room, but I am glad they are gone.

I quickly pack all my belongings into boxes. It's crazy that I pack everything up in just a couple of hours when it took me weeks to unpack them. I add the boxes from the dorm with the boxes that are still in my Jeep from Brookhaven. *Is it sad that I can fit my whole life into my Jeep?*

I walk back into the dorm building and check out with one of the dorm parents. I am definitely not going to miss them and their gloomy cloud of judgment.

I lock the Jeep and walk to Mr. Langston's office. He smiles when I enter the room.

"Are you all packed up?" he asks.

I nod. "Thank you for everything, Mr. Langston."

"Please call me Xavier. I won't be your teacher for much longer, and I hope you'll keep in touch."

I smile. "Of course. I really can't thank you enough for all you have done for me and helping me get approval for this last semester online as well."

Mr. Langston walks out from behind his desk and wraps me in a tight hug. I squeeze back and wish that he had been in my life sooner. I think both Gran and I would have benefitted from his calming presence.

I walk back out to the Jeep and pause to look at a group text Violet sent. I scroll through the pictures of our new apartment. It is small, but looks nice.

She is moving into the apartment this weekend. We are going to try and leave super early in the morning and get to New York as fast as we can to help Violet move everything in. A moving truck already came earlier this week and picked up all the boxes and furniture the girls wanted to keep from their house.

The house is empty, clean, and on the market. I hope it sells quickly for their sake, but like Violet pointed out, I worry that it will have trouble selling because of what happened there.

My phone vibrates with a text from Genevieve.

> We're already done with school.

> Should we leave tonight instead?

>> Fine with me.

>> Headed your way now.

With one last look at the beautiful Charleston shoreline, I put the Jeep in drive and head toward my future.

Chapter 49

Genevieve

I feel weird leaving. This is where I have lived my entire life. Sure, we went on vacations and we would visit Dad when he was deployed places we could visit. It isn't like I have never left South Carolina, but I have never lived anywhere else. I still feel like I am walking around in a dream and I will wake up any minute.

Violet, Konnie and I are orphans.

We are in charge of ourselves.

That is scary and a lot of pressure to take on all at once. I have always planned on going to college, but I always thought that I would have Mom and Dad to walk me through all the firsts that I wasn't sure how to handle. Strange that something I have been working so hard toward my entire life seems like a chore now.

I got WAY behind in my classes after everything happened, but thankfully my teachers are working with me so I think I will be able to keep my long track record of almost perfect grades. I probably won't be top of the class anymore, but I will still graduate with honors. I am hoping that maybe I can get back to focusing like normal next trimester. I have done some online work, but it will definitely be different.

It might be nice not having to be around people though.

I still struggle with all the concerned or compassionate looks I get walking down the halls. The teachers are the worst. I appreciate how much they care, but it just rubs salt in the already raw wound every time that look comes across their face, like I might break at any second.

Even though it is scary, it might be nice moving someplace new where nobody knows me. I haven't even decided if I will come back to Moncks Corner to walk for graduation, something I have dreamed about and envisioned for so long.

Livi tried really hard to convince Darla to let her come with me and finish school online too. Darla wasn't having any of it. She said that Livi would never graduate if she was in a new city and in charge of her own schooling online. I hate to admit it, but I have to agree with her.

Before I know it, Konnie and I are packed up, waiting in Livi's living room for Steve to come and pick us up and start the drive to New York. He got all his stuff done while we were at school and we decided that we might as well start on the drive so we could be there sooner to help Violet get all the moving done; Konnie won't be able to help much with her healing arm, but Steve and I should be able to help get a lot done. All the furniture and everything else we kept from packing up our house is in a storage unit in New York. So, there is quite a bit that needs moved into the new apartment. Hopefully we can get it all to fit.

A knock on the door breaks me out of my thoughts and I make my way to the living room and sit on the couch. Darla opens the door and Steve walks in. So many things have happened this last month that I have not been ready for.

I am definitely not ready for this.

How am I supposed to say goodbye to Livi and Darla? I don't know if I can. I freeze like a deer in headlights. Livi is standing next to her mom looking like she is about to cry. Steve seems to understand how I am feeling and comes to sit down next to me.

"Do you want to leave in the morning?" he asks quietly.

I shake my head. There is no use dragging it out. He stands up and pulls me up with him. Darla comes over and wraps me in a tight hug.

"Call me if you need anything, Sweetie! Our door is always open," she says before turning to Konnie for a hug. Hearing her call me 'Sweetie' reminds me of Mom and brings a fresh wave of pain with it.

"Thank you," I whisper and then turn toward Livi.

She rushes toward me and we both almost topple over from the impact. Livi starts sobbing, which of course makes me start sobbing and we just hold onto each other crying for who knows how long until Darla walks over and takes Livi's hand.

"See you later, Alligator," I say.

"In a while, Crocodile," she replies.

Funny how something we haven't said since we were kids is what comes out of my mouth now.

Steve and I start walking out the door with Konnie trailing behind us. I turn back and give Darla and Livi a little wave and then I don't look back.

I might never leave if I do.

The Jeep is nice and warm with the heat blasting. I climb in the front seat and put on my seatbelt. Steve helps Konnie into the backseat and makes sure she is comfortable. He starts to drive when I realize that I can't leave Moncks Corner just yet.

"Can we stop by my house before we leave?" I ask.

"Of course," Steve replies and turns, heading toward my childhood home.

Steve pulls up and parks on the street. I look at my house, and my grandparent's old house next door.

This small section of land, these two houses, hold so many of my life's memories within their walls. I open the door and step out of the Jeep.

I have always known I would leave Moncks Corner at some point in my life, but I never thought I would be leaving like this.

Konnie decides to stay in the warm Jeep and I walk over to the tree house, with Steve following behind. Climbing up the ladder and lifting the trap door to scramble inside, I sit on the floor and look around. Steve comes and sits next to me while I just stare around the small room.

At some point, he is going to think I am losing it if I can't stop silently staring at things all of the time.

Someone cleaned up since I brought Steve up here on Thanksgiving, the layer of dust and dried leaves gone. *Who would have been in the tree house?* I wonder and then it hits me.

Dad.

Steve startles as I jump up and rush to the other side of the room, finding the hidden pressure point that Dad made so we could hide our treasures.

The secret compartment on the other side pops open with a click.

I hold my breath involuntarily as I walk over to the compartment and peek inside and see three drawing tubes, a picture of Violet, Livi, and I last summer, and a notebook.

I lift the tubes out of the compartment and look at Steve. Shock and disbelief washing over his features.

"Are those what I think they are?" he asks.

I open the first tube and pull out the blueprints. Relief washes through me when I see the blueprints for the tree house. I quickly open the next tube finding the blueprints for my dream house.

Tears slide down my face. They aren't lost, I have them.

I open the third tube and find designs for some sort of weapon, maybe?

This must be what Mark and his Uncle Sebastian were after. I wonder if they will ever find the mysterious Sebastian who is responsible for everything that transpired. The link between Mark and Sebastian was easy for the detectives to find, but by the time they went looking for Sebastian he had disappeared. Steve peeks over my shoulder and stares at the pieces of paper that have caused so much pain.

"What should I do with these?" I ask.

"I have no idea."

I roll them up and place them back in the tube. I reach into the compartment and grab the picture and notebook before putting the tube back in and clicking it shut.

I don't want anything to do with those cursed blueprints.

I will call Detective McAllister in the car and tell him what we found.

I glance at the picture and notebook in my hands. Livi, Violet, and my happy faces last summer stare back up at me.

It seems like a lifetime ago that we took this picture in the tree house with Livi's Polaroid camera she got for her birthday last summer.

I open the notebook and see Konnie's messy handwriting inside. It looks like some sort of journal. I squeeze the notebook and picture to my chest and look around the tree house one last time before grabbing the blueprints of the tree house and the dream house I will build someday.

We climb down the ladder and as soon as I step down onto the grass, the dark sky opens up, and rain starts pouring down. We sprint toward the Jeep, trying to avoid getting completely soaked, but I can't leave yet.

I look back one last time.

Epilogue

The rain is cold and bites at my warm cheeks. The mist rising from the ground is so thick it looks almost unnatural and reminds me of the funerals. The mist, the rain, the hole in my chest, all of it is like reliving the day we put them in the ground. There are some mornings that as I wake, I am sure it was all a horrible nightmare, then reality crashes into me.

My life has been forever changed.

I am empty and full of pain at the same time. How is that even possible? Everything reminds me of them.

Standing on the empty street, rain distorts my vision of what was once my home. It looks exactly the same: still painted eggshell white with the big, happy, yellow shutters that Mom insisted the house needed. The lawn is still mowed and the beautiful flowers still bloom along the front of the house. More flowers line the stone walkway that winds its way from the front door to the driveway.

The gigantic willow tree in one corner of the front lawn brings painful memories: days spent climbing the tree, and the slumber parties with my friends and sisters in the tree house Dad built for us.

The tree house is still there, firmly attached like it has always been. Dad spent months making blueprints to build the perfect tree house for his daughters. Mom was so excited to paint it and hang curtains, but was so upset when none of us girls wanted to paint it bubblegum pink. After a heated debate, we all finally agreed on a lighter maroon. It was enough to satisfy Mom.

Memories continue to flood my mind, like the one hot day Konnie came up with the idea to make our own swimming pool. I wasn't sure we were going to survive when Dad got home from work and saw the muddy hole we had dug right in the middle of the front lawn.

I watch for any sign of life in the house now, even though I know there won't be any. There are no lights, no happy sounds of a family eating dinner together, no music coming from the garage where Violet had once tried to start a band.

The rain is coming down hard now. My sweatshirt hood isn't doing much to keep me dry and the cold, wet fabric clings to my skin. I try to swipe the wet strands of my long hair behind my ears, but they fall back across my eyes almost instantly.

The rain pelts my face like slivers of ice, which makes the hot tears sting my cheeks.

Wishing I could go inside and get a warm, comforting hug from Mom, or listen to one of Dad's horrible jokes, I turn my back on the only place I have ever felt safe and start toward the unknown.

I climb into the Jeep where Steve and Konnie are waiting. Steve grabs my hand and pulls out of the driveway onto the road.

Tears stream down my face, but I don't look back as we start our long drive to New York City. I squeeze Steve's hand. I don't have any idea what this new life will be like, but I know that I am going to try my hardest to be happy. It may take a while, but I know that is all that Mom and Dad ever wanted for their daughters.

I am determined to live a life my parents would be proud of.

A life I am proud of.

I won't let them down.

Acknowledgements

I can hardly believe that this novel is finally here. Fifteen years ago I wrote the climax of the story for the final in one of my creative writing classes. I always knew that it was meant to be more than that exciting short story, but life happened and there it sat at the back of my mind for years and it would not be here if I didn't have so many amazing people in my life. I am going to try my hardest not to leave anyone out. If I happen to miss someone I am truly sorry!

To my husband, for always pushing me to follow my dreams and who is happy to listen to nonstop chatter about my stories or the stories I am reading at the time even though he has no idea what is happening when I plop him right in the middle of a plotline because I need to talk about it. Also his willingness to fuel my addiction of buying and reading books. Even if I have TBR pile that will last me a lifetime. He is definitely a keeper!

To my wild and crazy boys that call me 'Mom,' for being just as interested in my stories as I am and cheering me on along the way. Also for understanding when Mom has to lock herself in the office and write.

To my parents, all of them, biological, step and through marriage. Thank you for showing me that the small moments in life are what mean the most and we should cherish them. Mom, thank you for being so supportive even though I haven't let you read a word of my manuscript yet. I guess if you're reading this now, you've finished the book, hope you liked it! Dad, I miss you every day, I have felt your encouragement from the other side throughout the whole process.

To my writing coaches, Ashley Mansour and Jessica Reino, for their amazing coaching, expertise and encouragement. Thank you for cheering me on and pushing me to continue even when life was throwing me some obstacles I wasn't sure I wanted to try and climb over.

To my beta readers: Susan, Tara, Carolyn, Joni, Nicky, and Diana. Thank you for reading my roughest of drafts and pushing me in the right direction. Also for your friendship and unwavering support.

To my editors: Melody Delgado and Erin Huntley for helping me get my first draft to this draft and all the versions in between. Thank you for your expertise, suggestions and comments that made the story what it is today. And thank you Erin for never making me feel like an idiot when I asked so many questions. One day all the rules will be engraved in my memory and your job will be easier. I hope, I mean it has to make sense to me at some point, right?

To all the authors in my Author Accelerator group, it was a pleasure to learn and write with all of you. Thank you for the constant encouragement and the friendships that we have been able to create. I can't wait until all of our books are out in the world. Know that when yours is, I will be one of the first to purchase a copy.

To my amazing book group, your excitement for my book to become a reality has been contagious and I love reading and discussing the books we read each month. But not only that, we have become a group that lifts each other up when needed and gives love and support when someone is in need. You are all some of my very favorite people on the planet, thank you for always being a bright light in my life!

To all of my friends and family who are just as excited to see *Haunted by You* out in the world as I am. From Ladies Nights where I get to get away from the stress for a while, to asking how my writing is going, to phone calls, texts and everything in between. The excitement you all have shown for every step I have taken along the way and all of your loving words and support have meant so much to me. Thank you.

To Susan and JoAnna, who are more than happy to brainstorm with me when there is a plot hole that I am having trouble with or anything else that I need another writer's brain for. Your countless phone calls, texts and Marco Polo's have kept me going through frustrating hang ups.

To Chantel, who's amazing artwork brought my characters to life. Thank you for taking the time and effort to make character art that so fit the image of the characters in my head.

To Nick and Diana, who answered all of my Navy questions and took the time to explain them to me—even when you probably felt like you were explaining things to a child.

To the whole Morgan James team for believing in me as an author, helping me make my dream a reality and supporting me along the way. Thank you for all of your hard work and dedication to design and create a book we can all be proud of.

To all of my animals who brighten my day with all of their antics, especially Jasper who likes to keep my feet warm while I write.

To all of you who connect with me on social media. Your kind words and support have made me feel seen and heard.

To God, for instilling in me the love of stories, the drive to write, and placing all the people and places in my life to help me along the way.

And last but definitely not least, thank you to YOU. Thank you for reading this book. Thank you for being a reader and keeping stories alive and thank you for making my dream of becoming a full time author one step closer to becoming my reality.

About The Author

Louise Davis is a powerful, up-and-coming, young adult author who has an innate ability to instantly draw readers into her stories with her dramatic realism. By combining a commercial and accessible writing style with highly-riveting and twisting plotlines, Louise's novels are truly unique works of literary art. Her recent book, *Haunted by You*, artistically showcases her wide-range of writing skills weaving in romance, mystery, and suspense all in one thrilling book. She has always loved reading books to her children and received

Photo by Kelsey Pease

a bachelor's degree with a focus in creative writing to write her own books, including her children's book, *Grandpa's Boots*. It is through Louise's profound character development and realistic storylines that she's able to not only entertain her readers, but also teach them valuable life lessons in the process. When Louise is not sharing her love for writing with the world, she loves to read, go on adventures and spend her time with her five boys, husband, and various animals on their peaceful 3-acre ranch-style home in Idaho.

Connect with Louise online: www.louisedavisbooks.com
Instagram: @louisedavisbooks
Facebook: @Louise Davis

A free ebook edition is available with the purchase of this book.

To claim your free ebook edition:

1. Visit MorganJamesBOGO.com
2. Sign your name CLEARLY in the space
3. Complete the form and submit a photo of the entire copyright page
4. You or your friend can download the ebook to your preferred device

Morgan James
BOGO™

A **FREE** ebook edition is available for you or a friend with the purchase of this print book.

CLEARLY SIGN YOUR NAME ABOVE

Instructions to claim your free ebook edition:
1. Visit MorganJamesBOGO.com
2. Sign your name CLEARLY in the space above
3. Complete the form and submit a photo of this entire page
4. You or your friend can download the ebook to your preferred device

Print & Digital Together Forever.

Snap a photo

Free ebook

Read anywhere

Printed in the USA
CPSIA information can be obtained
at www.ICGtesting.com
JSHW021516010424
60353JS00002B/37

9 781636 981727